SHAARA OF FREINANA

Book Three of the Shaarvan Series

Note: *To start at the beginning of this series, please go to:*

Scholar-Ship-Bound

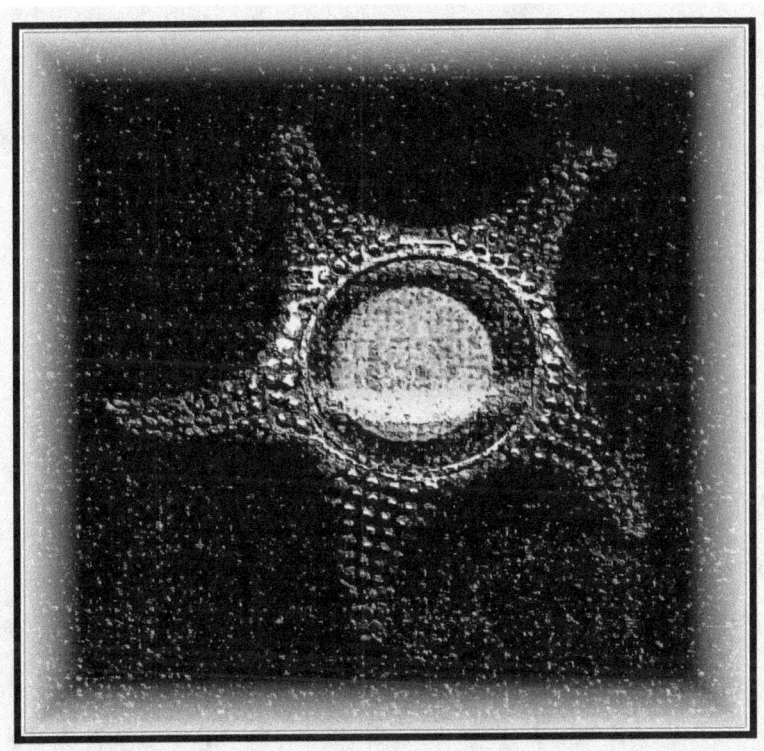

K. S. Riggin

Table of Contents

Main Characters & Places in the Shaarvan Series

Altar: Home of the Shapechanger & others. Altar is the name of the planet and is also the main city & capital.

Altarian: Those who live on the planet Altar.

Baltoff: The Old One on Westla who was manufacturing the drugs that Thenos used to overthrow the government of Altar.

Barquel: The main god worshipped on Freinana.

Blair: Owner of the landoor ranch. Good guy.

Brala: Shaara's friend on Westla.

Chaslow: Shapechanger working for Thenos, blew up a nursery on Westla & hunted for Shaara.

Clofa: One of Altar's two moons. It was where the old Shapechanger liked to retire. Thenos blew it up.

Crimson Black: The horse-like landoor Shaara befriends.

Flar: Freinana the housemaster that Shaara stays with. Husband of Frieda.

Frieda: Freinana housemistress with whom Shaara stays. Wife of Flar.

Goria: Pseudo wife of Pathe. Former lover of Shaarvan. Bad person.

Isandor: the commoner who owned Shaara on Freinana. Bad guy.

Landoor: An animal that looks like a horse.

Pathe: Son of Tevor & Teea (brother of Shaarvan & Thenos) Doctor, good guy.

Saberey: Symbol of the Shapechanger & their origin.

Shaara: College student. Wife of Shaarvan and later Stegthal (Thal) Renamed numerous times: Susan, Sletttha, Sleena, Skeva, Thalia, Thenosa.

Shaarac: (Thaarac, Thenon) Shaara and Shaarvan's son.

Shaarvan: Steals his wife, Shaara from a college campus, Altarian/Westlan Shapechanger.

Skeva: Name given to Shaara on Freinana.

Sleena: Name given to Shaara on Freinana.

Slettha: Slaver's name for Shaara on Freinana.

Spelon: One of Shaara's guardians. Shapechanger Warrior becomes Shaara's lover later.

Stegthal: (Thal) He becomes Shaara's Second Husband. Good & bad

Susan: Shaara's original Earth name.

Targone: Shapechanger who arrives on Freinana to verify that Shaara is Shapechanger.

Teea: Shaarvan's mother, lives on Altar, wife of Tevor (and later Starnkor).

Tem: Head of Westla, Uncle to Shaarvan, Tevor's brother.

Temina: Wife of Tem, mentally unstable.

Tenor: One of Shaara's guardians. Shapechanger Warrior.

Tessa: High Priestess on Westla.

Tevor: Shaarvan's father who lives on Altar.

Thal: Stegthal's name on Deathstar.

Thalia: Shaara's name on Deathstar.

Thandar: Shaara & Thal's son. Shaarvan adopts him.

Thedar: One of Shaara's guardians. Shapechanger Warrior.

Theinian: Another species, usually slavers and most often gay.

Thenos: Son of Tevor & Teea (brother of Shaarvan & Pathe), Bad guy.

Thenosa: Thenos' name for Shaara.

Tren: Owner of the casino and of Shaara. Good guy to Shaara.

Westla: Huge artificial satellite. Only Shapechanger may go there or girls and servants.

Additional Terminology:

Tide: Approximately one Earth day. Tides are usually grouped, as in a fiveTide, a twentyTide, etc.

Pass: Approximately one Earth year. A halfPass and quarterPass are common expressions.

Shapechanger: Never found in the plural. The Shapechanger are an artificially derived species that are capable of shape change, most often as a Saberey (tiger-like cat), This also includes many sensory improvements and abilities.

The Names of Shapechanger: Names beginning with T or S denote Power. Those Shapechanger are deemed Lords. Formal testing on Westla ranks them.

Warrior Shapechanger: Those who meet qualifications of specific battle readiness. Ranking is by formal tests on Westla.

Priestess: Females who have achieved a ranking on Westla denoting their ability to stand up against Shapechanger Power.

Chapter One

Shaara

Shaarvan was in a bad mood. The ship's cordor unit was acting up. It kept failing the circuitry test — which caused us to make a landing on a planet Shaarvan didn't want to visit. My husband kept pacing back and forth across the ship's control room like an angry tiger, eager to pounce.

"You assured me, Kada, that the unit was new when you put it a twentyTide ago," Shaarvan said, using his ice voice — the one that made me shudder when I was at the other end of it.

My husband, who also happened to be the captain of the ship, continued berating Kada, adding a look that cut through most men's excuses like a blade slicing skin. "A new unit would not have malfunctioned."

Shaarvan's words were as loud as a whip cracking the air. In the stillness of the control room, its echo was intensified. I wasn't the only one being extremely quiet in the face of Shaarvan's sub-zero rage. Three men sat hunched over, studying their panels so fixedly one would have thought the alarm system had flared blue with emergency warnings. Two other men were working under the panels, doing maintenance checks with such intensity it would seem the ship must have numerous problems.

Kada, the ship's main engineer (and the one getting the grilling from my husband), was beginning to smell like a sour orange. It was the peculiar odor of a guilty conscience. I was only a novice at recognizing the scent of emotions, but guilt was easily identified.

I used to be Terran — before my husband kidnapped me — and sniffing at people's emotions was not something I was really comfortable with. It seemed like an invasion of the privacy of their feelings, but for a Shapechanger, like I was now, it came without effort. Yet I didn't need to breathe in his odor. I could have easily guessed the man's feelings. He was wiggling like a caught fish, trying to get loose from the hook.

I felt sorry for the man, but I could have told him from my own personal history that my husband had no mercy — not for the guilty.

It had only been a scant two Pass (about a year and a half Terran time) since Shaarvan had forced me to become his wife. He had changed my Earth chromosomes so he could impregnate me. I'd had no choice but to adjust to being a different species. I was still adapting, and the training part wasn't getting easier. I knew all about Shaarvan's lack of mercy, and if I'd dared to interfere, I would have told Kada that resisting Shaarvan was useless.

"Kada, out with it!" my husband ordered.

Once again, I was glad it wasn't me Shaarvan was so angry with. Already, I could see the shadow of his fur. His cat eyes glowed yellow-green. My husband was on the brink of changing. I did not think he would complete the change and kill Kada in front of his crew, but I had long ago learned not to attempt such predictions. Shaarvan did what he pleased.

My husband was edging closer to Kada — so like a tiger — he did not need to Shapechange.

In a voice close to breaking point, Kada cried out. "Forgive my mistake, my lord. I am sorry." Then he fell to his knees, bowing his head like a man about to be beheaded. His legs were shaking. His knees barely supported him. The smell of fear permeated the control room.

Strangely, fear was not an unpleasant odor but rather similar to almond flavoring. For a moment, it drew me. My stomach rumbled. That broke my trance. I looked down at my sleeping son, fearful that the odd noise might have awakened him. His lips suckled for a moment, but he slept on.

"I did not mean to betray you, my lord," Kada cried out. "I bought the cordor from your brother, Lord Thenos. He told me it was a new unit he'd brought from your father's supply room."

Kada's eyes were dark with his fear. His pupils appeared overly large against the smallness of his eyes. His glance was shifting about the room as if he were looking for an escape door.

There was no smell of sulfur in the air, so Kada wasn't lying about that. I hoped he wouldn't suddenly spring up and attempt to flee. Shaarvan hated cowardice. He would be more lenient with a fool.

Kada saw, as I did that Shaarvan's pacing had stopped. My husband was assessing the man's statements, weighing the shifts of emotions in the air and in Kada's mind. My husband's rage was still present but lessening. Kada's life was no longer in danger.

Perhaps Kada sensed the change. His words continued, his voice lowered slightly from its former high-pitched hysteria. "I had no reason to distrust Lord Thenos. Not only is he your brother, my lord, but he is Shapechanger."

Kada was trying to honor Shaarvan with the compliment of honesty. He didn't realize Shapechanger were not moralists. It is true a Shapechanger does not lie, but that is because he cannot. It would make him physically sick to do so. Still, it was a political move on Kada's part. I watched curiously to see its effect on Shaarvan.

My son sleepily stretched out his fist. I tucked the blanket tighter around him and wondered idly what Kada was hiding. He wouldn't have smelled guilty if he'd been as ignorant as he claimed. Maybe Shaarvan would know, but the odds of his telling me were slim. He, like most Shapechanger husbands, did not include women in business discussions.

Shaarvan was no longer threatening Kada. I could tell the change in his intent. His body stance had altered. He was still Shapechanger, one to be feared, but he was no longer the hunting tiger.

"All right, Kada. Journey into the nearest city and find us a new cordor unit."

With one last glare at the man, Shaarvan released him from the inquisition and barked out, "Shaara, come here."

Shaarvan was calling for me. A Shapechanger always chopped off his own name and used it for the naming of his wife. Once upon a time, I'd been called Susan, but I didn't dare mention that name anymore. There were a lot of things about me that had changed. For one thing, I no longer attempted to argue with my husband.

I rose out of my seat. It was the one I'd dubbed the shaggy dog chair because of the furry material that covered its beanbag shape. It felt like a dog, too, because it shifted slightly whenever I sat in it. The first time I'd deposited my rear, it had taken my measurements for its memory banks, wiggling all about exactly like a dog's tail. I still remember how I'd started to jump out, frightened at the motion. But Shaarvan had turned his eyes on me. His look had changed my mind about moving. I'd sat in the shaggy dog chair as still as a deer when a light shone at it and just as frightened.

Remnants of anger were still floating about like wisps of fog. They coated the air in spots, non-existent in others. I could feel them and even see them if I looked from the corner of my eyes. Obviously, I didn't pause to debate whether it was a good time to get within close proximity of my husband. A Shapechanger wife learns to obey quickly. I walked forward — carefully, though, not eager to wake the baby I held in my arms. Shaarac was little more than a fortyTide (about a month and a half,) but he already had a Shapechanger's temper, just like his father.

My sweet little miracle woke up anyway. The angry words and the violence in the air had not made him twitch, but my movement, or his father's voice calling my name, popped open his eyes. He yawned and again stretched out his tiny arms. His blue-gray eyes focused first on me. The radiance of his smile made me give him one in exchange. A wave of love swept through me. I pressed my lips against the soft silk of his hair. But Shaarac was ignoring me. His eyes had found his father. Although he was the age now to laugh and string a gurgle of nonsense sounds, the eyes that studied Shaarvan were as contemplative as an adult's.

"Let me have him," Shaarvan ordered.

I handed Shaarac to him and began to edge away. My backward wasn't quick enough. Shaarvan's arms gathered up the little one, and as fast as a rattler's bite, his hand caught me.

"Where do you think you are off to my wife?" His words held the tiniest breath of warning, but his eyes were smiling. I breathed a sigh to see that Shaarvan's anger had left with Kada's departure.

I shut my eyes and then sighed with carefully suppressed irritation. Shaarvan's anger might have slipped away, but his intention to train me had not. The hand that halted my retreat was soon sliding snake-wise down to rest on my breast.

That's why I had tried to back away — training! I hated it when Shaarvan fondled me in front of the crew. But he was as intent on breaking my Terran conditioning as I was in trying to avoid a public mauling.

"You are a Shapechanger, wife," he'd told me time and time again. "You will make love whenever and wherever your husband desires it."

In general, I tried hard to obey Shaarvan, but I was far from comfortable with that part of Shapechanger etiquette. If there was anything I still dared to rebel over, it was public displays, yet I kept silent. The punishments of Shapechanger too often fit the crime. If I protested, it might cause Shaarvan to take me right there on the control room floor.

"Matop, take my son and entertain him," Shaarvan ordered.

Matop turned pale, but he did not argue. Not many people dared to dispute the wishes of the Shapechanger. Matop's arms scooped up my beautiful son. Shaarac gurgled in happy tones, pleased to be given the special treat of a new face and body to explore.

I couldn't stay quiet over it, though. "Shaarvan, Matop doesn't know how…"

"*Silence,* wife." The words were a command I'd be stupid to ignore. Shaarvan's eyes reinforced the warning. I sighed dramatically, but I kept still.

My thoughts were all mixed up with irritation, worry for Shaarac, and resentment, but when Shaarvan's lips began to ply my neck with kisses, all the thoughts whirling around in my brain disappeared, as did my inhibitions. I could steel myself to ignore Shaarvan's touch for a couple of minutes, but his lips never.

Eagerly, I returned his kisses. I was wildly in love with my handsome husband, and lust was his middle name. His tongue lit fires in me that raged like a Santa Ana wind. His touch on my back was fire. Shaarvan's tongue in my mouth urged me, teased me, and sent me into orbits of desire. Then his hands moved lower and pulled my body close. Once again, I was his.

It was the capitulation Shaarvan wanted. His tongue withdrew. Warm lips still entrapped me, but Shaarvan was letting the flames die. I knew then that my husband would not take me in the control room.

I should have been relieved. I would have if my heart were not beating the rhythm of lust and if I were not drunk with desire.

"Shaarvan," I cried out, the sound a whimpered protest.

"Easy, Shaara," he cooed. His lips sprinkled kisses across my face. "You have done well." His knuckles rose to soothe my face. It was a calming touch, a touch of approval.

He whispered in my ear, "I would like to carry you to the closest room and quench our fires, but it will have to wait, my enchantress wife."

My skin craved his warm, gentle strokes, but another fire inside me was flaming, too. As Shaarvan had eased my desire with his words and touch, my awareness of my surroundings brought me embarrassment. My face grew as hot as if I were feverish. I wanted to stamp my foot or scream.

It was Shaarvan's eyes that stopped me. They were not angry eyes nor even full of warning, just watchful.

I took a breath, as deep as when you plan to dive into the water and glide across the bottom of a pool. I held that breath almost as long, and when at last I let it out, I lowered my eyes, bit my tongue, and waited.

The moment passed. Shaarvan's hand had stopped petting me as his eyes observed.

One of the men dropped a tool. It clanged heavily on the control room floor. I didn't move. I scarcely breathed. Shaarvan reached under my chin and brought up my eyes for his appraisal. "Very good, Shaara," he said." You are doing well. When we leave here, I shall take you to the Old Ones."

I searched his eyes. The Old Ones? I'd thought we were on our way to Delor. It was what he'd told his buyers.

My husband was a trader. He went to backward planets, planets not in the League. He stole young women. Then he transported them in metal sleeping caskets to a score of different League planets. As if they were dry goods or machinery, he sold the women to buyers.

I was not proud of Shaarvan's livelihood. In fact, I hated what he did. But I was not allowed to speak of it. I held scars on both arms, in fact, due to my attempting to interfere with his business.

At first, I had not believed it when I'd first awakened to find myself onboard his ship. Shaarvan had frightened me, and he had angered me. It took me almost a Pass to discover that it was much safer to fear him.

"I own you," Shaarvan had told me, and for a while, I'd waged a stunted war that spurted little rebellions. He had squashed them with the same ease he did everything.

Once, I had been Miss Independent — a Californian, cocky, and sure that I had all the answers. I believed that I was in control of my destiny. I'd thought life was a train going towards the future of my dreams. I'd loaded my cargo and was meeting all my schedules. All destinations were on a route I'd carefully planned. It had been full steam ahead — but, in one odious moment, my train derailed.

"You will obey me," Shaarvan had commanded. He'd locked me in a room with no sound, no food, no water, nothing to do, and no one to talk to.

They call that sensory deprivation. I can tell you how easily it breaks you. Resistance crumbles like a giant wave against a sandcastle. When the only sound you hear for hours and hours is the loneliness of your own heartbeat, and you realize how isolated you really are something changes inside you. You discover that you have to make contact with someone, even if that person is your enemy.

My enemy, my friend, my husband, my lover — Shaarvan, who kidnaps women for buyers so that they can sell them to rich men wanting wives.

I understand why now. The biochemists made all the people in the League disease resistant. It was a lovely gift, but the people, free from cancer, cavities, and disease, found they could no longer bear female children. The men wanted wives, so they stole them from planets that were unhampered by such progressive gene therapy. A whole system of trade developed. The Shapechanger, in particular, grew wealthy and flourished as a breed of space traders.

I love my husband. I didn't at first. I hated him, and I needed him. But somehow, the need grew stronger than the hate, and a bond formed between us. I guess it's like falling in love with a criminal. I love Shaarvan, but I wish his livelihood were anything else.

Shaarvan's gray-green eyes were smiling down at me. I hoped my wandering thoughts were not being projected onto him. They often were. Yet he said nothing. His hand brushed rough knuckles down the side of my face. It was the gesture he used to tell me he was pleased with me.

"Come, Shaara. While Kada hunts for parts, I shall show you Watha." He led me towards the back of the room where he'd stored a blue felt hat. He lifted it up and placed it on my head. It perched there like a bird's nest until a strap was snapped together. I shook my head cautiously, but the hat was secure. It was light enough to ignore until Shaarvan pulled at the top, and a net sprawled down, covering my face. I could see through the veil, but the clingy fabric was an irritant.

"That's necessary?" I complained. Of course, I was sure it was, or Shaarvan wouldn't have positioned it there. He rarely allowed me to tie back my hair or to cover it with decorations. But, I felt the need at times to complain over such trivia. It was all I had left of my Terran heritage.

Shaarvan nodded. His eyes were firm and unsmiling. I said nothing more. On our travels, I'd often had to wear strange clothes to meet the customs of the culture. I was glad I didn't have to change my dress. Some of the outfits I'd been clothed in had been as ugly as the dresses made in junior high home economics classes.

I was eager to go planet side. In spite of the quirky customs, the adventure of seeing new places was always exciting. But — did Shaarvan mean we were going without Shaarac? Shaarvan's hand was already propelling me forward.

"I can't leave Shaarac here," I said, attempting to turn around and go back for him.

"Even when your husband orders it?"

Surely Shaarvan would not expect me to leave our son? My eyes begged him, but he was unyielding. I knew the answer then. Whether he was testing me or not, I must obey the Primary. Pleasing Shaarvan was always first.

"I will obey," I said and lowered my eyes appropriately.

For a second time that Tide, I had pleased my husband. I glanced back at Shaarac. He was sitting on Matop's lap. He seemed content. I knew he would not be hungry for a while since I'd just fed him before his short nap.

I sighed. Then I walked down the ship's ramp at the side of my Shapechanger husband, not even daring to look back.

Shaarvan

Shaara is becoming more submissive. She pleases me. It has been less than a TwoPass since I took her. How quickly the time has marched forward.

I do not like being stuck on Watha. It is not a planet on our trade routes, so we waste our time here. However, my wife is due a treat. It will pleasure me to see her eyes when she views the city's bazaar. I have seen it before. It does not excite me, but her taste for such things is avid.

Perhaps that will take the sting away when I order her to stay onboard at Delor. It would be better for her not to see the capturing of slaves. Even in all our time together, Shaara has not accepted what I do. I will leash her to a computer task, brusquely and demandingly. That will occupy her mind for a while.

Shaara

I loved seeing different planets, and being able to get off the ship was its own freedom. My eyes darted about like stones skipping over water. I'd seen the spaceport from the control room, but I was eager to catch something new. Unfortunately, most spaceports are all disgustingly similar. This one was no exception.

Strings of robots, unconnected but following each other in perfect columns, transported materials and supplies to various ships. Their dead-looking eyes, empty of thought, flashed in matching iridescent greens. As they passed us, their heads did not turn to glance at us. Their eyes flashed no interest.

A ship burst upward, almost soundless in its blastoff. A ripple of disturbed air brought a low-pitched boom as it broke the sound barrier. The planet's barrier unit muffled the rumble, of course, so we felt it more than we heard it.

Shaarvan had hired a bubble cruiser for the trip. Its sleek lines spoke of speed and a gentle ride. The metallic surface shone silver in the late morning sun. Streaks of black corton were embossed in the sides, a decoration denoting the cruiser's high price tag. It was a pleasure vehicle meant for a tourist or a wealthy spacer on leave. I smiled to see it. What fun it would be to coast through the lower atmosphere and gaze down on the planet below.

Shaarvan lifted me up into the cruiser. Then, he and the guards followed. I was placed in the back where the windows were most expansive. I was surprised when Shaarvan ordered Kay to sit beside me. My husband glanced back at me, told the guard to check my belt, and then lifted up into the sky.

"We are headed for the city of Cruegan," Shaarvan told me.

I didn't care. I was enthralled by the colors of nature. The trees were such a velvety forest green, and their branches held a splendor of hues and shadowed tones. Up ahead, a mountain loomed — its summit was a sharp peak of brown, rust, and coffee. Smudgy gray boulders, rounded and smoothed, were on one side. The other held twenty shades of green in grass, weeds, bushes, and trees, from autumn golden green and lemon-lime to a green so dark the black fought through.

I laughed out loud with the joy of it. It captivated me with its richness — such an overload of nature. I drank it all in with the thirst of a woman who'd too long gone without. Shaarvan glanced back at me, his eyes amused. "Keep breathing, wife. The trees will be here all day."

For a second, I passed him a smile, but I'd just seen a cloud that drew my eyes. What a puffball! It was a white so bright it hurt my eyes, yet shaded into grays along the sides. It was lusciously plump with moisture. How beautiful it was against the background of sky, a sky so cobalt blue it was like looking at a pristine mountain lake. Above my head, other clouds dotted the sky in swan-white puffs.

The sound of Shaarvan's laughter once more drew my eyes to him. He was handing the controls to Nester and moving back to me. He took Kay's seat, forcing the guard to move up front. Immediately, an arm was circling around my shoulders. One hand turned my face towards him. His lips pressed a kiss on mine. "Your rapture is contagious, my wife. You will have me giggling in delight in another moment."

Shaarvan's eyes held the soft gray of love. If I could have, I would have danced and twirled with the happiness I felt. Instead, I only smiled and hugged him back. It looked like it was going to be a perfect morning.

Shaarvan pointed to the distant right. "See there, Shaara, that mountain peak?"

I nodded, following his finger.

"That is the volcanic mountain of Teynor. Can you make out the black puffs just above it?"

"It's erupting?" I cried out.

"It flares up cyclically, but it is more or less harmless even when it erupts. The lava funnels into the sea, and its energy is harnessed by Watha to produce electricity."

I oohed and aahed as Shaarvan showed me other things. I couldn't believe how good a tour guide he was. He seemed more relaxed and gregarious than he'd been since we left Altar. I reached out and placed my hand in his. His large one gobbled mine up. The smile he gave me made my heart flutter like butterfly wings.

"On the left is the Forest of Thunoor. I shall take you through there, Shaara, on our way back. There are pine trees in that forest older than the volcano." He was silent a moment as if thinking. Then he continued. The long finger of his left hand pointed again. "In that forest lives the only bird on Watha. It does not fly. It is similar to your Terran wild peacock, but the feathers of the Migoot bird are far more valuable." Shaarvan leaned closer and whispered into my ear, "Its feathers are rumored to be tipped with magic. I have heard it said that to suck on the feather's point can give one the ability to read minds."

I whispered back, "Is that how the Shapechanger got their Powers?"

Shaarvan pointed his finger at me as a *sign of caution*, but his eyes were still smiling. Although he didn't answer me, I knew I was not in trouble. I was getting better at reading him.

Still, I nodded and lowered my eyes. I knew talking about Shapechanger in front of commoners was not permitted, but I was always so curious about them, and I rarely got to learn anything about their origins.

As we approached the city, the lights announced it. Miniature blinking white lights encircled every roof and window. It reminded me of Terran Christmases.

Other bubble cruisers were popping in and out of the sky. None of them were close to us, but I could tell that Nester was getting nervous. Shaarvan once more took over the controls. Without a word, Kay returned to sit beside me, his face as reposed and placid as always.

Shaarvan always said that the guards were paid to be obedient to his will, but I wondered if Kay resented having to move twice. My thoughts didn't dwell long on the guard, however. Not only would that have been unwise with my jealous husband so near, but there was too much going on below me. I had a whole city to absorb through my eyes.

The city magnified to full size as we lowered down to the roof of one of the tall buildings. The bubble cruiser, although it looked a lot like a Terran plane, landed like a helicopter — vertically. With Shaarvan at the controls, the touchdown was a bare tap on the roof, and then the motor was shut off. My husband was amazingly proficient at everything he did.

Several large cruisers were parked near us, but there was an abundance of spaces all around. Smaller crafts had their own spots in a section to the right. I wondered if the city charged for parking like they did on Earth, but I saw no one accepting payments.

We exited from the bubble cruiser and passed into an elevator that took us directly downward. Shaarvan stood beside me, of course, his arm draped possessively over my shoulder. Six tall guards surrounded us, blocking my view on all sides. I was disappointed that I was not able to see out the windows as we descended.

I stared instead at the wall in front of me. It was copper, so shiny in its newness that I could see the reflection of my face. It was the first time since I'd been kidnapped from Earth that I'd seen myself. How strange it was to feel so much older yet see the same face as before. Except as I stared, I saw differences. I knew my eyes were grayer. Shaarvan had told me that. Were my cheekbones slightly different, too?

I glanced at the others in the mirror image and stared at my tall, brown-haired captain. The copper didn't show off the golden streaks of sunshine in his hair. In the shimmer, though, Shaarvan looked like a statue I'd once seen of Apollo. Where were his golden steeds and the chariot he would drive across the sky?

The six guards, dark and ugly with their suspicious scowls, were just as tall as Shaarvan but without the look of the Shapechanger. They appeared to me to be underworld gods. Pluto's sons, if he had any.

Shaarvan let out a chuckle. His eyes crinkled with laughter. "It is amazing what goes on in that mind of yours," he said.

The kiss on my brow took away the sting of his knowing my thoughts, but my face heated, and I tried not to think about Roman gods.

When we reached the bottom, the doors of the elevator opened soundlessly. The guards exited first. Their eyes darted about like they expected trouble, but I saw they had not pulled out their pipe weapons. It must not be that dangerous here, or Shaarvan would be carrying one, too. As we walked to the left, we stepped onto the mossy pathway of the city's bazaar. I gasped at the sight, for all about us waged a carnival of color.

Peddlers were walking about with their wares bundled in huge, heavy bags carried draped across their fronts and backs. Jugglers and musicians strolled nearby, hoping to catch the interest of buyers yearning to see entertainment. One man was hitting a tambourine instrument against his leg. When it touched his thigh, it drummed a beat. As he lifted it, a melody whined out the spiral sides. He raised it slowly, high over his head, and then shook it twice in succession. Each time, the music varied in pitch, even when he was pounding it on his sides. I wanted to stand and watch and listen to his song, but Shaarvan pulled me forward.

There were numerous people, most of them dressed in outlandish costumes. Many of the women wore strange and colorful masks over their faces. Some of them wore netted hats like mine. Others had painted their faces with elaborate designs so their features could not be discerned. Everyone was drifting about, smiling and shouting like at a Mardi Gras parade. All about us was laughter and chatter.

I giggled as one couple marched nearer. The woman's dress shone in oranges and yellows but was striped in purple trim. The material flared about her in ruffles, layered to the ground. On her face lay a mask with outrageous purple and orange feathers. Only her eyes showed, dark with thick, black eyeliner, giving her an Egyptian-pharaoh look.

Her husband strutted beside her in a robe of the same fabric. His sleeves flared out in heavy ruffles and bagged at his elbows, then fell abundantly over his long, skinny arms. The man also wore eye makeup, but it was smeared on one side. It made him look like someone had cuffed him.

Shaarvan's hand squeezed mine. I knew he was sharing the thought of my giggle.

We wandered farther into the center of the festivities. A group of citizens was dancing a medieval dance where hands were held high, and people twirled and circled in and out. I stopped to watch, enchanted. "Shaarvan, do you know how to dance?" I asked.

"Of course," he smiled. "Would you like to try?"

"I don't know how," I laughed, but he was already dragging me forward.

"Follow the other women," he ordered, making it sound easy.

Skillfully, Shaarvan wove us into the ongoing dance. Without the music stopping, we joined into the circle. I stumbled several times. I didn't know what came next in the sequence, but no one seemed to care. I watched the ladies next to me, and soon, I was lifting my feet in and out of the pattern, shifting right each time the music changed. The ring opened, and the men danced off. We women formed our own circle, going faster and faster. The men on the outside passed by us, dancing even more rapidly in the opposite direction. A sudden note of discord in the music struck, and everyone stopped.

Shaarvan and the men raised their hands. The women all raised theirs. Shaarvan's hand touched mine. The men backed two steps, went forward two, and then each twirled his partner around. In a moment, we were forming the full circle again, and the whole thing repeated.

Shaarvan was right. The dance was not difficult, but when the note of discord came the second time, I was not paired with Shaarvan. I paused, looking for him. He nodded for me to continue, so I followed my partner's lead and twirled about. I ended up dancing with all the men and laughing with all the women.

The music went on and on, waving the tune into other melodies. The dance seemed to have no ending. New men with their partners entered. Tired ones left. The music continued, only stopping to mark the note of Discord each time the pattern changed. I was out of breath by the time Shaarvan partnered me again. Even so, when he danced me off the floor, I was still laughing, though I was grateful for the break.

"That was really fun," I told him, reaching up to kiss his cheek.

"You like touching other men?"

I gasped and backed away. "Shaarvan!"

"Be easy, Shaara," he laughed. His knuckles stroked my cheek. "I know you are innocent."

The guards still hovered near us. I no longer resented their existence, as I had at first, but it seemed to me that they didn't need to draw so close to us. I would've preferred to savor my husband's lips without their watchful eyes.

Shaarvan had often warned me that women were valued possessions that men fought and died for. I hadn't believed him, not until on Altar, Shaarvan's home world, when our guards had saved us from thugs. While I was thankful for the guards' protection, I could still never ignore their presence as Shaarvan seemed to do.

We soon strolled on, examining the sights and sounds and the myriad booths that were filled with everything imaginable. As we walked by one stall, Shaarvan stopped so abruptly that the guards almost rammed into us. We'd almost passed a cofora, a place where drinks and snacks were sold. In a flash, Shaarvan's little plastic card was inserted into the "taker." Shaarvan bought drinks for each of us.

My husband was not one to offer me a lot of choices. Today, it made sense. I didn't speak Wathan or know much about the native diet, so I wasn't surprised when he handed me a glass of green-hued liquid without asking my preference.

"Shaara," he said as my hand took hold of it. I froze, hearing a distortion in his tone, a warning that I must heed. Had I done something wrong? What had he found to correct me on?

"I have ordered you, Stuchor. You have complained so frequently about not being allowed to try it. This is your chance."

I waited for more. That was it? No directions, no commands, no lecture? I smiled, but I suspected something was up. Shaarvan's manner was too strange. His eyes held a hint of arrogance and sly mischievousness. Was he teasing me? I took a hard whiff. It didn't smell great, but it wasn't an awful odor. Besides, I doubted that I had an option. When a Shapechanger male hands you something to drink or eat, the choice is no longer yours.

I shrugged. No matter what he was up to, at least I'd finally get to try alcohol. Besides, I was proud of the way I'd learned to sample new things during my time with Shaarvan. I'd learned to gulp and swallow foods and beverages that were really bizarre. And I was so thirsty at that point I vowed to myself to drink it all, no matter how bad it tasted.

I poured the amber liquid down my throat like you do on a hot day when you're dying for an ice-cold soda. Glob! Glob! Glob!

Nobody had ever mentioned that alcohol burns going down. Stuchor was like drinking gasoline along with a lighted match. From my throat down through my esophagus, all the way through those roller coaster loop de loops, my insides caught fire.

I started coughing just to get air into my lungs. Something had to put the inferno out! But the air didn't help at all. My eyes went into overtime. Tears started splashing down — not that they landed anywhere near the blaze.

Standing next to me was my six-foot-four tree of a husband. Did he act concerned and pat me on the back or wrap his arm around my shoulder to support me in my time of need?

Of course not! He stood there laughing. The only helpful thing he did was to take back the glass of flame-throwing juice. He handed it to one of the guards and continued chuckling while I struggled to breathe.

Finally, I pulled myself together enough to speak. "Shaarvan, that was cruel!"

"Cruel?" His eyes were mocking me as he stood there drinking the same awful liquid. "I told you many times that Shapechanger females did not like it, but you always argued that *you* would. How like a woman to be unhappy when she gets what she has begged for time after time."

"But you never told me it would hurt!"

"You never asked. You assumed that what a male would like, you would also."

Darn, how I hated lectures! Shaarvan could make a male chauvinist throw up! I stamped my foot, but just mildly for emphasis. "Women on Earth drink alcohol!"

"You are not a Terran."

I sighed. "Shaarvan, I suppose you're trying to tell me that a female Shapechanger *never* drinks?"

"Careful."

I knew my voice had been too demanding the moment the words left my mouth. Early training dies hard.

I started to try again with a softer tone, but Shaarvan was already moving forward. Do you know anything more frustrating than unanswered questions?

Shaarvan once more inserted his plastic and purchased a second drink. The second drink I liked. My frustration slipped away as my thirst was quenched. I ignored the smug look in my husband's eyes. I could only guess why he had chosen to teach me a lesson at that particular moment. Shaarvan's thoughts were not open to me. His reasons for doing such things were almost always kept to himself. But my gulp of alcohol was a lesson I would remember. I would not ask him again to be included when he joined the other males in a drink.

When we were finished with our beverages, we moved on to walk along the avenue of booths. Some had been set up with displays of costly garments from across the galaxy. Others held exotic plants, pets, or artifacts. We examined framed paintings, curious specimens, collections of everything from plant pots to "magic" potions, and examined a group of chittering flibpons that reached out with tentacles of feathers. We walked amid the displays for hours, yet Shaarvan had to drag me away from almost every one of them.

Of course I never asked to buy anything, not even a mirror for which I yearned desperately. I did make sad, pleading eyes over it, but Shaarvan only shook his head and said, "You only need to please me, wife, and you do the way you are. A mirror makes a woman paint her face strangely, attempting to hide what is common knowledge."

I don't know where Shaarvan gets his ideas. How could I possibly use a mirror to apply makeup? My purse, with its lipstick and mascara, had been gone since I was abducted.

I would have loved to have the earrings from Sazor. They were like dew drops on a windowpane, iridescent with color as you turned them. The seller apparently saw the direction of my covetous eyes. He spoke to Shaarvan, saying, "Your lovely wife desires these." He dangled them before my husband. Of course, I didn't dare say a word to the man. My eyes dropped.

"Will you not add sparkle to her eyes by making her a gift of them?" the merchant continued.

Shaarvan laughed. "My wife's eyes always sparkle. She does not need baubles."

The seller said no more. He hung the earrings back up. They twinkled and glowed in the lights of the tiny white Christmas bulbs around the display. I sighed — and walked on.

But a moment later, Shaarvan's arm reached around my shoulder. He pulled me close. "How did that buyer know how lovely you are behind your face covering? Did you unveil your face?"

I stopped abruptly. "Shaarvan, I never touched it." I heard the alarm in my voice, but I couldn't calm it. Shaarvan was so easily angered.

"Easy, my wife. Forgive my teasing. I am well pleased with your conduct today." His hand rose to slide underneath the netting of my hat. "That seller would have called you lovely had you had warts on your face, Shaara. It is a seller's way to compliment."

I let out my breath and smiled again. The sun was glowing a warm orange-yellow. The touch of it on my back and Shaarvan's hand caressing my face made me feel limp and happy.

He laughed. "My sweet, sweet Shaara. Are you hungry?"

His hand had ceased its stroking to bring my eyes up to his. I nodded, but food was not my only interest at that moment. His voice and the touch of his hand had set my body aflame.

Shaarvan chuckled. "Shapechanger woman," he whispered with glowing pride. "We shall find a booth that serves *some* of our needs."

We walked forward, passing five or six more displays. Then Shaarvan pulled me towards a large yellow tent. We ducked under a net and through the opening. Inside, there were tables and chairs, and people were enjoying their meals. At the sight of the chairs, I suddenly realized that with the heavy gravity of the planet and the dancing and walking, I was tired.

"Stay here, Shaara," Shaarvan ordered the moment I collapsed into a chair. He motioned Nester to sit beside me and then directed Kay and Stal over to the side. Shaarvan spoke to them a moment and then left.

I was a bit surprised by that. Shaarvan rarely left my side, but there was so much to study. The marvel of it fled my mind as my eyes feasted. I ignored Nester beside me as I'd been trained and let my eyes take in the diners. There were Turkish-hatted traditionalists from Selters and Friedish traders with bright red Klafish blanket-shirts. Two Theinian slavers sat on my right. They had no women with them, but I recognized their banded heads. Several Wathan families were eating with their laughing children. It was a fascinating gathering. I tried my hardest to observe everyone without appearing to do so.

The Wathan family nearest us intrigued me the most. Two little boys were sitting on the edges of their chairs. They were clutching huge finger sandwiches, almost too big for the small-sized mouths. I wondered how old the boys were. Their father and mother were eating also, but they kept their eyes on the boys. The family's bodies emoted loud feelings of love and scented the air with grape bubblegum. It made me feel guilty remembering how I'd left my little Shaarac. He'd be hungry now. Would Matop know to offer him a bottle when he cried?

Shaarvan had made me take a pill before we left to prevent my milk from flowing. I would have been in pain otherwise. I was grateful he'd thought of that, yet at the sight and smell of the family, my breasts still ached.

The woman, the mother of the boys, drank from her cup. I noticed she'd lifted her veil over the hat so she could dine pleasantly. I was relieved. I'd wondered if I'd be forced to eat by slipping each bite under my net.

A gentleman nearby had ordered pasta. The sharply pleasant aroma of the sauce made my stomach growl. His meal had the unmistakable scent of bishtals, a garlic-like root, which I wasn't fond of eating but loved to smell.

The two Friedish traders suddenly began to argue. That drew my attention away from the man's food. The men's loud voices sounded angry. The trader in the reddish-brown robe and Friedish bright-red shirt bolted up. He slammed his fist down on the table. Plates of food jumped about with the vibration. A cup spilled as the trader's robe knocked it over with his agitated arm gestures. Orange liquid drooled down the side of the table.

The man's voice escalated in pitch and volume. His face reddened with rage. Then, he flipped his plate, food-side to the table, and stamped off. The other trader continued his meal as if nothing had happened. He was eating something flaky. The crumbs dropped on the table and down on his robe.

I was so engrossed in the drama of the two traders that I hadn't heard the approach of the strange man who suddenly stood in front of us.

"Altarian Master, may I sit and speak with you?"

I looked up to see who was addressing Nester. I knew I shouldn't have reacted. I should have kept my eyes down, but it was always difficult to act demure and shy when I wasn't.

The stranger was a Theinian slaver. The two-inch silver band that encircled his head was etched with writing proclaiming his lineage. Of course, I couldn't read Theinian, so his lineage remained a secret from me. As I stared, the man's eyes peered into mine, attempting to examine the face underneath my veil.

Almost in the same instant, Kay stepped up behind the Theinian with a drawn pipe weapon. "She belongs to a Shapechanger," Kay told him. Kay's voice was rough and surly. He sounded meaner than I'd ever heard him. "I would not stand there if I were you," Kay warned. His pipe weapon was sticking the slaver in the ribs, and with his words, I saw him jab the man again.

"My pardon," the Theinian replied, bowing briefly and carefully.

I could read the man a little, thanks to my increasing Shapechanger abilities. What I read surprised me. The slaver was neither frightened by Kay's viciousness nor the knowledge that a Shapechanger owned me. In fact, the Theinian was debating the odds of attempting to wrestle the pipe away from Kay. He would have tried had Nester not suddenly exhibited the one he was holding, the weapon also pointed at the Theinian.

The slaver gave me another quick glance. His eyes considered me.

Why wasn't he surprised by the information Kay had given him? How had he known my husband was Shapechanger? I was wearing a Wathan headscarf, and my eyes, although not truly yet Shapechanger gray, were covered. My dress could also have passed for Wathan clothing. In fact, there was nothing to give the slaver any indication I was other than I seemed.

Although my mind was pondering all these things, my eyes were steadily examining the tablecloth. Yet, I could feel the Theinian's eyes fastened on my face. If two pipes had not been pointed at his middle, I knew he'd have torn off my veil.

I felt Shaarvan's sudden return prior to my sight of him. He was there beside me, focused on the slaver before I had time to become alarmed as the man continued to stare.

I sighed, relieved. Then my eyes swung from Shaarvan back to the man. Why was he so shocked by my husband's arrival? The Theinian's scent had changed. The faintest touch of his almond-scented fear flavored the air. How did the stranger know Shaarvan was my husband? Shaarvan hadn't touched me or spoken.

"A problem?" Shaarvan asked in his commanding voice.

"Only a, a, a slight misunderstanding," the slaver stuttered out. "I was just leaving."

"You were unwise to approach a Shapechanger so closely. My wife is young, but her Power grows," Shaarvan said. "Luck was with you that, I arrived when I did. Leave before she changes to her cat image and rakes you with her claws."

I held my breath to keep from gasping. Shaarvan had said that in front of the guards. And how could he have lied like that? Shapechanger could not speak an untruth.

For some reason, it worked, though. The man waited only for the pipe to be moved from his back before he fled. He retreated very quickly, fleeing through the exit on the left. The tension in the guards eased at once. The smells of fear and the reek of mustard, battle-readiness, lessened.

Nester stood abruptly and gave his seat to Shaarvan. When my husband sat down, I plopped my elbows on the table and stared at him. For some reason, he was looking quite unbothered with what had just occurred. In fact, he was wearing the self-satisfied expression of a cat who'd just gotten away with the goldfish.

He ignored my eyes for a minute, watching the exit through which the Theinian had disappeared. Then he relaxed, waved the guards off to find a table nearby, and the two of us were finally alone — well, alone as much as anyone can be inside a tented restaurant filled with strangers.

"Why did you tell the slaver that about me changing into a cat. . . and. . . Why?"

"It served a purpose."

Shaarvan's eyes were still scanning the tabled groups around us, but there was nothing in his voice or manner that indicated concern. I shook my head. "But Shapechanger do not lie," I said, struggling to understand.

"No. We do not, my wife." Shaarvan's eyes returned to me. They mocked my puzzlement. I could tell that there would be no explanation. Unfortunately, it was Shaarvan's way.

"I thought you went to get food?" I said, changing the subject.

His eyes rippled with suppressed laughter. "Why would I do that?"

"But then why did you leave?" I was in the dark, flailing my arms about, trying to locate a passage I could safely walk. Why did he not offer his hand? Why didn't he explain what had just occurred?

The worst of it was that I knew now the guards had been in on the secret. They'd known Shaarvan's disappearance was a trap. How had they known someone would approach?

I should have suspected something was up. Shaarvan so rarely left me alone. Only on the ship in our room or once in a while on Altar when I'd visited friends in their well-guarded mansion.

There were so many puzzles. I could never hope to sort them out. "Shaarvan, will you tell me what that was about?" *Please,* I flashed using a hand sign.

Shaarvan lifted my right hand. His lips lightly touched my palm. "You have behaved well, wife. I shall explain after I order."

I saw the flashing eyes of the server robot then. It had arrived at our table. It was smaller than the spaceship's robots, tinier even than the cleaners. This one was only about three feet high. Its metal face held no expression as it waited for our requests.

Shaarvan ordered in Wathan. I listened, fascinated as always to hear him speak in different languages. When Shaarvan finished, the robot's eyes turned from green to blue. Its little server arm reached over the table. Its fingers sprayed liquid into the cups it had just set down. Its middle hand disgorged two chunks of ice into each glass. Then the hand withdrew, and it rolled away to another table.

My mouth must have dropped open while watching. I'd never actually been served by a robot. Usually, robots cleaned. How could liquid be stored inside its metal cavity? Wouldn't the robot rust? And the ice cubes . . . how were they kept cold?

Shaarvan chuckled. I pried my eyes away from the robot to glance at him. His gorgeous gray eyes were twinkling. I shut my mouth, picked up my drink, and began to sip.

Shaarvan had ordered me Krilla, a drink similar to sparkling cherry water. It was just right for my thirst.

I looked over to check on the Wathan family, but they had gone. Only the remnants of their meal were left to indicate their former presence.

"Why couldn't I have brought Shaarac?" The words were out before I had a chance to curb their disrespect. Would Shaarvan be offended? I hadn't meant them as criticism.

He put down his cup and reached out for my hand. For a moment, he played with it, massaging the skin and tickling my palm. I waited.

"You are a good mother, Shaara, but even good mothers need time off. Matop took care of a younger brother, born when he was sixteen. He will know what to do to entertain our son. Do not worry."

I would have said more, but the server arrived with our food. The little robot handed out our utensils, the tweezers we always used, and then placed two plates on the table. Shaarvan had ordered *storg*. It was a green noodle with green sauce that tasted pretty much like macaroni and cheese. *Storg* was one of my favorites, and the dancing and window shopping had made me ravenous.

Shaarvan had also ordered us dessert, *crub*, a pear-shaped fruit that was crispy like an apple but strawberry flavored. I smiled at him in appreciation.

Unfortunately, by the time I'd eaten what I wanted of the *storg* and finished every bit of my *crub*, I needed a bathroom. I registered my problem with Shaarvan, and we went off to find one.

Shaarvan

What was the Theinian slaver up to? He'd been following us since the dance. I had slowed our progression through the shops and even stopped to buy a drink for our group. But the man had tailed us in a nefarious manner. I'd let him bide his time, alerting the guards, of course, but otherwise not interfering. It is wisest to keep one's enemies where they are easiest to watch.

Why had his mind shield been impenetrable? I rarely had any difficulty assessing those who walked near me. I made a point of being conscious of the motivations and the emotions of such ilk. Yet his mind was blocked probably by drug or artificial enhancement. I couldn't tell. That, alone, raised the potential for threat. An honest

Theinian, if there were such a thing, would never trouble himself to shadow a Shapechanger. He wouldn't dare.

I had been tempted to stop him several times, but it was not wise to engage a citizen in battle openly. The Shapechanger are cautious of attracting such attention. Yet I itched to sharpen my claws on the man. The smell of him was wrong.

It angered me to see my suspicions proven correct. It was Shaara he was after, Shaara, he wished to see. But why? What would a Theinian want with a Shapechanger's wife? She could not be sold. Not anymore, now that she had born a child. But, of course, he might not have known that. Yet, why had he dared? He must have realized he could have forfeited his life, even approaching the property of a Shapechanger. It puzzled me. Something didn't mesh.

I warned him away most suitably, attempting to plant fear into him. But somehow, he knew that Shaara had not yet Shapechanged. Commoners did not have that insight. They assumed that all those connected with the Shapechanger were capable of horrific violence. It was a strange occurrence that gnawed me, but I could not allow Shaara to fret. She deserved her happy day.

Shaara

One thing I'd noticed about interstellar travel was that there were always more than adequate bathrooms. Women didn't have to wait in those long, long lines on Earth while men dashed in and out.

League planets had unisex bathrooms. Since a woman was never allowed to be alone in public, a man always had to accompany her, even inside a necessary. So all bathrooms were luxurious, with large waiting rooms for the husband. They were always clean, too. Robot cleaners kept them that way, and sterilizers at the door ensured hygienic exits. Everyone, therefore, had spotless bodies, clean fingernails, and sweet-smelling breath. What an improvement over Earth!

When we had finished, and while we waited for the guards to have their turn in the necessary room, Shaarvan sat me down on a bench and explained about the slaver.

"All right, Shaara," my husband began. "The slaver was following us since the booth where you admired those earrings."

"How did you know? I mean, about the man."

"I felt him, of course. I was surprised that you did not. You have been getting much more receptive since Shaarac's birth. I think you were too preoccupied with the newness of the city to notice."

"That's why we stopped to eat?"

"No, but that is why I left you with the guards. I knew the slaver would not dare to make an approach while I was present."

"I don't understand; what did he want?"

"You."

"Shaarvan, that's not funny."

Shaarvan picked up my hand and squeezed it. "A slaver buys, steals, or kills. He would have done any of those for you."

"But there are women everywhere. Why me?"

"I do not know the answer to that, Shaara. I had difficulty reading the Theinian, which is strange. But, for some reason, he had chosen you."

"Could we go back to the ship now, please?"

Shaarvan reached under my face net to rub his knuckles against my cheek. I knew he meant to reassure me, but the slave trader's eyes had not been kind. He had frightened me.

"No, do not fear him, Shaara." Shaarvan's eyes burned into mine. "Nester, Kay, and Stal would have protected you with their lives, and I would kill any man who touched you. And know this, my wife, what I told the slaver is no lie. Inside, you have the Power to kill. You are Shapechanger now. You have no need to fear a commoner."

The guards had returned, and Shaarvan said no more. As we left that area and returned to the main, I thought about my husband's words.

I think I understood what he meant. He was trying to tell me that I could change into a beast and kill with my hunter instincts. I had done that in my dreams. Together, we'd often prowled the soft, padded forests. We'd killed together and feasted. We'd drunk the blood of our kill. But that was only in dreams. I could never *really* do that.

"You could, Shaara," Shaarvan said, turning me to face him. Shaarvan's hand cupped my chin. "You are Shapechanger, my wife. When you wish to Change, you will."

He raised my chin. His eyes flared green. I felt his mind in mine. He was imprinting on me the knowledge of his words. For a moment, I felt the stab of its placement in my brain. Then, he retreated.

Shapechanger magic terrified me. I tried not to shake as his lips joined with mine, but I knew that not even my fear was an excuse to refuse him.

Shaarvan had trained me to submit, and I did. The lips burned with their own fire, but from the moment they joined mine, my fear, like cinders floating upward into the circling drafts of heated air, rose skyward and disappeared into the warm sunshine.

Desire flamed from where the fear had fled. One quick tongue thrust reestablished Shaarvan's dominion and then came a cooling down of sweet, gentle kisses, a teasing touch, and a caress of lips on cheek and throat. My mind analyzed, but I could not fight the Power.

I knew the hand that gentled, calmed, stroked, and relaxed me was the easing touch of Shapechanger ownership. But it held me spellbound.

Shaarvan had once told me I'd been branded with a label under my skin. With the right tool, the label could be read to state my owner, his home planet, and city. I'd been angry and rebellious about wearing a dog tag, proclaiming me a thing that could be owned. Shaarvan had laughed at my protests, telling me he didn't have any inclination to view me as a thing, but he'd restated that I was definitely well and truly owned. I'd ranted, fought him, struggled, and cried, but I had learned. A Shapechanger did own his wife — body, mind, and soul. Shaarvan hadn't wanted me to fear his touch, so he'd removed my fear. To be so Powerless was a humbling feeling. It had made me hate Shaarvan once.

When Shaarvan released me, we continued our tour of the city's fair — but only one booth drew me. It was a tent filled with play toys for children.

"Please, Shaarvan, please, may we go in?" I begged.

"Briefly."

I knew he was already thinking about returning, and I was ready but toys? I had to see what toys were available for children Shaarac's age.

There were push toys for toddlers, rubber balls, toy robots in all shapes and sizes, coloring mixes, supplies for assembling a variety of ingenious marvels, fantasy games that used holograms, and a whole section of toys for babies.

"Shaarvan, surely you won't refuse a toy for Shaarac? Please?"

"Shaarac has a mother and father for stimulation. Our arms hold him and rock him to sleep. Our fingers and faces draw his interest. He has no need for the junk they sell."

"Shaarvan, arms, fingers, and faces aren't toys. A toy is something that entertains without interference. Shaarac needs to learn to play independently."

"When he is older, there will be the twigs and pebbles in the garden. The garden also has a strong tree for climbing. He would lack for nothing if we never left the ship."

"Are you telling me that you never had a toy?"

"I had many. I had trees and sticks "

I couldn't help stamping my foot. There is a level of frustration we all reach when something has to let out the steam.

It was the end of any discussion. Without a word, Shaarvan's hand grasped the back of my neck in his infamous neck grip. He usually did that when I was in a lot of trouble, and it was excruciatingly painful if I tried to struggle.

Shaarvan wasn't angry this time, just giving a gentle warning. There was no pain in his touch, but I shut my mouth and walked out of the store without another word. About three booths down, the neck grip was off, and I breathed such a loud sigh of relief that Shaarvan stopped to look at me. Immediately, my eyes lowered to the ground. *No challenge* that meant.

Once again, we started forward, retracing our steps back to the ship. We passed the dealer with the dewdrop earrings. He hadn't sold them yet. I gazed longingly, but I was careful not to sigh.

Shaarvan stopped anyway and turned to me. "Shaara, study the earrings and remember them."

I couldn't gaze at them then. I stared at Shaarvan, wondering why he was being so cruel.

"You do not understand, Shaara. You think putting those earrings on your ears would add to your beauty. How could they? Your body and your face are already perfect. That is why I tell you to commit them to your memory. It is the sight of the earrings you enjoy. To own them would make them dull in familiarity, but in your recollection, they can shine forever."

I was speechless. Shaarvan must be part Irish the way the blarney rolled off his tongue.

He smiled at me and gathered my two hands in his giant ones. "Someday, the smooth skin on your hands will be lined with veins and wrinkles, and your face will sag and show fine, little pieces of life around your eyes. I shall still think you are perfect, my wife. But then, I shall buy you baubles to flash and shine so you do not focus on the lines you feel or the gray hairs you may find."

Shaarvan lifted my hands and kissed each one. "It will be a very long time before that happens, Shaara, but even then, you will never need a single shiny stone to make my eyes glow."

What do you say after that? I moved forward when Shaarvan did, but I was in a daze. I saw nothing the rest of the way back to the bubble cruiser. The earrings had already faded in importance. It was my husband's words that were the memory I would keep.

Shaarvan flew us through the forest of Thunoor, as he'd promised. There was a magical quality in the place where he set the bubble cruiser down. The trees breathed in sighs, whispering sweet secrets in the language of the pines. I was lost in it, hungry for their communion.

We walked around a bit, breathing in the smell of pine needles and the fragrance of decaying bark. The softness of the tree-shaded ground felt exactly like the forest paths of our home on the Altar. And even though the needles pricked through the material on the sides of my slippers, I wanted to run through its padded trails.

Shaarvan drew me close and spoke in my ear, "Shapechange with me, Shaara. I shall send the guards back into the ship, and together, we can journey deep into the forest. We shall sample the breeze and feel the joy of the hunt. We shall pleasure ourselves in a quiet and private glen." His eyes were urging me and the trees were crying out, "Come to us, join with us, run into our innermost parts."

I wanted to. I could almost see myself running through the forest, Shaarvan at my side. But I could not. It was fantasy, a dream only. I could not Shapechange. What Shaarvan asked was impossible.

"I can't," I whispered. Slow moving tears crept down the sides of my eyes. My desolation was beyond disappointment.

"Try, Shaara," Shaarvan urged.

"Yes," the trees urged.

"I'm not like you, Shaarvan. You can do anything!"

"My blood is yours. You are Shapechanger. Change, Shaara, Change."

I wanted to please him. I wanted to run through the forest on four paws, feeling the taste of the air on my tongue, knowing the freedom, but I could not. My body was Terran. It could not do the things a Shapechanger could do.

I collapsed onto the soft padding of the pine needles. They scratched and pricked, but it was familiar. My hand reached down and bundled a fistful. The smell was of Earth, of Altar — of home.

Shaarvan knelt beside me. "Shaara, it is all right. You are not ready yet. I should not have urged you so intently." He reached out and took my hands, attempting to raise me up, but I heard the disappointment and the loneliness in his voice. I sobbed from his frustration and from mine.

"Shaara, easy. It is all right." His arms gathered me up, but I had lost control.

"No, please, just a while longer," I pleaded, weeping with such wretchedness that Shaarvan broke off a pine branch and placed it in my hand.

"Shaara, feel this."

I opened my eyes and wiped them to better see the little branch. It was only about a foot long, but the needles on it were green, and the smell was of the forest.

I closed my fingers around it and breathed in its scent. I shut my eyes and wished again that I were able to do what Shaarvan desired.

"You may take it with you, my wife."

I opened my eyes to stare at him. "But you never let me keep anything. You told me that a Shapechanger does not own things."

"Ah, Shaara, it is a toy." His hand lifted to dry another tear. "It is a toy for Shaarac and for Shaarac's mother."

So, with my tiny branch of forest clutched in my fist like the most precious of all jewels, we flew north to the ship. I was worn out from the day, yet I needed to process what had happened. Shaarvan never allowed tears. He grew angry when I cried without reason. Why had he disregarded them and then rewarded me with my first souvenir?

And why had I cried? It wasn't like me. Why did a forest have such a magnetic pull on me? It wasn't like my home on Earth. I'd lived in Santa Barbara with my parents and then, later, after they died, in Los Angeles. Neither place was a forest. They were beach, city, and desert.

Obviously, Shaarvan understood more about it than I did.

Shaarvan

I pressed Shaara too hard with my desire for her Change. I must back away. Yet, she feels ready. Her Power is mature enough. It is only that she does not believe she can. Father says that it is rare for adapted Terrans to alter their shape. His wife, my mother, has never completed the transformation, and she is strong.

Yet, Shaara walks the Paths with me at night. She has gone further than Teea. And Shaara has been taken in the Old Way. The Saberey cat has given strength to her.

I shall give her time. But it is hard not to be impatient. My body craves the full acceptance rite.

Shaara

The bubble cruiser returned us swiftly. Shaarvan parked near the ship, and we had only to walk up the ramp. Shaarac's wails were the first thing to assault us on our return. He was in full strident yell. I started to go to him but realized I must let Shaarvan approach the man.

"Why does he cry?" Shaarvan demanded angrily of Matop.

"I do not know, my lord. Shaarac was good all day. Then, when the bubblecruiser arrived, the young lord began to scream, and no bouncing or soothing quieted him."

"I see." Shaarvan reached for his son. Abruptly, the wails stopped. The little hand fastened into his mouth, and blue-gray eyes stared into his father's face.

I wasn't surprised. Shaarac had always been like that, even before his birth. When he'd kicked restlessly inside me, Shaarvan's hand on my stomach or the quiet tone of his father's voice had stilled our unborn child.

My husband turned to hand me my son. It felt so good to hold Shaarac once again. I planted kisses all around his head, but it was not kisses that Shaarac wanted. I looked up to see if I had permission.

Shaarvan nodded, and I went to the fuzzy dog chair. I was unsure if my son's suckling would bring down the milk. The pill was supposed to hold me for a full day, but I knew that Shaarac would not be content until he'd tried.

Altarian nursing dresses were cleverly designed. A meal was just a fold away. Shaarac's insistent mouth soon brought the milk forth. I felt Shaarvan's eyes and looked up to meet his smile. Gruffly, he turned away and became captain of his ship.

Shaarac was not as hungry as he'd pretended. He lost interest almost at once. I moved him to the other breast, and he suckled a moment, but he had not really been hungry. His eyes were studying me.

I started to move him away from my breast, but he fretted crossly. I let him stay. Once more, his mouth suckled, but he was done. His mouth blew bubbles in the milk, dribbling out. I burped him and lay him across my lap. Then, I showed him the forest branch. He gurgled happily. His tiny hand stretched out to hold it. The hand opened and closed several times as if Shaarac could not quite believe the feel of the branch. He wanted desperately to pull it towards his mouth, but I would not allow it.

He protested loudly. I looked up to see Shaarvan frowning at us. I shifted Shaarac, hoping he would forget the branch, but he was turning fussy.

"Give him to me," came his father's sharp order.

I did so, but for once, Shaarac was irritable even in Shaarvan's arms.

"Hand me the branch."

"He wants to put it in his mouth, Shaarvan. I took it away."

Shaarvan's hand reached out. The command was still in force. I handed over the branch.

"He must taste it, Shaara. It is his nature. It will do him no harm. Thenos 'cut his teeth' on forest branches."

I watched Shaarac draw the branch to his mouth. The soft, green needles surprised him. He didn't like the way they struck his lips. He examined the branch once more. Again, he brought it towards his mouth.

I held my breath, full of a mother's list of things that could happen — like germs and poking himself in the eyes. I wanted to pull Shaarac to the safety of my arms and feel his soft, warm body cuddled against me, but I was still.

Shaarac's mouth once more rejected the branch, and his tongue poked out as if he didn't like the taste of it. He popped his tongue against the roof of his mouth and was scared by the sound. For a moment, he sucked away on a finger. Then he reached out and touched Shaarvan. His tiny fingernails scratched at his father's shirt. He liked the sound of that. His tiny mouth cracked open into a toothless grin.

"Do not prevent him from tasting the new and strange, Shaara. Shapechanger must do so." He handed Shaarac back to me, but his arm pulled me close. "All Shapechangers are extremely tactile."

Shaarvan's hand caressed my cheek. One finger moved to stroke my lips. It pushed into my mouth and stroked my tongue. Shaarvan had never done that before. I didn't like it, but I felt the flush of wanting him.

"I, too, have waited too long," he told me, with that certain look in his eyes that sent a charge through me. "I had planned to wait for Kada to return, but I think there are better things to do. Come."

I wondered what we would do with Shaarac. Our son's eyes did not look the slightest bit sleepy. Through the maze of the ship's long halls and turns, Shaarac was bright-eyed and curious.

When we returned to the chamber, I pointed out the situation. Shaarvan smiled and took Shaarac from me. He rocked our son high up into the air and then low, almost to the ground and between his legs, and then swung him once again up into the air.

Shaarac did not cry out, but he seemed uncertain as to whether this was a fun activity. His little fingers flew to his mouth. He sucked and thought about it. Shaarvan continued until Shaarac's tiny mouth grew round with laughter. Once released, the laughter grew and grew.

Then, Shaarvan rocked Shaarac gently, close to his body, and my husband began to sing to him. It took four verses of the *Shapechanger's Lore of the Galaxy* before Shaarac closed his eyes and slept.

"Sing to me," I laughed when Shaarvan joined me in the bed.

Shaarvan's eyes were smiling as he strode towards me. "I shall sing to you, my wife; I shall sing with my body."

Shapechanger are the lovers of the Universe. With the touch of his tiniest finger, Shaarvan could make me soar through the winds of fire. With his lips and his tongue, he could nova all my stars.

This time, my husband was not content to make love, even with the skill and finesse of a Shapechanger. This time, he was not satisfied until he drove me wild. His tongue seared my skin with rivulets of desire.

"Shaarvan," I panted in desperation. "Why are you tormenting me? Please take me. I need you."

Suddenly, the tongue stilled, and gray eyes peered down at me. "Remember the dance? A score of men touched your hand. I must burn their memory from your mind."

I tried to sit up, but his body pressed me down. "You gave me permission. I would not have danced with them if you had not."

Shaarvan did not speak again, and I could not. When I could once more breathe, I said, "I will never dance with anyone else again."

Shaarvan chuckled. "You will, my wife, because I like to watch you dance. Your eyes light up, and you toss your head. Your thick curls of hair frizz into ringlets around the heat of your face. Your laughter complements the music with a melodious counterpoint. You will dance, Shaara, whenever there is dancing, but the memories you have after will be of me, and your dreams in the night will be of my hands, my tongue, my lips, and my possession."

I lay there, remembering the words of Teea, his mother. She had warned me that Shapechanger had a stronger sex drive than Terran men. She wasn't kidding! If Shaarvan told me he had any more burning of memories to do, he'd be making love to a corpse.

Shaarvan began to laugh. I rose up to look at him. "What's so funny?"

"You would never be a docile corpse, my wife. Even if you were dead, you would be asking questions."

"You're not supposed to read minds. I've heard you tell people you can't." I sat up in irritation and glared.

"Shaara, I have told you before. Sometimes you project images so clearly I cannot help knowing what is on your mind."

His hand circled behind my neck to urge me down to him. "Like now, when you are wishing you could kiss me. It is just little wisps of thoughts you send out that I catch."

I tried to pull back. Gray eyes were staring into mine. I knew he was urging me to try it. I leaned forward and met his lips. No arms circled me, but his lips and eyes were definitely willing. He let me kiss him. For the first time, I slipped my tongue into his mouth.

Afterward, he smiled at me, not in mockery but playfully. His smile reminded me of the time we'd walked in the forest, and he'd pretended to engage a dragon in a swordfight. He'd fought bravely with a branch and cavorted about just to please me.

My hand stroked his face wonderingly. The strong, hard jaw and the feel of his bones above his cheeks amazed me. "You are all bone and muscle, and there is such firmness, even in the angles of your face. It is strange how different your body is from mine."

The amusement was back in Shaarvan's eyes. "Who taught you to analyze everything?"

"My father."

"Tell me about him."

"My father was wonderful. He was a high school chemistry and physics teacher, and he knew absolutely everything."

"And your mother? How did you feel about her?"

"I loved her, of course, but she was the one who always made me deal with reality. It was my father who made up all the science fiction stories and taught me about nature and the world. Mom only taught me the practical stuff."

"So your mother stayed at home with you?"

"No, she was a kindergarten teacher."

Shaarvan shook his head as if something had just clicked in his mind. "When they died, whom did you live with?"

"My grandmother."

"She was not a teacher, too, was she?"

"No, she never worked. Grandpa worked. He was a small town lawyer. But he had a heart attack and then died. Poor grandma had no one, so she came to live with us. When she passed on, I had no one at all."

"Why did your parents choose to have only one child?"

"Mom couldn't have anymore. Grandma told me that once."

Shaarvan's eyes grew thoughtful. I wished I could read his mind.

"Why don't Shapechanger men love?" My question came out of nowhere, unrelated to our conversation — except that thinking of my folks always reminded me of how much they had loved each other.

"Because the word has no meaning. What do you think your word 'love' signifies?"

"It means you care about a person, and you're emotionally involved, and you want to be with him or her forever and ever."

"By your definition, Shapechanger men do love their wives."

"Then why don't they say it?"

"Because love also means — if you love me, you will do this, or buy this, or allow me to do…"

"That's not love, Shaarvan."

"A Shapechanger male is bonded forever. He will give his life for his wife. He will nurture, provide, and meet all of her needs. Is that not enough, Shaara?"

"Not unless he tells her he cares. I don't mean you, Shaarvan. You are generous with your words. I feel your love, even if you won't call it that, but someone like your brother, Pathe — he never tells Goria that he cares, and that's their problem."

Shaarvan sighed and shook his head at me. "You waste my time discussing 'love' when it concerns Goria and Pathe. I should turn you over my knee for that."

He couldn't. There wasn't time. Shaarac started fussing himself awake. I laughed and smiled cockily. Then, I walked over to Shaarac. I checked to see that his potty pants were functioning properly and carried him back to his father's arms.

Shaarac was positive that he was hungry. He did not fuss over being handed to his father, but when I lay down beside Shaarvan, our little one let out a sharp cry of unhappiness. Shaarvan laughed, startling his son quiet. Then he handed our son to me. At once, Shaarac found my breast and began to nurse. The slurping sounds of his contentment made Shaarvan, and me exchange a smile.

I settled back on Shaarvan's arm and continued my questions. "When does a Shapechanger first change shape? I mean, at what age?"

"At puberty, around eleven or twelve."

"Is that when you did it first?"

"At ten."

"Puberty at ten?"

"I did not take my first woman until eleven when my father bought one for me."

"Your father *bought* you a woman?"

"As I will do for Shaarac when he is ready."

"Not at age eleven!"

"I know you are not prepared, but I must caution you, Shaara. You will not be allowed to interfere with my raising of Shaarac."

"I thought I was raising Shaarac."

"A wife may be the principal caregiver in the nurturing years, as long as she does an adequate job."

"Shaarvan, you would never take Shaarac from me just because I made a mistake or I didn't know your protocol?"

"I predict no problems, my wife. You are a good mother. I shall allow you to foster Shaarac on Terran tales and songs — as long as he learns Altarian and Shapechanger ones as well. When he is five, I will allow you and my mother to teach him English, French, and Spanish

— if you still remember them by then. They are obscure languages, but they will prepare his brain connectors for more useful ones. I shall instruct Shaarac in the useful language of trade, as well as with his other training. All the males in our family will take part in his instruction."

"There are no schools?"

"No. The school is the family. Testing and instruction for all grades of piloting, professional status, and higher learning, such as medicine, is done on several planets near Altar, but most of the preparation Shaarac and our future sons will need will be obtained by the family."

Talks like the one we had that day were not frequent. Sometimes, Shaarvan could be so nice, but on other days, he was shorter in temper than Shaarac.

We dined in the cafeteria later. Several crewmen entered and left. Shaarvan asked each of them if Kada had returned. He had not. We spent half the night in the control room, with Shaarvan pacing. I knew Shaarvan was angry because he hadn't put a watcher on Kada. I also wondered why the man had not returned. Did he not realize that a Shapechanger would kill him if he failed to report back?

It was late when we finally retired, and Shaarvan was up early the next morning, dressing for Watha.

"You are going to look for Kada? Please, may I go with you?"

Shaarvan looked at me. I saw that he would say "no."

"Shaarvan, I promise not to cause any problems. I won't talk if you say not to talk. I won't ask for anything. I won't do anything you don't want me to do. Please let me go."

I knew when he smiled and shook his head slowly, like he didn't quite believe my promises but that he'd permit it. I jumped up and threw my arms around him.

"You will keep *all* your promises?"

I nodded my head.

"Wake up Shaarac and feed him. I will program you for Watha clothes this time. No complaints about the color, the style, or the veil."

"I promise."

Shaarac was handed over to another of the crewmen. I felt like a neglectful mother. For a moment, I almost didn't go.

Had I stayed, would the history of Altar have changed? Would Thenos not have become the villain of our tale? Would I not have become...?

Chapter Two

Shaarvan

I remember almost nothing of what occurred. Her laughing eyes, the way her small hand rested in mine, the delicious excitement in her mind — they were the flavor of my last thoughts.

The crew took me to Westla, the center world of the Shapechanger. They did it to save my life, yet I would have refused to leave Watha had I been conscious. The Theinian stole my Shaara. I am sure it was him. I had thought I protected her. I had doubled the guards, but the thieves were prepared for us in ways I had never imagined.

The moment we exited the ship that day, they attacked. When we reached the dirtside, and the ramp shot up behind us, our assailants struck us down. Gases stunned us. Shaara fell without a word, and I turned to help her. And then, I knew nothing more. While I was out cold, the bandits injected me with poison, and I was left to die.

All our outbound cameras had been disabled. It was not until the guards awoke that the deed was discovered. My guards took me back to the ship. They said that I was barely breathing, and a fever raged within my brain. In fear for my life, they flew the disabled ship to Westla. They risked their lives to save mine, and I should have been grateful, but when I regained consciousness, I could only curse them for leaving Watha, for abandoning my Shaara to those thugs.

My poor little wife — where is she now? What have the ones who took her done with her? Is she hurt? Have they beaten her? Is she dead? My cherished one, my soul mate, my wife. A part of me has been ripped away.

I shall find you, Shaara, I promise, and I shall never allow you to be endangered again. Be safe, my little love. Wait for me. I shall find you if it takes a lifetime.

But where do I look? Already, the Shapechanger have searched Watha and could not find her. She has a *flaorth* under her skin, of course, as all women do. That unit should have made her traceable, but the lords believe it was removed. If that is true, how can we ever locate her?

But I shall. I shall look in every tent that sells girls, in every trader's line, in every ship that passes with cargo, and I shall search in every Wathan home. I shall find my Shaara. I must have confidence that I shall because losing faith would kill me faster than the poison that almost did.

Slettha

I don't remember how I came to be in a slave trader's possession. When I woke, I found that I was tied to the pole of a tent — sagging against it — the weight of my body supported by my wrists. The gloves on both of my hands were fastened together somehow. I could not wiggle them off, and a silver chain connected them and formed the manacle that secured me to the post.

For a while, I was occupied with changing my position. The cramps in my legs held most of my concentration. I was quickly able to figure out that I could lie down with my hands over my head, or I could curl around the pole beside the handcuffs if I held my hands upright. Later, I figured out how to sit up if my legs circled the pole and my hands were in my lap.

I think my mind was still numb to the reality of my situation. I was in shock. I didn't even notice that I was naked underneath my dress. It was only after I had finally maneuvered my body into a sitting position, and my poor bottom discovered that the sandy floor contained small pebbles, that I looked down and discovered the absence of panties. Even then, it didn't bother me as much as it should have. I was only somewhat astonished.

I did not have long to ponder it. The slaver soon entered. He was a tall, thin, middle-aged man. His face was bristled with small black hairs. His chest was bare, but he wore a metal band around his upper arm and a silver strip of metal around his head, full of scratches etched in black.

I cried out when I saw him and begged him to free me, but he pointed a long black stick at me and soon demonstrated its use. All too quickly, I learned about the pain stick. When it touched me anywhere, ripples of agony stormed through my body. Soon, I did not plead for my release. Nor did I argue. Obedience comes rapidly when pain is the teacher.

My second lesson was in oral responses. When my master demanded answers from me, I found that I could not give them to him, no matter how painful it became. I could not remember anything: not my origin, my history, not even my name.

"Good," the slaver said when I told him I did not know. Then, he gave me the answers he wanted me to have. "You are a slave," he said. "Your name is Slettha. You are Altarian. Your master is dead. Another trader sold you to me. Understand?"

With the pain stick in the man's hand, raised to touch, I understood perfectly. I nodded, but I continued searching for memories to match his words. They were not there. There was only a black, solid wall in my mind, darker than the space between stars.

The slaver's eyes were squinty and full of coldness. His eyes were green — a dirty, dull green. I sought a hint of mercy or understanding in them, but there was only an unfeeling indifference.

"Please, will you unchain me? I will not run away," I told him.

My words brought a sneer to his lips. "Don't snivel, woman devil."

He pointed the pain stick at my thigh and ordered me to repeat the story he had told me.

"I am Slettha, an Altarian slave. My master is dead. I was sold to you by another trader." I blurted out the words quickly to avoid another poke.

"Good. Stand up, woman."

I pulled my gloved hands upward on the pole and stood. I attempted to hide my fear. For some reason, I thought that was important. Why? There was no answer in my brain. Why were my memories gone? Why hadn't I even remembered my name?

The slaver inserted a key into the glove lock. His hands touched my body, but they were inhumanly impersonal. The gloves retracted, and I was free.

I had been bunching up the muscles in my legs. I was ready when the slaver dropped my hands. I bolted to the right, but the pain stick was there. It hit my arms and then my legs. I ran to the left and then backward, away from him. The pain stick was always there. I could not get around it. I stopped, panting from the exertion.

"You will learn to do as you are told," the man said. His eyes made me shiver.

I watched the man's Adam's apple bob each time he swallowed. I thought how sweet the revenge if I could only grab the pain stick and touch him there.

"Strip."

"What?" I shrieked and backed away. Once more, the pain stick prodded me. This time, the slaver hit me in the stomach. I dropped to my knees from the pain of it.

"Get up and strip."

I stood up, but I was thinking about another place I'd like to place the pain stick.

I raised my dress above my head. It surprised me that I wore no bra. Hadn't I always worn one? I tried to picture it, but the memory blurred.

One glance at the slaver's narrowed eyes, and I pulled the dress the rest of the way off. Then, when he indicated it, I bent down and removed my shoes and stockings.

"You will toss those things into the fire," he ordered, motioning me to go through the doorway of the tent.

I did not want to go outside without clothes on. I knew that was wrong to do, but another look at the hard face of the slaver convinced me that I had no choice. I stepped through the opening and out into the sun. The area was empty of people. I was glad to see no leering eyes to view my nakedness, but there was also no one to beg for help.

As I moved towards the fire, I glanced about. I was in a desert clearing, with nothing around but sand and short, spiny trees. The sun blazed down on my skin. I knew I would burn if I remained outside long.

I tossed my dress into the flames and watched the material turn liquid before it reddened and was gone. The fragments changed to cinders and rose up into the warm air above the fire.

"Come here," the slaver ordered.

He was bending over a trunk filled with clothes. I looked around, thinking about running, but where would I go? It was a desolate, uninhabited region, and I was naked.

I walked towards the trunk and the slaver and watched as he pulled out a garment and shook it. It was a short top with puffs of sleeves. The material was a golden yellow.

"Put this on," he ordered.

I took it from him and slipped the blouse over my head. The material was thin. My breasts were clearly visible through the fabric. It was too small for me, and the edges cut at my skin. I didn't have a lot of plumpness there, but bulges at the top and bottom, where the material cut into me, emphasized what I had.

"Good," said the slaver. "Now this."

I looked to see what he was holding. It was a pair of pajama-like pants in a pink silky material. I pulled them on. The pants, like the blouse, were far too small for me. I could only pull them as high as my hips. The legs stopped at mid-calf.

"Perfect!" the man said.

I didn't know what they were perfect for. It was obvious to me that they didn't fit.

The man reached towards me and took my hand. Then, he led me toward a smaller chest. He let go of my hand to open it. I stared into it. It was filled with golden chains and jewelry that flashed in the sunshine.

"Oh!" I gasped. The slaver ignored me.

He pulled out one of the many golden chains and secured it around my waist. Where it latched in the middle, he placed a shiny disk of metal. It had glue on the back, and he pressed the disk into my belly button.

"That comes back to me when you are sold," the man ordered sharply.

I wondered if I should care.

The top of the slaver's head was going bald. A small round patch had only a few strands of brownish hair across it. I hoped the sun would burn it crimson.

"Put your right foot here," the slaver ordered.

He placed a similar disk on my middle toe. Next, a chain fastened around my hair, and a disk dipped down to be glued to my forehead.

"Yes, I like that," he said.

Then he reached over and slipped my top up. I jerked backward.

"Shall I get the pain stick?" he demanded angrily.

"No, please," I begged.

"Then stand still, woman."

He was muttering in a language I didn't speak. I listened hard, but no words seemed familiar.

The man turned away to look for something. When he found it, he seemed excited. He returned to me and jerked me close. Then, he began to rub some kind of salve on my nipples.

I wanted to pull away, to run and hide, to go back to sleep and never wake up. This couldn't be my life. It was too horrible.

The stuff in the pot made my nipples burn for a minute, and then they turned deep, dark red. The slaver nodded, "Yes. That should do it."

He jerked my shirt back down and studied the result. "You should sell quickly, little Slettha. Smile at the rich ones, no matter how big their paunch is. The fatter ones are easier to please."

I didn't think I was required to speak. I listened, trying to comprehend what the slaver was talking about. He didn't give me time to think about it. He yanked me about and then began pulling at my hair, teasing it, curling it, puffing it out.

"Turn around," he ordered.

I obeyed, spinning slowly as his finger indicated. I kept watching the slaver as I turned, wondering if I'd done this before.

Again, the man took my hand. He walked me over to the table and ordered me to sit. I was given a drink. He plopped food on my plate and then handed me a wooden spoon.

"I have to go pee," I said, embarrassed by my need.

"Over there," he told me gruffly.

His skinny finger pointed towards a boulder. I walked to the place he'd indicated. The sun overhead beat down on me. The intensity of it was already making me feel flushed, but I crouched down by the boulder and left out my water.

The slaver's eyes never looked away, and the pain stick was once more in his hands. I returned and sat down. He relaxed then and placed the stick beside him on the bench.

The wooden spoon felt awkward in my hand. I knew I'd used one before, but I also had a vague memory of another utensil and eating in a different manner. When I tried to call up the memory, there was only blackness. It seemed that life had started with the slaver. There was no last Pass, no Tide before.

"Why do I not remember my master?" I asked.

"You grieved so at your master's death you asked to be mindwiped."

"I loved him?"

"It doesn't matter. He's dead. Now shut up. Girls only speak when spoken to."

"Why?" The question was out before I thought.

The back of his hand across my face was his answer.

The slaver didn't let me finish eating before he grabbed my hand and led me to his bubblecruiser. It was old and scratched. The motor burped and coughed, but it flew. We were up in the air over desolate land for hours. I did not speak, and the slaver was silent. The motor groaned on and on.

Then, the land below us grew greener. The bubblecar began to grumble and shake like an old man, and I saw that we were descending. The slaver wasn't much of a pilot. His landing felt more like a crash than a touchdown, but surprisingly, we made it.

We climbed out of the bubble car, and the slaver led me to the only building in sight. It was a long olive-brown tent, as drab on the outside as the site where the slaver had dressed me. The man lifted up a flap on the side and jerked me inside.

It was cool under the tent and elegant, with the trappings of wealth. Exquisite carpets lined the floor in hues and patterns so vivid I wanted to stop and stare. There were men everywhere in all kinds of costumes. Some of them towed girls in colored outfits similar to mine. One man led a whole line of girls. The women's hands had the same gloves I'd worn before, and they were chained to a long pole carried by two men with muscles the size of rounded stones. My slaver and I soon joined the rows of people waiting.

My slaver turned to me and began to whisper in my ear. His mouth spit as he spoke, and I wanted to wipe my ear, but I didn't dare until he was finished.

"This is the line for the ramp," he told me. "When we reach the top, the buyers will look at you. Sell yourself well, girl, or you will feel the full intensity of the pain stick."

There were girls all about me. Some were crying. One wailed as her master beat her. Others were limp, passive slaves waiting for the next torture that life would inflict. Only a couple of the girls primped and readied themselves for their display. I wondered which of the approaches should be mine. Without my memories, I had no idea what kind of person I was.

The minutes dragged into longer segments. I don't know how long we waited. The line seemed endless.

The wailing girl was whipped onto the stage. Her screams carried over the noise of the clamor of voices. Two of the girls in line launched into a fistfight. Their master had to tear them apart, cursing loudly in an alien tongue.

My slaver, in general, ignored me. His eyes were fastened on one of the helpers, a young guard with hair that draped like golden wheat down his back. There were only wisps of tawny hairs on his well-muscled chest, but his skin glowed vibrantly. My master ogled him as if he'd found true love. I knew then why I had not been taken by the slaver back in the tent in the desert.

Eventually, there was only one girl and her master standing in front of us. I watched as the girl's eyes became fearful, and she began to sob and wail. I could not understand her words, but I thought that she was scared about being sold. Her owner used the pain stick on her. Why did she believe that her new master would be worse than the one she already had? What did she know that I didn't?

They left, and I was next. There was a sudden nervousness in me that had not been there before. My legs felt wobbly, and I wished that I had not eaten. Pain ripped through my stomach, and nausea threatened. What would I encounter beyond the heavy drapes?

Cheers from the crowd behind the curtain burst once more through the din. My legs refused to go forward. I knew at that moment that I could not go out there. I could not face the hordes of males I heard beyond that curtain.

An ugly, crooked little man urged us to advance through the curtains. It was my turn to be sold. I knew it was unwise, but I darted backward, away from where I was ordered to go. Once more, the pain stick licked at my legs. I hopped away from it, avoiding a second stroke, and thus was swept forward through the curtain. The pain stick stopped beating me, and I looked up to see that I was on a stage in front of hundreds of screaming and cheering males.

I stood frozen in disbelief. They were jeering and taunting, urging me to come closer.

"Dance for us, girl!" they yelled. Some called out commands I blushed to hear.

"Move forward, girl," my slaver ordered from behind me.

Forward? There was a plank laid, like a model's walkway. It led directly amid the staring, gaping eyes. Walk on that?

Again, the pain stick found me, and I moved against my will. The slaver drove me on, down into their midst.

I shivered as heavy waves of lust stabbed at my soul. Eyes, filled with the heat of unconcealed desire, surrounded me. Men salivating and slobbering like hungry animals prepared to feast on my nearly nude body. The coarseness of their calls and gestures appalled me. I felt raped by the onslaught of their need. I had to escape, to hide from this depravity.

I looked about me frantically, but there was nowhere to run and no one to help me. The slaver held up his pain stick, threatening me again. I turned around and cowered before the mad beasts that encircled me.

I had been covering myself as best I could, one hand across my painted breasts, another over my private parts, where the darkness of my hair showed clearly through the thinness of the material. My actions angered the men.

"Bind her hands. We cannot see her," the leering voices bellowed.

One man leaped up on the stage. I was frightened. I backed away from him, but my slaver blocked my retreat. The man held up cords and offered to tie my wrists. My owner nodded.

The slaver held me while the man bound my wrists behind my back. Then, he was given his reward. Eager lips claimed mine, and his hand squeezed my breast. I shut my eyes and tried to pretend I could not feel it. I imagined that I was in a forest of trees so thick no eyes could find me, sheltered within the softness of their warm, inviting branches.

It almost worked. I hardly felt the rough hand milking my breasts as if they were cow's udders. The alcoholic breath of the man gagged me as his tongue forced its way deeper. That I could almost ignore, but when his hand lifted up my chin and commanded that I look at him, the forest could no longer offer me a safe retreat.

I opened my eyes and stared into the man's face. A sudden wave of nausea made me stagger. I almost fainted. It was not that the man's face was so awful. His jaw was firm, and time had not yet sagged his wide lips down into a scowl, but there were no laugh lines around his eyes. And they were liver-colored eyes with red streaks from his drunken state. He was not an ugly man, I suppose, but he was not the right one, and the shock of the wrongness of his touching me made me want to die.

The man's eyes widened as he stared into mine. He backed away, cursing me. "Spit in the wind! She is Shapechanger!"

A hush froze those close enough to hear. Then, all about the vast hall, the words were passed, and silence spread like a plague.

"Get her out of here," shrieked one man. "Shapechanger revenge their own!"

"This is bad luck!" another hollered and bolted from the room. "I don't want to die!"

"Do you know what they do to people?"

"Take her away."

"She's death to us!"

"Bring on the next," someone yelled brazenly.

Applause wiped out all the angry and fearful words. A chant started, "Bring on the next, bring on the next, bring on the next . . . "

The ugly little man, who'd directed us in, came rushing out, demanding that we leave. He and my master stood there arguing a moment, ignoring the yells and jeers of the herd of males down below us. At last, my slaver gave in and agreed to lead me off if he could have a room from which to sell me. The little man glanced around at the riotous crowd and nodded his head reluctantly.

I was led away in disgrace. The men booed and hissed as I walked down the long, wooden walkway. Someone threw a tega fruit at my owner. Someone else tossed a plastic jug full of drink. It bounced off the slaver's thigh, jostling liquid across his pants.

We continued on through the curtain and to the right, where the inner rooms lay. The smell of the drink on the slaver's pants and the noise of the hecklers followed us. I could feel the anger of my owner growing thicker than the flies on a dead man. I cringed for my future.

He pushed me into an empty room where we were to wait to see if any buyers came. My master sat down in the only chair. I hovered in the corner against the wall, praying that someone would come before the pain stick beat me again.

We did not have long to wait. Single buyers entered, looked at me, and then left. Some of them cursed my master. They all looked at him strangely and shook their heads. Most of them crept away like thieves discovering a well-protected house.

I felt my slaver growing more and more enraged. "No one wants you, girl," he screamed at me. "You're too ugly."

He was going to punish me. I saw it in his eyes. The pain stick was just ascending when another knock pounded on the door, and a man entered. He, too, came close and stared at me. But, instead of retreating, he raised up my chin.

"How did you come by a Shapechanger?" he demanded of my master.

"She's not Shapechanger. You don't see her changing shape, do you? I've beaten her with the pain stick, and she never even growled."

The man felt my hair. His fingers rubbed at the curls, stretching them out. His eyes seemed fascinated by the way each strand sprang back into place when he let it go. "How much do you want for her?"

"Twenty qwai."

"Forget it," he said, turning away. "No girl's worth that."

He took two steps toward the door before the slaver called out, "Wait."

The man turned around. His eyes circled back to me.

"How much are you offering?" my slaver asked.

"Twelve."

"Twelve! She's beautiful. You can see that. Her body is tight. She is young. Her face is perfect. Surely you can go to sixteen."

The man shrugged and turned to leave. "You're right. She probably is worth sixteen, but I've only got twelve."

I sighed. The stranger wasn't young. He was probably in his early fifties, but he didn't look cruel, and he was better than a beating.

"Sold," my master said.

"Spit on my...! You wait a minute," the man said, turning completely around to stare at my breasts. "I never said I'd buy her."

He walked back over to me and stretched his hand out to cup my chin again. "Where you from, girl?"

"I do not know."

"What do you mean? You stupid?"

My master spoke up. "She's been mindwiped. She remembers nothing. I have named her Slettha, but she will answer to whatever you call her. I have trained her to obey. She knows nothing other than that."

"Are you a Shapechanger, Slettha?"

"My master says I am Altarian."

"What do you say?" the man persisted.

"I do not know."

The stranger's hand slid up to caress my face. It was a strange sensation, neither painful nor pleasurable. I knew that his touch was wrong. He didn't know how to wake my soul.

"How used is she? She can't be much older than a farder's orchard."

"She has known only one master. He is dead."

"I'd need to try her."

"You try her, you buy her."

The man's hand moved down to touch my breast. It was a different touch than the man who'd caused me pain on the runway. This man did not hurt me with his hand. His fingers played with my nipple. I thought he must be skilled. I felt my nipple grow hard.

"All right. I'll buy her, but as I said, I try her now, with you present, if you like. I don't care. But if she isn't tight, the deal's off."

My master nodded.

"Lie down, girl," the man ordered me.

I looked at the slaver. He raised the pain stick threateningly. I lay down, but I trembled. I could not remember what was to happen next, but I was afraid.

The man pulled off my bottoms and stuck his finger into me. He twisted it around a little, then grunted and stripped off his own pants.

In a moment, he was on top of me, trying to ram himself in me, but he wouldn't go in. I was glad. His hardness hurt me almost as much as the pain stick.

"She's dry as a drought!" he yelled at the slaver.

"She's frightened. Prepare her."

The man began to rub his tool up and down, but I was about as interested in his taking me as having an arm removed. My mind was in the forest.

At last, the man gave up and lowered his mouth to me. That I would not allow. I burst into a fury of wildness. I fought him with teeth and nails. The man forced my hands down at my sides. He was very strong. The sinewy muscle in his arms flexed once, and his hands bound my wrists. His mouth then lowered and plundered me. He didn't linger long. His saliva allowed him speedy access.

I lay there with my eyes shut and thought about pine needles, soft and cushiony but slightly prickly, like a pinecone softened by the rain. The rhythm of the man's body pumping into me was the swaying of a tree during a winter storm.

It was over quickly. The man seemed pleased. "Get dressed," was all he said to me, but his walk was cocky, and he was bloated with his satisfaction. I felt his mood even before he turned and paid the money he had promised. The slaver counted it out, then slipped it into his robe and took back his shiny ornaments.

Thus, did my new master buy me.

Thenos

I have succeeded. All went as planned. I shiver with anticipation. My little princess, wife of my dear brother, is mine. (May Shaarvan suffer greatly from the Krieger poison he was given. No, I did not wish him dead. Although that would have been easier to arrange — but one should always have an adversary to spice up life. What would be the joy of victory if my dear brother were gone?)

I have seen to the departure of Kada. He served me well and now feeds the Croota fish on Altar. Pity, he was a corrupted, submissive man — just my sort. But I shall leave no trail for Shaarvan when he finally rises from his bed of agony.

I hired a Theinian slaver to seize my little Shaara from her nest of comfort. I supplied him with a quantity of Norgota gas to disable the army of guards Shaarvan always protected her with. (Drat, those guards. I almost captured the girl in Altar.) The gas took out the guards and Shaarvan, and the Krieger poison, an easily administered injection, disabled my brother for a more than an adequate time.

How delightful it would have been to see him lying limp onboard his ship. And should the crew have mutinied, it would not have been my fault had they not rushed dear Shaarvan to Westla for the antidote . . . Of course, as the good brother I am, I would have destroyed the crew for their treachery or cowardice (it must be remembered that the cordor system was faulty). But, unfortunately, or is it fortunate, I have not yet decided, Shaarvan had hired dependable men who saved his life.

I would have been delightfully content to see the antidote administered to my brother on Westla. Ah, how Shaarvan must have writhed with the pain of it. How sweet the thought — Shaarvan, helpless as a baby, in agony. How delicious is the thought.

And, when he wakened, weak and pathetic and found that his precious wife had been stolen . . . Oh, how good that was. His pride must have burned him. His guilt must have stung. I can imagine the way he flapped about like a landed Croota fish: glaring eyes, teeth clenched, whipping back and forth in a struggle to breathe, but utterly powerless.

The thought of his pain makes my organs ache. I can appease it if I like, my hardened tool of pleasure. I have a cargo of fresh girls in the tanks. Shall I ride one as she sleeps or awaken some beauty and enjoy her terror? The latter appeals most. Why should I not enjoy the rest of my trip with a cringing, trembling slave?

Perhaps I shall find one that looks like my princess. But is that wise? No, I shall choose the opposite. The purity of my little Shaara should not be soiled by a slave girl. I must remember that my princess will soon become my wife. I must learn to treat her softly.

I close my eyes. I can see my little Shaara. Those curls with gold, those flashing eyes — eyes that dream and probe deeply within me. What an intimacy is found within her eyes, eyes the colors of my soul. Those eyes were changing each day when I saw her. By now, they must be gray as the shadows of mystery. Those eyes, they call to me.

Let me drink of your mystery, Shaara. Let me absorb you. Let me enter into your mind and dwell there. In return, I shall fill you with my throbbing organ, and you will feel the great size of me. You will moan and cry for mercy, and I shall grant it. Sweet bliss, my lovely princess, I shall grant you the delights of a feast you have never known.

I made sure to use the Theinian, Megloztar. He has worked for me before. He holds no interest in females. I chose him for that extra assurance. My little princess must be safely rendered to me, uncorrupted by the touch of any but Shaarvan. I shall keep her innocent and pure. She will know only what I choose to let her know of me. Is it not a good thing to foster a spot of morality within my rampant debauchery?

Megloztar will bring my naive princess to Casam, the first of my destinations. There, I shall take possession of her, deliver the slaver to his just and suitable reward, and sell my first load of girls. Then, Shaara and I shall journey on, sprinkling the delight that females offer to many planets. The slave girls in my hold will be the sweet incentives to my supporters, who will then assist me in my ousting of the Elders of Altar.

And I shall have my little Shaara to warm the coldness of my soul. I know that I shall need to weave the patterns on her the first time. Every innocent girl requires that, but soon she will no longer need them, and then she will beg for my arms about her. My lips will hold her spellbound with desire. Sweet, sweet little sister, come to me quickly.

Chapter Three

Sheena

My new master led me through the long halls of the tent. I was embarrassed because his semen was dribbling down, wetting my pants with a darkening stain. He seemed not to notice. His arm swung around my shoulder, and he strutted along like a man does when he's had a girl, and he wants others to know he's possessed her.

He led me outside to his bubblecruiser. It was dented on the side and encrusted with dried mud and dirt. The writing on the sides had nearly been rubbed out by the wind and dust of the plains and desert.

My owner helped me up, fastened me in, and then went to the other side. He stood a moment checking the vehicle, testing the wings, and kicking the tires. Then, he climbed up. The motor started the instant he pushed a button. That surprised me. I'd expected the bubblecruiser to cough and sputter like the slaver's had.

"I'm called Isandor," the man said. "I shall call you…" His eyes narrowed in thought. I watched him, waiting for my cue.

"I shall call you…" Sleena. I like that better. It means diamond eyes. Your eyes are like diamonds, Sleena — green, gray, and blue. I like the color of your eyes and the way the light makes them sparkle."

I guess the bubblecruiser needed to be warmed up. I thought it strange, otherwise, that the man would just sit talking to me.

Isandor opened up a box beside him. It was filled with drinks. He handed me a bottle of liquid. "Here, girl. Drink this. It's dry as a deftop's gizzard out there."

He watched me for a moment as I struggled to open the container. "Here., I guess there'll be a lot of things you don't know how to do, huh?"

He handed the drink back to me opened. I didn't know if I should speak to say thank you. I kept silent.

Isandor opened up a compartment on the panel with rows of small, colored buttons. Then, he took a plastic disk and studied it. His fingers pushed a series of buttons. He inserted the disk into an opening in the panel, pulled it out, and then flipped the panel closed. The disk went back into his pocket.

He turned his body to face me. "I'm your new master, girl. I've been saving up for you for a long time. I plan to treat you real well. You just obey me, and I won't have to go out and buy one of those pain sticks like your slaver had. Do you hear me?"

He looked at me like he expected me to say something.

"Yes," I said, still keeping my eyes down as I had been taught.

"You sure don't talk much. You just scared?"

I looked up. "Am I permitted to talk?"

"Well, spit in the wind. Why wouldn't you be?"

"I was told not to speak."

He patted my leg. "You talk all you want to, you pretty little thing. I'd like to hear you talk."

My new master had a strong jaw, slightly overpronounced. It made him look stubborn, but I wasn't sure he was. His bone structure was rough masculine, but not handsome. It was like a face carved in stone that had been weathered by the rain and wind.

The eyes that were examining me were hard, but the soft brown of them reminded me of the shell of a nut or a hot beverage with a touch of cream. The man's bushy eyebrows held a hint of red, although his hair was as grayish brown as the prairie dust.

Isandor was big all over, with a strong, hard body. I thought about how roughly he'd taken me. I hoped he wasn't going to do it like that always. Somehow, I knew my other master had been slow and gentle.

"Please, could you tell me what a mindwipe is?"

Isandor's eyes flashed a startled look, but he nodded. "I guess you have a right to be curious, girl. A mindwipe is a chemical that blocks all your memories. Your memories are still all there. You just can't get to them. It wears off sometimes, but it takes Passes."

"Only sometimes?"

"It doesn't make a lot of difference, Sleena. Your old master's dead, and your new one is sitting here beside you, ready to make you forget him."

He sounded irritated. "Do you mind if I ask questions?" I asked anxiously.

"Had a hard time getting you to say anything," he said, brushing my hair back from where it had fallen over my face. "And now it seems like you're full of questions."

I lowered my head and stared down at the floor. The mats were as filthy as the outside of the bubblecruiser.

Isandor reached over and raised up my chin. "Nah, it's OK, Sleena, as long as you know when to shut up."

He was still holding onto my chin, but his eyes did not appear to be angry. I was getting very confused. "But I don't know the rules here," I told him. "When am I supposed to be silent?"

Isandor pushed another button on the panel of the bubble cruiser, and the vehicle began to lift up. He positioned us in the sky and then verified that we were headed correctly. Apparently, he did not need to keep his eyes on the bubblecruiser's passage. He turned once again in his seat so he could look at me.

"Well, girls aren't supposed to do much talking, Sleena. They have to answer a question, of course. But if you want to talk when we two are alone, I think that's just fine."

"How do girls find out anything if they cannot ask questions?"

"I guess they listen and watch."

I thought about that for a moment. I hoped that I could learn enough from just listening and watching to be able to please my new master. "What will you want me to do?"

He laughed. "Be available for you know what. That's what I bought you for. Other than that . . . I guess you'll have to learn how to do everything. If you're really from Altar, you'll be used to robots and stuff like that. We don't have many of them here. Servants do that kind of thing."

I had an image of what a robot was, but I did not have the memory of seeing it do chores or providing other services.

"What do you do, Isandor?"

"None of your business, girl," he barked at me. His annoyance was almost a physical slap.

I dropped my eyes, alarmed not only by his sudden rage but because I did not understand what I had done wrong. "Please, forgive me," I said meekly.

He chuckled, readily appeased. "Oh, heck. Don't start to blubber on me. Spit in the wind! Are you one of those girls that cry every time a man looks at them with spit in his mouth?"

I wasn't crying, and I had no idea what he was talking about. I stayed silent with my eyes down.

"Oh, spit, I'm a gambler, girl. Now look up and give me a smile."

I obeyed him, but I was astonished that he'd told me what he said he didn't want me to know.

His eyes focused on mine. "That a girl. You're a real sweet thing. I'm real glad I bought you."

He was smiling again. Was it safe to question him? I risked it. "What is a gambler?"

He let out a loud guffaw. "Well, wipe my spit! You don't know much, do you? I make bets with people, and I'm always lucky. That's how I earned the money for you."

"Will I go with you when you gamble?"

"Spittin' heck no! Why would you think that? A casino is no place for a girl like you. You'll stay at the house. I have a room there I rent. You can clean or something. Maybe I won't have to pay for my room, then."

The bubblecruiser was beginning its descent into a town. I could see houses and buildings. There wasn't much to the town.

"What are those?" I cried out excitedly.

Isandor looked to see where I was pointing. "Those are landoors. Men ride them. Man who owns all that's named Blair, not that you need to know that."

I stared, fascinated. "They are like horses."

"What the Spittin' heck is horses?"

I just looked at Isandor. I couldn't explain because I couldn't remember. Where had the word come from?

Isandor seemed to accept my sudden silence. He was preoccupied with landing. I waited until we were down before I asked, "Do people ride landoors for pleasure or for work?"

"Spit, Sleena. Why this interest in landoors?"

Automatically, I dropped my eyes as his voice grew loud.

"Ah, Sleena. Look up! I don't want no tears now."

He was unbuckling me and, for some reason, decided to answer my question. "Yeah, people ride landoors for pleasure. I mean, some men do. Women, of course, don't ride."

"It's against rules or laws for females to ride a landoor?"

Isandor had been gathering up his things. He held the two empty bottles from our drinks and was just turning to open the door. With my question, he swiveled around. "Do you always ask so many questions?"

His voice did not hold a great deal of irritation, but I still wanted to placate him. "I can be quiet if you wish."

He examined my eyes. "How come you can remember that and nothing else?"

He was correct. I wasn't positive about it. "I think I can be quiet."

His finger tapped me on the nose. "I suggest you better start making sure of it."

I sighed. Somehow, the concept felt familiar.

Isandor exited and came around to help me down. He told me that he had already paid the owner before he'd taken the cruiser out, so we didn't need to wait. I did not understand why he gave me so much information, but I listened greedily.

We started to walk away, but the owner came out anyway and insisted on checking over the cruiser. I didn't see how he'd notice any new scratches unless he spotted a layer of dirt that had been scraped off.

Despite his words, the owner made no pretense of checking the inside and outside of the cruiser. He paid more attention to my breasts than to his bubblecruiser. Isandor got red in the face, took off his shirt, and threw it over me.

"Spitting fool! I nearly killed him, looking at you the way he did," Isandor muttered at me as we walked away. "I'm going to have to spend some money on clothes for you. I don't want every man's eyes raking you over."

The idea of a different outfit delighted me. I hoped Isandor dressed me in Pilgrim clothes. I had a flash of a woman in brown from her neck to her ankles, her hair tied back modestly. The image fled when I tried to examine it.

As we walked to Isandor's house along a hardened strip of dirt, I could see a patch of green that was the edge of the landoor ranch. It was a lovely pasture with shade trees bulging with fresh green leaves. A silver metal fence several posts high circled the pasture. I couldn't see the landoors from our path, but I vowed to myself that somehow I would manage to get a closer look at them.

The house where Isandor lived was a three-story residence that had once probably been a wealthy man's home. It was snug in a district that had gone slightly seedy — not unpleasantly, just from lack of attention and money. The town, so far as I'd seen, had the general feeling of a farming community that wasn't prospering.

The sides of the house were peeling paint strips, and the rain gutters were warped and full of holes. Garbage was piled up on one side, leaning precariously against a rickety, old chair. The refuse was overflowing from wooden boxes, and the smell of it was potent from the well-worn path we walked on. Even the weeds, taller than my knees, could not hide the mess that lay strewn about.

"Here it is, Sleena. It's not much compared with Altar. That's a rich man's planet, but you'll get used to it."

I started to remind Isandor that I had no memories of Altar to compare anything with, but I let it slide. I felt like it was probably best to tiptoe into my new life until I had a better idea of where not to step.

We walked through the outside door. It wasn't locked. Isandor merely pushed it open. I looked back and saw that there was no lock. The discovery startled me.

There were stairs leading up to the upper floors. They were curved irregularly like the builder hadn't quite figured out how to stabilize them. The steps creaked as we ascended.

The top floor had doors painted in different colors. We passed a blue door and a green. Isandor stopped in front of the red one.

"I painted them for you, Sleena. I figured it might cheer you to see a fresh coat. I thought red would help you remember which door was ours."

I looked around the hall. There were only two other doors. I didn't think I'd get confused.

Isandor opened the door and almost shoved me in. His hands were sliding all over me before I'd taken more than that first step inside. Without a word, he removed my top and bundled me up in his arms. Stumbling over some discarded clothes on the floor, he almost dropped me. My hands reached out and grasped his neck. His hair was long, covering his neck, drooping down over his collar. It was stringy and greasy, but what surprised me most was the texture of it. For some reason, I'd expected it to be soft as a quagmire's pelt, but Isandor's hair was scratchy and bristly.

Isandor tossed me onto the bed roughly and laughed when I bounced. The smell of the sheets and covers made me wrinkle my nose. I did not think Isandor cared much about cleanliness.

"You sure are a little beauty," he said as his rough hands fondled my breasts. His lips descended to suck and bite.

My eyes roved around the room as I lay there. I wondered if joining had always been like this. Had my first master been so oafish? Had I always been so disinterested, so detached from the whole process? Was this what serving a man was always like?

"Spit in the wind, girl. You make me harder than a fence post."

Isandor rose up and yanked forcefully at my pants. I heard them rip as he pulled them off. He didn't seem to notice. He tossed them onto the floor. His clothes now started falling, first his pants, and then whatever was underneath. He left his shoes and socks on and pounced once more back onto the dirty bed.

"You going to need me to help you get ready with my mouth, or are you as horny as I am?"

I didn't want Isandor near me. His breath was hot and smelled of unwashed teeth, and I shuttered to think how long he'd gone without a bath.

He sat up for a moment, admiring what he'd bought. For the first time, I saw the fence post he'd talked about. It was almost as wide as one.

I flung myself out of the bed, wiggling away from him when he reached out for me. The door had not been locked. I threw it open and rushed into the hall. There, I stopped and froze.

I was such a fool! I was standing, naked as a baby, shivering as the breeze blew in through a crack in the hall window. What was I doing? Where was I planning on running to? Isandor owned me. He had paid for me. No one would help me, even if I knew where to go.

I turned back. Isandor was standing there in the doorway, watching me. His fence post was falling, and the anger on his face was rising.

"I'm sorry, Isandor," I said. "I got scared." I lowered my eyes and walked back towards him.

"I ought to beat you for that, you know."

I nodded. I kept my head down.

"Ah, Spittin' heck. You're just a girl. Guess I shouldn't expect you not to get scared a little. I am mighty big. Is that what frightened you?"

Again, I nodded, and Isandor seemed pleased.

"Get back on that bed real quick, and I won't beat you, girl, but hurry. I don't feel much like waiting."

I climbed up on the bed, wondering if I should have kept running. If only I had my memories, I'd know what to do. I'd be used to this, or maybe I'd like it, but at least I wouldn't feel this panic and the hollowness inside me.

Isandor's hands once more attacked my breasts. He must have thought they were bread dough that he had to knead to make them rise. His lips again slurped and gulped like he was drinking me. I shuddered.

"You like that, huh! Don't worry, little girl. Your man's going to take real good care of you."

"Take care of you." The words echoed in my mind. I'd heard them before. Who had said them? My parents, my former master? Why hadn't they taken care of me? Why was I here in this rundown house with this awful man?

Isandor started sucking away at the other breast. He was like a baby, pawing and squeezing, playing with me with his huge, coarse hands.

One of his hands was stroking the skin on my belly. The hand began moving downwards. I wanted to slap it, but I knew I couldn't. Again, I shuddered in distaste.

"Spit and fire, that's you! You're a hot one. I can tell it."

"Full of fire," another reminder. Stars, it plagued me not to recall.

"Ah, Spittin' heck. You're still dry as a drought. I thought you'd be all ready by now."

"I'm just scared, Isandor. I'm sorry."

That brought a smile back to his face. "It's OK. I'll help you for a while."

Again, he sank his face into me. I wanted to throw up.

It was then that I started thinking about killing myself. I couldn't endure this. It was wrong. Life wasn't worth it if I had to service this man.

Isandor was Mr. Quickie. I'd expected the torture to go on and on, but he was in me and finished before his spit dried. One huge grunt like he was in pain, and then he lay there like a dead thing, sprawled across my body.

I was beginning to think he had died, he was so still, when an odd little snort of a snore vibrated through his nose. I tilted him sideways and slid him off me. He stuck slightly to my body from the sweat of his motion, and I felt a chill as the cold air of the room hit my nakedness, but it was a relief not to feel his weight on me.

Isandor snored away, and I lay in that dirty bed, thinking about ways to die. How would I find a weapon? What poison could I use? Would there be a knife in the kitchen?

The snore peaked and woke up Isandor. "Ah, that was good. You're a sweet girl! You'll learn. I don't think that old master of yours showed you how to do it. He was probably too old to wet your juices."

Isandor stretched and vaulted up onto the floor. I was amazed at how rejuvenated he seemed. One moment, I'd thought he was dead, then he was snoring like a pressure cooker on full steam, and next, he was pulling on clothes like he was racing to be first at the dinner table.

"You going to lie there all day? Get dressed, girl."

I tore the sheet off the bed and wrapped it around me. "May I take a bath?"

"A bath!" He chuckled. "Girl, you'll be lucky if you get a bath once a month. They cost extra. You don't smell yet, anyway."

I stepped over a pile of discarded clothes and found my blouse. I pulled it down over my breasts, wishing greatly that I had something else to wear. I looked around for my pants. They were in the corner on top of a pile of dirty dishes. I picked them up, trying not to look inside the bowl filled with the remnants of a long ago meal. The green and white mold that had formed on its surface probably held back some of the stench.

My pants smelled of Isandor's seed and the mold from the dirty dishes, but I would have put them on anyway. I tried, but the rip up the side would not allow it. The pants were ruined.

"Isandor, I cannot dress. My pants are torn."

"What!" He turned around to look. "Oh, heck! Guess I was kind of in a hurry."

He walked towards me. His eyes fastened on my breasts. "You can't go out like that anyway. This is a respectable house."

He reached down and gathered up some dirty clothes. "Here, put on this shirt and pants. I know they're a bucket too big, but you got to wear something, girl."

The shirt reached down to my calves. I rolled up the sleeves over and over, and then I pulled on the slacks. I sat down on the bed to roll up the pantlegs, but when I stood up, the pants fell down. Isandor cut a rope and tied it around my waist.

He laughed when his eyes traveled across me. "No one will bother you now, girl. You look like a boy." His eyes considered me a moment. "Maybe that's not a bad idea. Come here."

He twisted my hair tightly and crammed it into an old hat that had been lying on the floor. "Yeah, I think I like that. If nobody knows you're a girl, nobody's going to cause trouble over you.

"I'll get you clothes that won't fall off you when you walk, and I'll dress you like a boy. Then, only I can benefit from the fact that you're not." He began to chuckle. "Stay here, Sleena. I'll be back with clothes for you."

He shut the door, and I heard what sounded like the rattle of a lock being fastened. I waited until I heard the pounding of his feet going down the stairs and then the heavy thud of the front door closing. I tried the door. As I'd guessed, Isandor had bolted me in.

Without my master in the room, worrying me with his needs, the smell of dirty clothes and decomposing food nauseated me. I went to the window and unlocked it. It pushed outward with a high-pitched squeak. The clean smell of the breeze washed away some of the foulness of the room.

I was on the third floor. There was no way for me to get out through the window. It did not even open sufficiently. Nor was there anything to break my fall if I managed to crawl through it.

I gazed down towards the ranch. Two of the landoors were grazing in the thick grass. I studied them a moment, but I was too far away to see more than their general shape. Their heads seemed slightly elongated and broader than what I felt they should be. I wondered where I'd seen animals like them before and why they seemed so familiar.

I turned around and once more viewed the room. It was to be my home. Even if my life was only for a day or so, I could not live in this squalor. I reached down and picked up Isandor's dirty clothes and began piling them in a corner.

Isandor lived simply. He had only his clothes and a bed. There were no other personal belongings, and I could discover no knives or weapons of any kind.

Before long, I had to stop rooting around. My kidneys were dying for relief, and there was no facility within the room. I sat in a chair and crossed my legs. I was afraid to bend over for fear I could not hold in my water. The minutes dragged painfully.

Isandor's key in the lock was such a welcome sound. I barely let him step foot through the door before I began begging to be taken to the bathroom.

"I told you there is no bathroom in this house, girl."

Isandor was getting angry, but I was desperate. "I have to go. I can't hold it anymore."

"Oh, you mean, you need a pot. Come."

He led me down the hall to the green door. I rushed in and found the hole. My relief was so great that I sighed loudly.

Isandor was waiting for me at the door. "Move aside, Sleena. I got to go, too." He held me there by my wrist while he sprayed his water. The sound was disgusting, and the smell made my stomach roll with distress.

The clothes that he had bought me fit much better. The pants were still a little long, but rolled up, they were fine. The shirt wasn't much smaller than the one I was already wearing.

Isandor shrugged. "It was all they had. It will do. I didn't know what size feet you had. You'll have to go barefoot for a while. Those sandals of yours are too feminine."

Obediently, I removed them, placing them against the wall. I followed Isandor down the stairs.

Downstairs in the kitchen area, I met the couple that owned the house. The woman was tall, almost as tall as her husband. She was thin as a bamboo stalk and walked with a swaying motion as if the wind rocked her back and forth.

Her husband was almost the opposite. He was shorter than Isandor but almost twice as wide. His body swayed, too, but his movement was accompanied by a rippling of the mass around his waist and stomach. It jiggled rhythmically as he breathed in and out.

When the couple's eyes turned to regard me, I saw the husband's eyes open wide, and I swear the pupils darted inward in astonishment.

"What in spit's name are you doing with a Shapechanger?" the husband yelled at Isandor.

"She's not Shapechanger. Her master died and left her unchanged. All she's got of it is the eyes."

"I don't want any trouble."

"What trouble? She's as helpless as a babe. They mindwiped her. She doesn't even know her name. I call her Sleena."

"What language does she speak?"

"Altarian."

"A rich Shapechanger? Isandor, you're a fool."

"I'm a gambler, and I think I made a lucky strike."

The man kept shaking his head. "I don't know about this. Shapechanger watch out for their own. If anyone finds out . . ."

"Oh, Flar, quit worrying over it," the woman said. "What's done is done. The girl can help around the house. Why have you put her in men's clothing?" she asked Isandor, wrinkling up her nose.

"I'm going to keep her like that. She's too pretty a packet dressed like a girl. I'd be afraid to let her out of my sight. This way, with her hair tied up in a hat, no one will even look twice."

"Better make her keep her eyes down then," Flar warned.

"Hear that, Sleena?" Isandor turned back to Frieda. "If you use Sleena for chores, I expect to get free rent. You can make her do anything you want, except servicing your husband . . ."

Frieda chortled and slapped her husband on the back. "You can bet Flar isn't going anywhere near a Shapechanger!"

Isandor continued. "When I'm home, though, she's mine. She has her own chores to do for me."

Flar laughed mockingly. "Enjoy her quickly. A Shapechanger's death is not pleasant. I've heard it said that if a man dares to touch a female Shapechanger, the razor claws of the beast slice through the man's vocal cords. That way, he cannot scream as the beast eats away at his heart."

I couldn't wait for permission to sit. I collapsed into the nearest chair. My brain could no longer focus on the words that were buzzing around me. My head was aching as if someone had pounded in a nail.

"xxxxxxxxxxxxx," Frieda said, handing me a bread roll. I took it from her, thankfully, and nibbled at the hard, crisp, rounded edges. I wondered why I could no longer understand her words.

Isandor came and stood beside me. "xxxxx xxxxxx xxxxx xxxxx," he said. I just stared at him, too exhausted to struggle to understand anything.

"What's wrong?" he asked me in my own language.

"I am tired."

"Of course. You aren't used to all this. I even forgot there for a moment that you didn't speak our language. You obeyed just like you did. I'll speak your Altar speech for a while, but you better learn ours real fast. Chow down. I'll take you back upstairs after the grub."

The meal was so greasy I almost couldn't eat it. The sight of the tiny white flat globules floating around in the soup killed most of my appetite. I finished my bread and drank the cold water they had poured for me. The soup could congeal without me.

After the meal, Isandor kept his promise and led me back to our room. I lay down on the bed and was asleep before he joined me.

Shaarvan

Who did this monstrous deed? Who has stolen my Shaara? I have no enemies. Nor does my father. Who is it that seeks revenge in such a way? In all the cities of our world, men steal females, but they would not take a Shapechanger woman. One look at Shaara's eyes, graying darker as her Power grows, and no slaver would try to capture her. No sane man would buy her.

Was it the Theinian who followed us in Watha? But I warned him that Shaara was Shapechanger. He would not want her. He would never dare to war against us, knowing the revenge we would demand. We are secretive, we Shapechanger, but we let small pieces of information escape. It is common knowledge what happened to Serrqwel when he raped a newly taken Shapechanger girl. Saberey claws ripped and slashed, and the owner of them ate Serrqwel's heart. Those who watched were not all Shapechanger. The deed was told, and the punishment circulated. No, not even a Theinian would be so foolish as to steal a Shapechanger woman.

Was it Kada who took Shaara? He did not return to the ship, and I had threatened him. Could his fear of me have turned to hate? Desertion is a death sentence, but if Kada truly took off, perhaps because he was unable to find another cord or unit, I do not think he would have stayed in the area. He would have fled as far as he could run. I do not believe that it was Kada who did this, but perhaps he was a part of it. A new cordor unit should not have failed.

Which leads to Thenos. I do not understand my brother, but to suspect him of this? Besides, Thenos was on a ship bound for the primitive Melo, a planet far in the opposite direction. And Shaara has not turned up in Altar. Both Westlan and Altarian officials have insisted on checking (an insistence that has displeased the Elders of Altar greatly. They always resent any interference from the Westlans). My father is still searching the distant cities of Altar — those not associated with traders or Shapechanger. And he has sent ships with full crews and additional men to scour neighboring planets.

But the odds are good that Shaara was not stolen for the girl trade. She has been taken to get at me, but why? Who would hate me enough to do this? And where would they have taken Shaara?

Sleena

The next morning, I woke to find Isandor groaning in his sleep. "What is wrong?" I asked him.

"Go away. Go down to Frieda. She will work with you. I don't need you this morning."

Isandor's eyes were blood-red and pulled down at the corners in the agony of a hangover.

Gently, I withdrew from the bed and made my way down the stairs.

Frieda saw me the moment my foot touched the ground floor. "Good," she said. "I would have gotten you up an hour ago, but I did not have the courage to awaken Isandor after one of his binges. He'll not be fit to be around until the sun peaks in the sky.

"There is bread to knead and butter to prepare. We will not miss him."

Frieda kept me busy, but she was not unkind. She kept up a constant stream of talk. At times, I found that my mind could tune in and understand her, but the effort strained me. Mostly, I let her words flow about me like the sweetness of ocean waves tumbling at my knees.

Isandor crawled in even later in the day than Frieda had predicted. His breath was as sour as his dirty dishes, and his clothes gave off a stench of alcohol, sweat, and vomit. He plunked down on a chair and demanded a spoge. I brought it to him in a cup. Frieda had sprinkled it with a powder she stirred in. It seemed to help him. A short while later, his head lifted, and he demanded bread.

As he ate, I mixed the batter for a cake Frieda was making her husband. It called for five hundred licks, as Frieda called the mixing. I would have finished, but Isandor's bear hug swooped me up from behind. He tossed me across his shoulder and carried me up the stairs. He only made one flight before his breath grew ragged, and he set me down. "Climb, girl. I'll save my breath for better things."

Again, I was dry when Isandor thought I should be ready, but he laughed and brought out a spray of lubricant. "Picked this up yesterday. I'll be spitless if I keep having to juice you up."

Once more, he entered and squirted. "The quickest gun in the west," I thought and wondered where I'd heard it.

That evening, Isandor disappeared again. Frieda told me he spent every night at the casino down the road. I did not miss him. Before leaving, he had given his permission for me to stay downstairs for a while. I watched Flar and Frieda play a game with cards. They did not ask me to join them, and they talked around me, accepting my silence.

It was pleasant to be with them. I was glad they owned the house I lived in.

The next day, I was up earlier. I helped Frieda before the sun was up, and our work was finished before Isandor arose. Frieda asked me to sit down and chat with her.

I drank the bitter spoge and attempted to sort out Frieda's words. She was speaking of her religion. I listened, fascinated by her animation.

"Barquel rules the stars. He paints pictures in the sky to tell us how to live our lives. When we look up and see the Marong tree, we must bow three times each day and bake fresh Marong cake until the tree fades away.

"The Sky Demon comes then. He demands our sacrifice. All women must allow their husbands to visit other women during the Sky Demon's reign. Many interesting men have come to see me, and I have visited their households during my sacrifices.

"Next comes the Golden Chair. It is the most demanding of all. During its reign, no woman may cook. Our food must be raw, or a man must prepare it.

"The Wheel slips in mysteriously, blending with the Golden Chair for weeks. It demands strong drink to be consumed by those who do not drink and abstinence from those who do. It is a time of riot in the streets, and many find their fortunes overturned."

I never heard the rest of the long saga of Barquel. Isandor had awakened and slipped in to hear Frieda's words.

"No more of that spit in the wind garbage! Sleena, I forbid you to listen."

I wondered why he thought I'd understand Frieda's words. She spoke in Freinan. I wondered, too, why I did.

Frieda was silent about her religion after that, but I knew when she baked the cakes each day that the Marong tree hung over the sky.

I was curious about the Sky Demon. Was that the reason Isandor did not wish me to learn her religion? He did not need to be concerned — the Sky Demon had already demanded my sacrifice. That was Isandor.

Frieda often let me use knives to cut the meat and vegetables. I cut my finger once, curious to see if I could slice my flesh as easily as a *cabo* root. The blood welling out from the cut seemed to flow so eagerly. It asked me to cut deeper. For a long moment, I stared at the blue veins in my wrist. I saw two of them so near the surface. One slice would cut through them both.

As I stood there, examining my wrist, Frieda walked in. She saw the blood dripping down from my finger and screamed. Her husband came waddling in faster than I'd ever seen him go. He stared at his wife, and then his eyes moved to me.

The knife was still frozen an inch from my veins. It thirsted. I felt the urge of the metal to lap up the sweet redness of the river of my soul. I heard it plainly, and I was listening to the whispers of its voice. The screams of Frieda had distracted me from the knife. Then, the eyes of another drew me, and I paused, wondering at their interference.

Faster than I could have believed possible, Flar's arm flashed out and up. It was not forceful enough to make the knife take flight, but it released the spell. I placed the knife down and backed away.

For days after that, Frieda and Flar watched me carefully. I felt their eyes on me wherever I moved. They never spoke of it with Isandor. He would not have been so silent. Having spent his money to purchase me, he would've been angered by my wish to escape his bondage.

Flar waited three days before he brought it up. "Sleena, you will talk with me."

"Isandor forbids it."

"My wife stands there watching, so your honor will not be broached. I am the housemaster, and you will obey."

I looked up. I knew what he wanted to say. I had been there for thirteen days; I had discovered it was not their language I understood but their thoughts.

"You almost took your life, Sleena. Is Isandor that bad?" he asked in Altarian.

I answered him in the same language. "What could you do, Flar, if I told you, yes? Would you buy me from him? Would you attempt to protect me from his demands? I thank you for your concern, but there is nothing you can do. Isandor does nothing that it is not his right to do."

My answer relieved their minds. I meant it, too. I liked them. How could I burden them with my belief that I was dying a little each time Isandor touched me?

The power of the knife had been partly due to my disbelief that there was still life in my veins. I had thought my blood had frozen into solid tubes of ice, as empty of life as my soul. But I had seen that the blood still flowed warm and liquid as a red river. I knew how easy it would be now to end my life. The knife would talk to me again, and I would let it drink, but curiosity was stirring within me. A new world was calling to me, and landoors waited for me in the green, sweet-smelling pasture beyond my window. I would wait for a while before I answered the call of the knife.

Shaarvan

I have had our son put into deep sleep. It will not harm him, and Shapechanger will surround him. There are those who would expect me to send him to Altar, to my mother. She would willingly care for him, but I shall not do that. Shaarac is safer here on Westla. In a deep sleep, he will not be aware that both his mother and his father have deserted him.

Forgive me, Shaara. That is false. You did not desert him. I know that you have not gone willingly, wherever you are. There is no treachery in you. There never has been, not even on that day when you were accused of it, and I took you as a Saberey. You were as true then to your heart as you have always been. I am sorry, Shaara. Perhaps I should have returned you to Terra as you begged me to do so many times. You would have been safer there.

I wallow in my guilt. All the occasions when I was harsh with you, my Shaara, curse me now. The many times when just a smile, a word, a gentle touch would have eased your fears — those moments point their finger at me and reproach me. My remorse grows heavy, but it serves you little good. I shall be a different husband when I find you.

I see I have lapsed into talking to Shaara as if she were here by my side. It is difficult not to. She is so much a part of me. But I cannot live on memories of our past together. I must get out of this bed. Stars, how I miss her!

Every day while I lie here, I send out a mental call. If only she were more mature in her Power. If only she had Shapechanged. But she has not been of the blood long enough to channel her resources.

She is still ignorant of the ways of the Shapechanger. And she is still so young. Soaring Eagle, watch over her from above. Do not let them hurt her.

Chapter Four

Thenos

Imbeciles! I have ordered them to find the Theinian, Megloztar, and they dare to inform me that he has disappeared! I know he has disappeared. That is why I sent them to find him!

Megloztar was supposed to have come to Casam. He was to have met me at the spaceport and handed over my little Shaara, but he did not come. I took my precious cargo, and I distributed the girls to the buyers. I performed like the perfect son of Tevor, but all my plans have gone astray. Why did Megloztar betray me? Did he sense his doom? Did he find out the fate of Kada? What has gone wrong? And, more importantly, how can I fix it?

First, I must find Shaara. If she is still with Megloztar, she is safe, but if he has sold her . . . Who would buy a Shapechanger woman? Only a fool. and it would have to be in some small settlement of an unvisited planet, a planet where Shapechanger do not normally go.

My little princess, where are you? Have I taken you away from the heavy guards and safety of Shaarvan to cast you out to the Croota fish of men? I have made a grievous error, but I will rectify it. I shall find you, my little innocent. And then, I shall rip the tongue from Megloztar's throat and dine on his liver as he watches. You will be revenged, my future wife.

Sleena

Frieda was sick one day, and I was finally allowed to leave the house. The day was fresh. Buds had sprouted, even in the squalor of neglect. The grass and leaves were a blending of greens and shadows richer than the morning sunrise. I breathed in deeply and felt my feet, bare against the cool, hard dirt of the path, reaching down into the planet's life force. The power of it surged through me, tingling my deadened soul.

My lungs drew in the morning's crisp air. They expanded wider in the vibrant quality of spring's renewal. My heart, too long suppressed by the misery of my endurance, opened, awakening to the sweetness of life, and inside me, a voice, so long silent, sang of the promise of tomorrow and of possibilities.

What a self-indulgent baby I had been to hang my head and seek an end because life was difficult. It was a coward's avenue to stroll with the tip of a knife. Where there is life within and without, there is hope. I must remember that.

The market where I had been sent was further down the way. It was clearly visible from where I stood, but on my right, the green pastures and the landoors called. I ran down the path, feeling the freshness of the air against my face, feeling freedom like a drug, pumping me full of the euphoria of existence.

As I reached the ranch, I saw men crowded about a large arena, sitting on the top fence post, watching. I sneaked towards the offside and peeked inside the arena. In the center stood a maddened stallion, flaring his nostrils and snorting challenges. He faced the men, daring them to enter. One hoof struck the hard dirt floor of the arena. So angry and so violent was the force of his pawing that it sparked the ground. The stallion wheeled around, turning his back to the men. His black skin flared red in the light of the sun, crimson-red on black.

I must have sucked in my breath at the beauty of him. His eyes darted towards me. He bugled his challenge.

"I offer you no threat. I have only come to worship your beauty," I whispered to him.

For a moment, his ears flicked forward, and I thought perhaps he understood, but once more, he flexed his neck, tossing his head with the pride of a king. His eyes met mine, and he snorted his disdain.

"Get away from there, boy," one of the men yelled at me.

I backed away slowly, but my eyes had found the reason for life. It wasn't springtime or the greenness of the grass and leaves, nor of tomorrows and possibilities. It was a landoor I would call Crimson Black.

I asked, from then on, to be the one to shop for fresh vegetables each day. Frieda agreed readily. I wasn't sure if it was because of her avoidance of an unpleasant errand or because of what she saw in my face as I returned to the house. I was convinced that the joy I felt must be reflected there.

Frieda and Flar stopped guarding me. They seemed to think I'd grown resigned and had accepted my life. I had done neither. I still hated my existence, but I had found a reason to continue it.

For days, I stalked the arena, attempting to stay downwind of Crimson Black, but the wind was frivolous, and he always knew. His eyes were relentless in their hate.

Blair, the owner, caught me on the fourth day of my adulation. I knew who he was. I'd seen him working the landoors and giving orders to the men. His graying hair, thick and handsome with its silver highlights, had first caught my eye. I liked the way his long, regal nose, with its creases and lines etched in deeply by the sun, told of a life lived outside. His clear, smooth skin, darkened to a saddle-colored tan and beaded with shiny drops of moisture across his forehead, had a shine that glinted like pearls in the afternoon sun.

But it was his posture that held my eyes spellbound. Erect as a military man, he sat on a landoor like poetry. His hands, covered in brown leather gloves, barely moved as he guided the animal. I had never seen him jerk at a landoor's mouth or carelessly lose the contact the animals so depended on for guidance.

I knew who he was. I admired him, adored him, and worshipped him. He was everything clean and good in the world, and when he yelled, "What are you doing?" I froze. My world was spinning as he came near. I waited too long to try to bolt away, like a frightened animal, too panicked to run.

Blair caught my arm as I turned to flee, and he swung me back around to confront him. Muscles, heavily toned by years of lunging landoors, gripped me to a halt. The sudden jerk was too much for my hat. When I stopped abruptly, it didn't, and my hair came tumbling down like leaves in a windstorm.

Blair released me as if he'd touched a poisonous snake. I turned and darted for my hat, still hoping for a clean get-away, but his foot tramped down on it and held it there.

"Are you Isandor's girl?"

I kept my eyes down, but I was pretty sure it was too late. Blair had probably had a good view of the grayness of my eyes.

"Answer or I shall tell Isandor that you come here."

That jerked my head up. "Do not tell him, please."

"So I was right. Why do you come here?"

"Because of Crimson Black."

"Crimson Black?" Blair's eyes followed mine to the stallion. "No, that's High Mountain Peak. I named him that because I knew he'd be the best jumper anyone's ever seen."

"He's got the legs for it," I agreed, forgetting that girls should not speak freely.

"What do you know about landoors?" he demanded.

I hung my head. "May I have my hat back?" I said to the ground.

Blair stared at me for a moment. "If you tell me why you said that about the stallion's legs."

I kept my eyes down and my head at a humble angle. "Well, he's also got the heart to be a jumper. His chest is wide and deep, and the muscles in his flank ripple with his spring, but none of that would help him jump over obstacles if his legs weren't long enough to spread and give the height he needs."

Blair reached down and picked up my hat. He held it a moment and studied me. "Here," he said. "I suggest you cover up before you are seen. Most of the guys know Isandor well."

I shoved my hair down under the rim in the back and pulled the hat down low over my face. Then, without a goodbye, even to Crimson Black, I raced the wind back to the path.

I stayed away from the landoors for a whole day. It was all I could hold out for. I had to go back. The call of Crimson Black was too strong for my fear.

I arrived just in time to see one of the trainers enter the arena with Crimson. The man had a whip in his hand, and he cracked it into the air. The sound frightened me. I knew it would lay open Crimson's skin if it touched him.

The stallion was terrified of the whip. He reared and blew loud bursts of rebellious protest, but he did not go close to the man.

The trainer hunted him like a lion with its prey, backing Crimson into a corner, but the arena was round, and the stallion would not be trapped. The two continued like that for an hour, and the stalemate persisted. I knew I must go. It was dangerously close to the time that Isandor would be awakening, and I still had not purchased the day's vegetables.

One last kiss I flung at Crimson, and then I turned and ran. The vegetable mart was busy. I was forced to wait. My position on the scale of priority was low. Wives came first, and slaves were only served after the others had been supplied with their needs. My disguise hampered me there. I appeared even younger than my years and so was afforded less prestige than the other slaves.

The sun was well past its midday point when I reentered the house. Isandor was not only awake but had eaten and was waiting for me at the doorway.

"Where have you been?"

"I was purchasing vegetables."

"Where else did you go?"

I looked down. "There is nowhere else to go." The words flowed out easily, but a wave of pain and nausea swept through me. I sagged against the wall, doubled up in pain.

"I'm going to be sick," I cried out, and I rushed out through the doorway to vomit into the dirt.

"What ails you, woman?" Isandor asked, following me outside.

I couldn't speak. I was too sick. I collapsed on the ground and tried to catch my breath. Again, the nausea swept over me, and the spasms wrenched up every drop of spoge and bread I'd eaten for breakfast.

Flar came out at Isandor's insistence. "She's been poisoned," Isandor was shouting at him.

"Did you eat anything in the market?" Flar asked me.

I shook my head. That brought on another burst of vomiting.

Flar's bulk blocked the sun. Lying there in the dirt, I felt the chill in the air that the sun's rays had formerly warmed.

"What did she say before this started?" Flar asked.

"Say? What do you mean? She said she'd only gone to the market."

"Sleena, a Shapechanger cannot lie. If you said something false, you must renounce it, or your vomiting will continue."

I was in the midst of the dry heaves, but I heard Flar. "I went to the landoors," I said the moment I could speak.

At once, I could breathe again. The nausea was gone as instantly as it had begun. I lay there, grateful to be done with heaving and coughing up my insides, but then I began to feel the anger boiling inside Isandor.

"So you lied to me, did you?" The flat of his hand came down on my thigh. I cried out more from my fear of what would follow than the pain of his hand.

"Get upstairs, you worthless spit."

I ran like the Star Demon was after me. I took the steps two at a time and made it to the top of the third floor before Isandor arrived at the second. I rushed into our room and began to disrobe, hoping my nakedness would distract his anger.

I cursed my stupidity for being so late. I'd known that the anger had been building up in Isandor. It had been seeking a release, and I'd handed it to him.

The room smelled sweet of fresh air, clean clothing, and freshly washed sheets. I had done everything Isandor could wish for except the one thing he wanted most. I could not warm to him in bed, and that was the root of his anger.

Every day, his temper had grown worse. "You're cold as the butt of an iceberg," he'd told me over and over. "I find about as much pleasure in your icicle of a womb as I do in losing in the casino," he'd yelled at me the day before.

I lay on the bed, waiting for his violence or his joining. I wondered, for a moment, which was the more repulsive.

Isandor stormed into the room. The door slammed behind him. He towered above me. When his hand began to slap my breast, I had my answer. The pain of it was much harder to block out.

Shaarvan

As I lay on the bed, forced to endure the healing process, I began to have dreams of Shaara. Sometimes, I could almost see her, but she did not hear me. She turned away from me, and then the dream always faded.

Where was she? Even the dreams, if they were true sendings, gave me no information. And the Shapechanger on Watha had still not found a scent of her. I believed they were ready to give up.

My uncle visited each day. He brought me reports from the searchers. Kada had disappeared, and the Theinian slaver had probably returned to his homeland. We had searchers in Theinia as well. We would find him.

The other suspect who was at the top of my list was my brother, Thenos. The reports had come back that he had left Melo with a shipment of girls. Father kept saying that Thenos could not be blamed for Shaara's disappearance, but I had lain here thinking for many days, and my suspicions always returned to Thenos.

I have claimed "a need for justice" with the Altar Elders and with the Westlan Courts. I have demanded an investigation by all who share the blood of the Shapechanger. It is not enough to satisfy me, but it is all I can do until I can leave this bed.

Tem, my uncle, scolds me often. "Shaara is but a woman. Be sensible. Another will take her place in your heart. You must declare her gone and start again."

He, of all people, should understand. He has held steady to Temina, although her mind wanders with sickness, and she has never given him a son. She is not even Shapechanger, yet he honors her as a husband.

"I shall find her," I tell Tem each time, not even attempting to explain why his guidance is faulty. I think he does not entirely believe his words, either. He may be the Highest of Westla, but he cannot convince me (or himself) that one can ignore the bonding of a soulmate.

"This bed has been my jailer far too long," I complain to him, changing the subject.

And it is true that I can barely tolerate it. Yet, I am still too weak to sit up and must be fed with bottles of a sweet substance that I find almost impossible to swallow.

Tem attempts to distract me, but his words miss their mark. He speaks of the end of my suffering. He does not comprehend that it is only the agony of my slowly healing body that I find agreeable. I am glad for the pain. It is my constant reminder of my failure.

I have displeased Tem again, or perhaps it is merely time for him to depart. The medics insist that I sleep throughout the day, even though I would prefer never to close my eyes again. The medics do not understand that my sleep tortures me. They do not see the nightmares — those far worse than seeing Shaara turn away from me.

In those, I am searching for Shaara in tents that sell the same innocent girls that I peddled for Passages without the least bit of guilt or trepidation. So far, Shaara's lovely eyes have never matched those of the scores of girls who look up at me with expressions of misery. But one night, I might see Shaara's eyes, and the horror of that haunts me. And, so it is that my imaginings torment both my sleeping and waking hours.

Where is my Shaara? Where have they taken her? Is she all right? My beloved Shaara, wife of mine, I vow in the name of the Somber Tree, the Saberey, the Soaring Eagle, and the stars above that I shall find you.

Sleena

I was more cautious after the beating — but the ranch was my life. I could not stay away.

Blair came over to stand beside me when he saw me. I think, at first, he came to protect me, thinking that the others might chase me away. Or, perhaps, he felt my hero worship and was warmed by my adoration. Sometimes, he spoke. It wasn't that he talked to me. It was more a musing sort of speech as if I were the sounding board for his thoughts. The words darted about like thoughts often did, shifting and percolating. Sometimes, there was only silence as we watched Crimson Black.

"That darn colt," he said one day, referring to a brand new gelding that had unbelievably unseated him. "What do I do to stop his shying at every paper and everything that moves? He's useless as a jumper, the way he is now."

Blair had asked me a question. He hadn't meant to. His words were only the frame for his thoughts, but he had stated it as a question, so I was free to answer.

"Tie him to a rail from which he cannot break free and fasten papers to the posts. After a while, he will become so accustomed to the movement of the papers in the wind that he will no longer shy at the sight of them." I rolled the answer off my tongue as quickly as I could. I knew that a slave should not give advice, but I also knew it was the correct solution.

Blair's eyes grew stern. For a moment, his muscles twitched, and I thought he would slap me for speaking so freely. I closed my eyes and waited for the blow.

A moment of silence passed, and then he spoke. "I will not hit you, Sleena. Isandor does that enough, doesn't he?"

I didn't answer. My eyes went to the ground. I had told no one, not even Flar and Frieda, how lately, Isandor's hand had grown harsher. He seemed to need to slap me now before he hardened. How had Blair known? Isador left little evidence that was not covered by my pants and shirt.

"It is why I allow you here. No animal should be beaten senselessly," Blair said, sighing.

I felt his eyes once more move to the stallion. "I suppose I did ask you a question, but you knew I did not expect you to respond. Why did you speak?"

I drew a quick breath in case he changed his mind and I must dart away to safety. "Because I knew the answer."

Blair turned to look at me, but he was not angry. "How could you possibly know the things you know? Where have you learned about landoors?"

"I have no memories of before. The slaver who sold me to Isandor said I was mindwiped."

"But you have knowledge from before? That is interesting." He shoved his boot over the bottom rail of the fence, loosening a layer of stable muck. Then he shifted and looked at me again.

"You better get on home now, girl. I will think over what you said about the colt."

I ran all the way to the vegetable market. The smile on my face made the seller stare. I had to wipe it clean, but I could not hide the smile inside me. My feet danced me home.

Blair did try my suggestion on the colt. He found it worked to calm the young gelding, and his tone was full of amazement as he told me the news of it later.

As the days drifted by, sometimes more questions sifted into Blair's musing. I answered them when I could, and he began to accept my knowledge. My speech no longer angered him.

One day, Blair granted me more than that. I was worrying over one of the young animals I'd seen trained the evening before. Isandor spent his evenings and nights in the casino. He was always gone then. That evening, Flar and Frieda had been fighting. I went over to the ranch and watched as a gelding was being worked over jumps. I'd noticed at once that he shouldn't have been.

I was wondering how his leg was this morning, wondering how I dared to ask. I did not hear Blair when he asked a question. "Sleena, wake up. You haven't heard a word I've said. What is wrong?"

The opening I'd waited for! "You know the brown colt out of Spitfire. He was off last night, and the trainer jumped him anyway!"

"How do you know?" I felt Blair's anger. I stepped back and prepared to run.

"Sleena, easy, child. I told you I don't hit girls."

His manner with me was just like with the landoors I'd seen him work. I relaxed with the words and the gentleness of his tone.

"Good girl. Now, answer me, Sleena. How did you know about the colt?"

"I came last night."

"Sleena," he sighed. "You have no more sense than a *trida*. Do you think that pair of pants you wear will save you from the lust of a man? Some men prefer boys."

I kept my head down. My face grew hot with embarrassment.

Blair sighed and was silent for a long time. I decided that I should probably leave before it grew late, but he started to speak again. "Sleena, I gave one of my men money to buy you last week. I told him to offer double what Isandor had paid for you, 24 gwai to be precise, but Isandor refused."

My eyes rose to Blair's. He wanted me? He read my question.

"No, Sleena, you do not need to fear me in that way. My wife and I are well-matched. I certainly do not crave a girl hardly old enough to spit. I thought we could take you in. I know you cook and help with the house. My wife could have used you. You would have been safe, and you would have been near your precious stallion.

"I'm telling you this, Sleena, because I worry about you." Blair's eyes, as they looked at me, were soft and full of concern. Then they hardened, and he turned back into the stern owner of a landoor ranch. "You must not visit here in the evening. If you journey here in the nighttime, I will forbid you to come at all."

I had a friend! How sweet the knowledge was that someone cared. I smiled. "I will obey," I told him.

I saw him relax. For a moment, he almost touched me. I felt the impulse in his mind, but he knew he could not. Instead, he talked. "The colt you saw last night is Stardust. You are correct. He was off in his hind right. The stupid groom never even felt it. Riding Stardust over the jumps last night was a big mistake. The vet was here this morning checking the gelding's lameness."

Blair turned to watch me again. "The vet also told me, Sleena, that I should put down High Mountain Peak."

"No!"

"I did not have him killed because of you, but that horse is not going to make a jumper, Sleena. It's a waste of money feeding him."

"I could tame him!"

"Sleena, you're a girl. Have you worn those pants so long you've forgotten?"

"I can ride. I don't remember when or where I learned, but I do know how. And I have the knowledge of how to train a horse like Crimson, too."

"No, you don't, and you will not go anywhere near him. Nor do I wish to hear any more talk of riding. Girls do not ride."

He'd taken off his hat to scratch his head. He used it to swat at a fly that buzzed too near.

"I could tame him just by talking to him if you'd let me."

"Ah, Sleena. I know you love him, but you're wasting your time. Choose another landoor to to invest your heart on."

"Love isn't a choice. It just happens. There is only Crimson Black."

Blair's eyes studied me. He was silent so long I wondered if he'd speak again. "You're a stubborn one, Sleena. I'll think about it."

I turned around and galloped on feet that flew over the ground. I had a friend who cared about me. I could talk to him. Life wasn't really so bad after all.

I arrived home with my hands full of vegetables. The sales had been great that day. I knew just what I'd cook for dinner, and my mind was sorting through the steps.

Unfortunately, Isandor was waiting for me. "I bought you a present, my cold one. Come see. It's in the room."

It was late morning, but Isandor was drunk, drunk, and dangerous. I did not want to go with him, but his hand lashed out and twisted mine behind me. The vegetables dropped at my feet.

I did not struggle, but as we climbed the stairs, Isandor hurt me anyway. I saw that it pleased him.

He locked the door behind us, a habit he'd developed of late. Then he tossed me on the bed and ordered me to strip.

"Now, tell me where you've been."

"I bought vegetables like I do every day."

"And?"

He knew. I read it in his eyes. "I went to watch the landoors."

He pulled out the surprise then. I recognized it at once as a pain stick. The slaver had introduced us adequately.

"So it's you and Blair. Isn't he a bit old for you? Do you have to prop him up? Or maybe you ride *him*."

The pain stick touched my leg. It was a wave of torture, intensified by the length of time a man held it there. I writhed and cried out. Isandor laughed.

"Are you as cold with him? Do your juices flow at the sight of wrinkled skin? Do you savor his kisses?"

"I only watch the landoors," I sobbed.

"Everyone knows about you two. The men jeer at me, asking if Blair pays for it or gets it free."

"I only watch the landoors," I cried out again, trying to make Isandor understand.

He didn't listen. His fist slammed into my arm, and then he set to work with the pain stick in earnest. I retreated to the forest. Its branches held my tears. The breeze tousled my hair, entreating me to forget. I sheltered there, at peace in the storm that ravaged my body. I was surprised when the door slammed, and Isandor left. My body ached from the spasms the pain stick had caused, but I had felt almost none of the abuse.

Isandor was never sober after that. His body plagued me less and less, and the pain stick could not reach me. Then, Isandor began to experiment with different kinds of pain.

Once, he cut me with his knife. I watched the blood spread over the sheets, and I laughed. "Do you think I care if you kill me, Isandor? Let the blood flow, and with it, my life will be released from your torment." He did not cut me again.

It seemed to pleasure Isandor most greatly when the blows of his fist caused my body to turn blue and purple. Those marks fascinated him. He often stood over me, staring at the record of his violence.

I did not care. Isandor was like a pebble thrown on the surface of the water. For a moment only, he disturbed my calm. Then he sank to the depths of his wretchedness, and my soul was left untouched.

Shaarvan

I have searched Watha from its forested outskirts to its clusters of cities. I have carried the *flaorth* tracker everywhere with me. I have two teams of men led by Shapechanger scouring the settlements. We have gone from house to house, bazaar to tent. We have cross-examined every slaver, every trader, and every dealer in girls. Yet, how can I be sure that Shaara is not on this planet? I could spend years combing each dwelling and still miss her. It is an impossible task.

My father transmitted several lengthy messages. His communications discussed the searches of his men on Altar, Despega, and Cinder, but it is evident that he has been as frustrated as I by the lack of information we have to go on. He gave me his promise that all his ships and resources would be at my service, but he had the gall to urge me to set a time limit for my pursuit. "Dedicate a thirtyTide, or a fortyTide, if you must," he implored me. "But, then, concede that Shaara is lost if you have still found nothing."

"Is that what you would do if Mother were taken?" I lashed out at him angrily.

"Yes," he answered me, and perhaps it was true. But I knew that I could not stop. I could never disregard the promises I had made to my wife. I could never halt the dreams that still plagued my sleep, and I would never be able to stop wanting her in my arms at night. Her eyes would always haunt me, even in the day — her eyes so watchful for my mood, so curious, so joyful, so Shaara. She was my chosen, my wife. How could I listen to my father or to Tem? How could I ever declare that what Shaara and I had together was over on some named date of the future? How could I stop this pursuit, this obsession? I could not. It was impossible to give Shaara up.

Chapter Five

Sleena

Blair cooped up Crimson Black in a stall, and I was given permission to try to calm him. Blair stood watching me the first time like he was afraid I'd disobey and attempt to touch the stallion. I had promised him I would not. I did not understand why he did not accept my word.

"Hi there, beautiful one," I greeted Crimson Black. His low blast of warning was almost a growl. I stayed silent. The stallion put his ears back and trumpeted once more. He knew I was still there, and he cautioned me not to come closer.

I froze, waiting for him to get curious. When at last he stretched his head through the opening, again I spoke. "I've been watching you for weeks, Crimson Black. You're smarter than all the others. That's why you're in so much trouble. I understand you."

Again, a loud blowing through his nostrils was a warning given. His back hooves kicked at the stable door. I waited, silent as a listening forest. I heard Blair slip away, but the stable was so quiet, then that I could hear the sound of Crimson's breathing as he tested the air.

Once more, the horse couldn't stand his curiosity, and his head poked out to look at me. "I respect you, Crimson, for your intellect, but they want to kill you because of it. You have to listen to me."

He paid enough attention to my words to kick at the door again. His bugle once more challenged my right to stand so close.

"Please don't let them kill you, Crimson," I said when his long neck poked around the stall to look at me. "You're all that keeps me alive. If they kill you, I will go, too, Crimson. Maybe somewhere else, there's a better world."

Crimson's ears were flicking back and forth, listening to the sounds I made. I knew he could not understand my words, but maybe something filtered in. Already his interest in what I was doing was overcoming his fear. He was blowing at me, but he was also sniffing the scent of me in the wind.

"Do not touch him, Sleena."

Crimson wheeled back into his stall and sounded off about the second voice. I glared at Blair. Where had he come from? His feet had made no sound.

"I gave you my word."

"Does spit fly?" he said.

I wasn't sure what he meant by that. I'd never understood the men's fascination with spit.

Blair's eyes met mine. I knew then he'd heard my words to Crimson. There was a sadness in his eyes that shouldn't be there. He cleared his throat, grinding away his pity, but had the good sense not to mention what I'd said. "All right, Sleena. That's enough for today. Run on home before Isandor comes looking for you."

I started to go, but Blair called me back. "Sleena, I've been meaning to ask you. He hasn't gotten any worse, has he?"

I kept my eyes down. "I'm OK," I told Blair. It was the best I could do without lying.

It's funny how something good is always followed by something bad. Did Frieda's god, Barquel, up there in the heavens, make sure to balance it all out like she said he did? Did he weigh the wonder of being given permission to tame Crimson Black with the horror of

Isandor in a rage? What would happen if sometimes Barquel let slip two goods in a row? Would the heavens burst and the stars fall?

I won't go into details. Isandor was drunk and angry. He rotated his methods of beating me, so it was harder to shut him out. My body felt like a punching bag. It was a blessing when I passed out. I woke to find that Isandor had raped me while I was unconscious. There was semen on my thigh, and I hurt all over.

The pain stick, the beatings, and the rape — the highs were not nearly high enough, and the lows were too quickly following. I wasn't willing to endure it anymore. If it was a coward's way, then let me be a coward. Even with Crimson Black, the price of living had become too great.

Methodically, I dressed and hobbled downstairs. The knife was calling me. I would listen this time to its love song. Quietly, I pulled the drawer open. There it lay, gleaming silver, clean and strong. I lifted it up and touched the blade lovingly. I pressed the sharp edge of it against the blue of my veins. Would I be able to slice two wrists or only one?

"Courage," I said out loud. "The pain of it can be no worse than Isandor."

Should I sit down? No, there would be more strength in my arm if I stood. I raised the knife and lay my arm against the table. I was sorry Frieda and Flar would find me. I wondered if they would miss me. Would Blair? I sighed one last time and lowered the knife to let it drink.

"Drop it."

The voice startled me. I obeyed without thinking. Then, I turned around to glare at the man who had stopped me. It was the cycle of the Sky demon. Frieda and Flar were both sacrificing themselves in the arms of a lover. Had this man expected Frieda to be here? I didn't know why else he would have come. Why had he interfered?

"Who are you?" I demanded.

The man didn't answer. He reached down and picked up the knife. He placed it high over my head on top of the cabinet.

"I think you know," he said.

"Why would I know?"

"Because it is obvious that Isandor told you."

"Do you always talk in riddles? You have come into this house, stolen the knife . . ."

"It's not stolen; it is only put away from little girls."

The way he emphasized girls made it sound like he wasn't sure I *was* one. I turned my back to him and attempted to walk out of the kitchen.

"Turning your back on a man is an insult in many cultures."

"So is calling me a 'little girl.'"

"I see."

"I'm glad one of us does."

"Sleena, did Isandor name you that?"

"Yes."

"I shall call you 'Lea.'"

He wasn't easy to read. His mind was more complex than the others, but I stared into his eyes and sought the core of him.

He slapped me. "No, you will not read me. Lead me to your room. I am your new master."

He wasn't lying. I could tell that.

"Isandor gambled me and lost?" It wasn't difficult to guess my change of fortune. I'd often wondered how he could gamble at all, as drunk as he was lately.

"Correct," the man verified.

I took a deep breath for courage, but I couldn't move. The man reminded me of someone. Stars, I wanted my memory back!

"I see you are a difficult slave," he said.

One arm swung me around, and the next instant, I was draped over his shoulder like a Puda's toga. I was so startled that without thinking, I punted him with my knee.

"Lea, if you kick or hit me again, I will be forced to thrash you."

I lay still after his words. I had already been beaten once that day. I did not relish another go. The man carried me on his shoulders the whole way up the stairs. When we reached the top, I was certain he'd be winded, but his voice was even as he asked, "Which door?"

"The red one."

Like Isandor had often, the man tossed me onto the bed. "Strip," he ordered.

It was too much. I'd been raped, beaten, and I'd almost succeeded in killing myself. Why wasn't Barquel doing his balancing act? Didn't I deserve a little good now? But what would a male god know of justice?

I felt so sorry for myself that I started to cry. I grabbed at the sheets to hide my face, and I let it happen. All the pain and the wretchedness of the day poured out until I was drained of it.

The man said nothing, just stood there watching me. "Are you finished now?" he asked when I'd quieted.

I wanted to throw something at him. I reached over to the other side of the bed for one of Isandor's shoes. I grabbed at it and raised it up. The man's hand clasped mine like a vise, squeezing. The shoe dropped to the bed with a dull thump, and the man tossed it away from me.

"I am not a patient person, Lea. Stop your games and undress."

I was only making him angrier. He was not going to go away. Resigned to what was to come, I stood up and unbuttoned my shirt. The pants had ties in the front, which I attempted to unfasten, but I ached from the earlier beating, and a sudden surge of anger made me say, "You want them off. You take them off."

"For such a little girl, you sure use powerful words," he warned me. The expression in his eyes made me change my mind, but it was too late. "All right. I will," he said, and he lurched towards me.

I jumped over the bed to the other side. "I've been raped once today. Don't you think that's enough?"

He stopped. "Lea, last chance to avoid punishment. Come here."

I studied his face. The chin, hard and muscular, and the set of his jaw told me that this was a man who did what he said. It was a stubborn chin, and the clench of his teeth in the jawline showed determination. His eyes were capped by ridiculously thick eyebrows, dark as the midnight sky, darker than even the blackness of his full head of hair. One of his eyebrows raised slightly in warning. His deep olive-green eyes, hard and as resolute as the set of his jaw, narrowed as he watched me.

I sagged and crept around the bed. My eyes lowered in acceptance. I was through challenging. I knew this man. His soul was tempered, cold, hard steel.

I stood before him. His great size dwarfed me. He was massive, solid as the boulder I sometimes climbed to gaze out into the field of landoors. His hand raised my chin, and he stared into my eyes. "You do not feel exactly like a Shapechanger, Lea, yet your eyes are gray like theirs. There is a mystery here I do not understand, but I shall soon find out."

His hands smoothed the shirt off my back. His eyes widened at my breasts, but he did not touch them. He pushed me down on the bed. He wasn't as rough as I'd expected, nor did I feel any anger from him, although I had given him cause to be furious with me.

His hands pulled down my pants, and he lifted them off of me and tossed them on the floor. I watched them as they fell on top of my shirt.

"Lie down," he ordered.

I lay back on the bed. I wondered when he would disrobe, but he did not seem inclined. He stood there drinking me in, his gaze traveling up and down my body. I shivered under the intensity. I knew that his eyes took in more than the sight of a warm female body lying there. His force was penetrating.

"Please," I began, but I stopped, not knowing what I wanted to say. Please, don't rape me? Please, let me go? Please, let me cover my nakedness? None of them would I say, for the answer was in his ownership. It was his right.

The man's eyes had moved up to study my face. "I have seen many girls, but none has been more perfectly shaped than you. Yet you hid it so successfully. I doubted you even had a figure."

He spoke as if to himself. I did not answer, but I felt his mind grow hot with his desire. I was amazed when he lay down beside me, still fully clothed.

His hand reached up and touched my face. The fingers were roughened like Isandor's but somehow gentle in their caress. "Why did Isandor hate you so?" he asked, examining the bruises on my shoulders and breasts.

"Because I am cold."

The man shook his head as if it confirmed one more thing in his mind. "He is an oaf, Lea. Forget him. If you are a Shapechanger, you will always be cold, except to your bondmate. If you are merely frigid, I will teach you to respond."

"Isandor could not." Once more, my eyes raised in challenge. I would not be cursed again for what I couldn't change. If I were unable to respond to a man's touch, I would not be beaten for it.

"I like your spunk, but I will punish disobedience. Do not think to be the rider with me. If I ride you, it will be me on top, Lea."

He was a different man from Isandor. The depth of him astounded me. His control scared me. I could not peer inside him.

"Good. Your eyes tell me you understand more than words can paint. There is a keen intelligence there. We shall get along fine, my little hidden jewel."

I looked away. He had not won more than my body in the casino. Isandor, I had endured, although I had been nauseated by his touch. This man, who probed my soul, I was beginning to hate.

He did not allow my withdrawal. His hand moved and stroked, sketching odd patterns on the skin of my cheek.

"Stop!" I said, "Rape me if that is your will, but do not play with me, tormenting me like that!"

"For a slave, your mouth is far too liberal. I will do as I wish."

My hand attempted to brush his fingers away as it would a spider's web that clung to me. I did not consciously seek to fight him.

He jerked my hand above my head and secured it. The force of it hurt my wrist. My eyes watered, and a whimper slipped out.

"I warned you. I am not a patient man. If you struggle more, I shall bind you." His eyes backed up the threat as his hand released me.

I would not resist again. I shut my eyes and searched for my forest. I saw the trees with their branches stretched towards the sky, but they did not call me. The hand with its patterns held my mind. I dropped down to the forest ground to smell the pine fragrance of the needles. The sharp pungency of the odor drew me. The needles pricked my knees, itchy, yet comforting, and the hand on my face with its caress…

"No!" I cried out, and my tears once again began to fall. "Don't do this!"

But it was too late. He had opened my defenses. My hands reached out to touch the man, to draw him down. *Kiss me,* my mind called to him. *Claim my mouth, and you will know me.* His lips drew near. I could almost taste the fullness of their lusciousness. I rose to meet them, arching with my need.

"Hold!" he cried out. "Shapechanger witch. I have learned what I wanted to know. You will not woo me with the magic of your Power."

He sat up and threw his legs off the bed and down to the ground. Then, he stood there watching me. I had no idea what he was talking about. I was ready for him. Why was he leaving me?

"I did not fight you," I said.

"You are not Lea. You are Shapechanger. Tell me your name."

"I do not know. Isandor bought me from a slaver who called me Slettha. Isandor named me Sleena."

"Two times your name began with an 'S.' Coincidence? I think not. Stranger things have happened with Shapechanger. I will not call you Sleena -- diamonds are cold and hard. Your body speaks of neither. Nor will I proclaim your Power in a name. It could endanger you. Skeva — 'Tiny One' — I will call you until your people come."

"My people?"

"You are Shapechanger. It would be dangerous to own you and death if I gave in to my desire for you. I will contact Altar. Perhaps they can trace you."

"But the slaver bought me when my master died."

"He lied. Shapechanger are never sold, nor would you have had a master. A Shapechanger does not change a slave into a Shapechanger unless he takes her as his wife. If your husband were dead, another would have claimed you. Once of the blood, you are always Shapechanger."

I did not understand. Why had I been sold to Isandor then? Maybe there were exceptions. "What will you do if the Shapechanger do not want me back?"

For a moment, the man's eyes surveyed my body. "You belong to me until you are claimed. I will not make decisions on what is wishful thinking."

Then, as if storm clouds traveled with the wind across his face, Tren grew dangerous. He sprang at me, grabbing at my wrists to pull me up. I could not fathom his sudden anger. The numerous beatings of Isandor had robbed me of my courage, and like a coward, I fell down to my knees, covering my head with my arms.

"Stand up, Skeva. I'm not going to hit you," he yelled at me. The anger in his voice was full of exasperation.

I opened my eyes to study his. Obediently, I stood. There was no longer any defiance in me.

"You will *not* keep your appointment with the knife. Promise me, or I shall lock you up until your people come."

He meant it. I stared into his eyes and attempted to read him.

"Promise," he ordered and his will prevented me from knowing his thoughts.

"You will not beat me?"

He shook his head. "I am not an Isandor."

"Or rape me?"

Again, he shook his head, but his eyes smiled. "I do not think it would have been rape, Skeva, but you are free of me. I will not touch you unless the Shapechanger deny you."

I blushed at his eyes, the way they had looked into my soul and the frank way they appraised me now. "I promise," I said.

"Good."

He turned to go, but I cried out. "Wait, please."

Once more, his eyes returned to mine.

"You own me, but I do not even know your name."

"Tren."

"You will leave me here?"

"You are better off here than with me. Keep your disguise and walk with your eyes down. I will pay for your board. You may continue as you were before I won you. You glow with good health, so I know they are feeding you sufficiently. Isandor seemed your only problem. He cannot bother you now. Your bruises will heal. You are young."

"But what about Isandor? This is his room."

"He will have to move elsewhere."

"But, if I need you — where do you live?"

"You can find me in the casino."

"No! You will gamble me off like Isandor did."

"I will not risk you, Skeva. I would lose the casino itself before I dared barter you."

"Lose the casino?"

"I am the owner."

I nodded. I understood, then, that I was probably safe for a while. "Thank you, Tren."

He turned again to leave. He pulled the door open, and I stared at his tight, hard buttocks.

"Tren."

He stopped, but he did not turn back towards me.

"You were right, Tren. I was not cold like Isandor said I was. I was ready for you."

He did not answer but continued out the door.

Thenos

This imperfection of my plan is upsetting. I find that I cannot concentrate properly. How can I conquer Altar if everyone around me is an idiot? Some thirty of my peasants have gathered to tell me of their inability to locate my Shaara. Their excuses anger me. If money and girls will not unveil Megloztar's hiding spot, then violence must flush him out. I will not tolerate the failure that these commoners cloak their explanations in. They will find my Shaara or die.

The thought of their death pleases me. Too long have we Shapechanger hidden in the shadows. Why should we not proclaim the feats that we can do? Why should we camouflage our strength? I shall use these peasants to build my realm. But, afterward, they will view the true sovereignty of the Shapechanger, and all these dirt-infested commoners will cower before us.

Perhaps a touch of fear will guide their success in the endeavor I have set for them. I shall allow my face to shadow with the patterns of my fur and let my teeth grow long and sharp. My claws will extend.

They who serve me will be the first to witness my Power. Perhaps I shall rend a commoner or two so those around me will know that what I demand, I expect them to achieve.

Seeing me begin the transformation, one of them whimpers. My tail thumps on the ground. The man's fear reeks of almonds. What a delicious morsel he would be should I choose to dine. Pity that I need these peons.

"Hear me, my associates, my noble followers," I say, feeding them the words they want to be told. "We are almost there, the victors of the richest planet in our space. We shall be great!"

They cheer as if I have said something new. They are like spellbound children in their one-dimensional beliefs.

"The Elders are weak and ready to be conquered. I have done that for you, my devoted supporters."

Once again, I pause to allow them to gloat over their intelligence in being connected with me.

I continue as they quiet down. "But you must aid me in my line of attack, my colleagues." The man in the second row, with the pale face, appears to be thinking about my statement. How unwise. I shall watch him closely.

He feels my eyes on him, and the almond scent grows stronger. I smile and curl my lip up slightly to show my teeth. He trembles. A growl would send him tumbling to the ground in abject terror. I am pleased.

"A necessary component has slipped away from us."

They are mine now, these commoners. I have emoted successfully. Their devotion will not be uncertain again. What contentment it brings me to curl my tail around their thoughts so masterfully.

"You think I desire the wife of my brother because I lust? Do not be foolish. I have a shipload of girls. Any one of them would serve that need. Shaara of Shaarvan has other value. She is intimate with the Old Ones, having been taken in the Old Way. You do not understand the significance of that, my cohorts, but it makes her the most Powerful of all Shapechanger females. At the side of Shaarvan, she and my brother may be able to defeat us. Whereas, if she is owned by me, the balance is on our side."

The peons are easily impressed. With that input, they are eager to support my desire for Shaara. But I am not through with them. I will not have them harm her in their zeal.

"Imagine her Power co-mingled with mine. Picture the sons she will bear me, the sons who will make you great. Altar will have a throne again, and we will rule. Bring me the woman — bring me Shaara of Shaarvan."

The cheering goes on and on. I am bored. I turn and walk away. Not even the smell of almonds entices my appetite. The thought of Shaara hidden away from me by the treachery of a Theinian peasant thwarts my contentment.

Skeva

I worked the next day in the kitchen as usual. I liked to make the bread, kneading it with my hands, punching it, and poking at its fullness. I had taken over the rest of the cooking, too. Frieda had been in the Sky Demon's influence for a week, and she was more often in her room with a man than in the kitchen.

I heard them that morning in the peak of their joining. Their moans of completion sent ripples of desire through me. My need urged me to go to Tren, but I did not. I wanted him, but not enough to bring his death, if what he said was true. Or had he only said that because he was afraid to join with a Shapechanger?

What was there about me that so many people feared? My eyes of gray had not kept me from being beaten by Isandor. They had not kept me from being sold as a slave. What was there about Shapechanger that frightened people? It had frightened all those buyers, Flar and even Tren, right out of my bed. Were Shapechanger not just people like everyone else?

After my morning chores were done, I went to the stables, as usual. I wouldn't say that Crimson acted really glad to see me unless you call three bugles, two blasts, a kick, and a stomp a greeting. I ignored his anger and told Crimson everything that happened at the house the day before. I don't know if he was interested, but his ears flipped back and forth, and he only snorted once as he listened. I was almost finished telling him my woes when Blair stormed up.

"Sleena," he said with a heavy sadness. "You must not come to the stable anymore. Isandor was here last night, storming about how he'll kill you if you come here again. I'm sure he wouldn't really kill you, but he'll sure beat the spit out of you if he finds you disobeyed. You had best stay away, at least until he cools down."

"He already beat me, Blair, but it doesn't matter anymore because Isandor doesn't own me anymore!"

I figured that Crimson's training was all ruined by Blair's yelling. One more weird sight couldn't bother his mind any more than it already was, so I cartwheeled across the lawn, yelling, "Isandor doesn't own me!"

"What in the spit was that?" Blair asked when I returned. His eyes were almost as wide as Crimson's feed bucket.

"I was celebrating. Haven't you ever seen cartwheels before?"

"The wheel of a cart? Did Isandor hit you in the head, Sleena?"

"No! And I feel wonderful!"

"All right, slow down, girl," Blair said, shaking his head and deciding to ignore my gymnastics. "What do you mean Isandor doesn't own you? I told you he *refused* to sell you. Why would he suddenly change his mind?"

"He didn't sell me. He *lost* me in the casino. Tren owns me now."

"Oh, spit and double spit! Sleena, I'm so sorry. Maybe I can buy you before Tren pulls you into that whorehouse of his." Blair suddenly turned red as a radish. "Sorry, Sleena. I didn't mean to say that. Don't worry about it. I'll do my best to get you out of his clutches."

"Sorry? Tren is great!"

"Who the spit told you that?" Blair looked like he wanted to grab me and shake some sense into my head. I almost giggled at the vision of Blair shaking me with his teeth, like one of the rubber toys we gave the colts to play with. As if he sensed my laughter, he flicked his riding crop at my leg. I didn't feel it, but I knew the warning.

"Tren came to the house last night, and he didn't beat me or anything, Blair. He was nice! He said I could do whatever I wanted to do."

For a moment, there was only puzzlement on Blair's face. "Tren? The Tren-who- owns-the-casino Tren?"

"Yes."

Blair laughed. He brought the crop down on his own hand several times as if the motion helped him think. Then, he shook his head at me. "Tren would be just as happy to kill a person as to smile at him. He eats little girls like you and swallows them whole, Sleena."

There was a ring of truth in his statement. Something about Tren had told me that he was dangerous. "He could have last night, Blair, but he didn't."

Blair just stared at me, and then he shook his head. "Well, if you think you're going to spend time here like when you belonged to Isandor, I'm afraid the answer is 'no.' "

Blair's voice was gruff, but I knew it hurt him to say it. "Listen, Sleena, I'll try again to buy you, but I can't stand up against Tren. He's got friends I don't want, understand?"

Blair was almost pleading with me to agree. What would he have me do — walk away from everything that made life tolerable? I couldn't leave Crimson, not now.

He could tell from my face just what I was thinking. "I like you, kid. You've got spunk. But I don't need problems with Tren."

I sighed and thought about solutions. I watched a spider in the corner of Crimson's stall. Its four legs were busy threading the straw from Crimson's stall into a pattern. I wondered if the spider's web would be able to withstand the slight breeze that was waving it back and forth. The spider was riding it like a sailor on rough seas.

"What if Tren would come and tell you that it's OK for me to be here?"

Blair laughed. It was so robust it set Crimson off into a snorting, kicking rage. Blair backed us further away. I noticed he didn't touch me. He used his crop to push me back.

"If Tren comes here in person," he said, chuckling like I had told him some wonderful joke. "If he comes here and tells me that he will permit you to play around with the landoors, dressed like a boy, then I'll say 'yes.' " Again, Blair burst into laughter. "And I'll eat straw, too!"

I ignored his scorn. I raised my head and looked Blair fully in the eyes. "OK, then, I'll go ask him."

The crop barred my way. "Hold it, child. You stay away from that one."

"I can't. He owns me now. Except . . . I don't really know where to find him."

"Sleena, nobody wants to *find* Tren. He usually locates *them*, and what he does to people isn't friendly. Listen to me. You don't want to go looking for him."

"You're the one who said I had to. Where would I find him if I had to find him? He said he's usually in the casino. But where's that?"

"That's easy, Sleena. It's the tall, black building over there. It's the only tall building in town. It's where Tren and every foul smell on the planet can be found."

"Then that's where I'll go."

"Sleena, if Tren *really* owns you, I can't tell you what to do. But my advice is that you stay away from the casino. It's not a place for a kid like you."

"I'm not worried about that. I just hope they'll let me in."

Blair laughed. "If Tren owns you, they can't keep you out. But getting in is not the problem — it's whether they will ever let you out again. Even Isandor, as bad a master as he was, would never let you near that place. It's too dangerous for a girl. In fact, maybe you had best just disappear, Sleena. I could give you some money. You could leave here and find someplace safer."

"No," I said, shaking my head. "I told you — Tren was nice to me. He said I could do whatever I wanted. He'll let me come here, and he won't get mad at you for letting me be near Crimson."

Blair shook his head. "Does spit fly? You were almost safer with Isandor."

"Right!" I said sarcastically.

I set out searching for the black casino. It was just around the corner, but I'd never seen it. I'd never gone farther than the landoors.

As I walked, I mulled over the things that Blair had said. He had made me doubt my memory. Had Tren really been as nice as I'd recalled?

I tried not to let Blair's words scare me, but he *was* pretty knowledgeable, and I'd never known him to be wrong. The walk to the casino was a lot farther to go than I'd been before — not in distance, maybe, but in courage.

At the front door, the biggest man I'd ever seen tried to bar me from entering. He was as tall as the doorway and had to stoop to come out. He was almost as broad, too, but his broad wasn't at all like Flar's. His "broad" was all muscle.

"I have to see Tren," I told the giant.

"Sure you do. Come back later, like in a couple of years, when you're grown up."

"No! I have to see him right now!"

"Look, kid, Tren doesn't want to see anyone right now. Take my word for it."

"Tren is my master, and he said . . ."

I didn't have to finish the sentence. The door opened like magic. The giant stepped back and bowed me in. His bow was a mockery, but I ignored it and raised my chin.

I couldn't believe the inside of the place. Thick, red carpeting, laid across the floor, covered the entire area. It was so soft that it was like walking on piles of green leaves, but there was no sound as my feet passed over it. The walls of the room were decorated with huge murals that moved and looked like real people. I gaped at it, trying to figure out how something so animated could be fake. It was a moment before I realized that in the murals, the men were doing things to women I didn't think I should see. I carefully averted my eyes and looked towards the people standing all around me. They were watching me like I was a rare kind of creature.

I glanced back at the front door. The giant had disappeared, and the door was once again bolted shut. I turned all around, viewing the inside, making sure that I looked away from the murals and the wall of eyes staring at me. I scanned for Tren. A crowd of people was lined up around a big machine. I didn't think any of them were Tren, but I walked closer to make sure. The strange, noisy thing that all the people were watching had twirling lights in greens and yellows, and it was spinning so fast it hurt my eyes. I wondered how the people could focus on it so intently.

One tall lady with a huge spiked helmet was resting her leg against the side of the thing. Her leg was painted green with some kind of glittery frosting that perfectly matched the plume on her helmet. I approached her and waited for her to look at me. The woman shoved her leg down, ran her fingers down the sides of her outfit, and lifted up her naked breasts. Then, she looked at me.

"Baa! You stink, kid. Don't you ever take a bath?"

I ignored her question. "Do you know where Tren is?"

"Kid, you don't want to know." She laughed at me and placed her other leg up on the machine. Her tight, very short shorts barely covered what they were supposed to cover, and she had nothing else on. I tried to keep my eyes from bulging at the sight of her pendulous green breasts.

"Tell you what, kid." Her helmet bobbed back and forth as she spoke. "You barge on in, and I'll buy you a drink . . . if you're still alive afterward!" Her laugh was infectious. The others nearby joined in. Their eyes were all watching me curiously.

I ignored them, but I couldn't pull my eyes away from the green woman. She was bobbing her head up and down as she laughed. I was afraid that her helmet would go flying off at any moment. At one point, when her laughter had bobbed the helmet far too forward for it to stay on, I reached out to catch it.

The green woman fell over the machine in a spasm of laughter, causing a couple of the men to swear heavy oaths at her. Everyone else snickered. My face turned hot, and I looked down at the ground, mortified that everyone was laughing at my mistake. The woman righted herself and took another look at me. Then she started to hoot and chuckle harder. "Well, spit on my boobs! Will you look at that! The kid's blushing."

I started to move on, but the woman whirled up and grabbed me by the arm, swinging me around. "Hey, kid," she said. "The helmet never comes off. I had it attached permanently. It doesn't even come off in bed. Want to watch? Hey, Gipa, want to ruffle my plumage a little and show the kid?"

A huge man with an ugly, red-scarred face turned to look at us. He growled something at me. Then his arm reached out and twined around the green woman's neck. "Bola, you are irritating me. Shut up," he said.

I thought the woman would be frightened, but she just laughed and grabbed for Gipa's manhood. "I don't always irritate you, Gipa. How about we entertain the kid for a while?"

I backed away from them and moved further on into Tren's casino. Behind me, I heard the woman continue to laugh. Her voice sounded like the high-pitched screech of someone on drugs. Somewhere, I'd heard a similar speech pattern. The memory drifted off before I could catch it.

I kept walking, dodging drunken men and women and hands that tried to grab me as I passed by. A man erupted a belly full of booze that almost caught my shoes. I backed up too quickly and fell into another man's lap. He wasn't pleased. I was saying I was sorry while he was roughly throwing me off of him. His toss landed me in the hands of another. That man breathed his sour breath on me and threatened to cut me up. I was shaking when I wiggled away from him.

I began to wish that I had taken Blair's advice and stayed away from the casino. But all the faces around me were angry, and I couldn't see the green woman anymore. I nudged and pried my way through a group of males until I reached the wooden booth where a serving man was doling out liquor. "Please, could you tell me where Tren is?" I asked.

The bartender's eyes narrowed as he examined me. Then, a corner of his mouth lifted, and he shrugged and pointed upstairs. "Only one door up there, kid. You'll find him there, but he's not going to like it. If I were you, I'd wait here. It's a spit and a heck better than having him tear your ears off, boy."

A dirty-smelling, heavy male moved closer. "Need some help, little man?" he asked. His mouth was smiling, but I didn't trust his eyes.

I shook my head and turned to move towards the stairs. The man with the shifty eyes reached out and grabbed at me. He caught my shirt and pulled me towards him.

"Let me go," I said, keeping my voice low and gravelly so he wouldn't know that I was female.

"How about I buy you something to drink, my little friend? What do you think a kid his age would drink?" he asked the others, who had all clustered about, laughing and jeering as I tried to wiggle away.

"Give him some *urgul*. That'll quiet him down," said the big gorilla on my left.

"Let the kid go," the bartender said. "He's been asking for Tren. That could be trouble for you."

"Ah, since when does Tren bother with runts like this?" asked the ugly one holding me. He still had my shirt all twisted at the neck. I couldn't move enough to even fight him.

"I belong to Tren," I said. "He's going to be mad if…"

"What you saying, boy? You trying to tell me Tren…"

"I told you to let the kid go, Bebor. This is your last warning." The bartender had pulled out a pipe weapon and was aiming it at the man holding me. The jerk let go of me so quickly that I almost fell. I regained my feet, threw a thank you over my shoulder, and ran through the crowd without stopping. I was almost surprised when I reached the stairs without further problems, but I looked back and saw that the bartender was still holding the weapon. He nodded to me, slipped the pipe gun under the counter, and went back to serving drinks.

I ran up the stairs without pausing and flung open the door. It hadn't been locked, but it should have been. I froze as I realized what the others had all been talking about. Tren was in bed with someone. He was on top and very in the middle of actively pursuing man's favorite sport. I felt my face turning red and started to back away.

"What in Barquel's butt, Skeva? Get back in here." Tren's voice was firm and as icy as the frost I sometimes scraped off the top of the landoors' water buckets. I knew I'd better not retreat. I stopped and waited.

"What in the name of Barquel are you doing here?" he cursed at me as he disconnected himself and crawled off the woman.

"You told me I could…"

"I told you to come here? I thought I told you to stay away."

I was trying not to watch Tren, but his body was beautiful. It was difficult not to be fascinated by the hairiness of his chest, his hard, flat stomach, and the rest of him that was just as magnificent.

Tren didn't attempt to cover himself, but he glanced over at the woman beside him. "Malla, pull the sheet up over yourself." Then, he glared back at me. "Get in here and shut the spittin' door." He watched me a moment as I obeyed. I leaned against the door, and my eyes continued to assess Tren's firm, hard body. I wondered if he'd get angry if I walked forward and touched him.

"Seen enough?" He laughed at me and added, "Turn around pest. Your eyes are too inviting."

"I'm sorry," I said quickly, looking down. He was silent a moment, still watching me. I darted a glance. He didn't look angry. "I thought you said I was Skeva," I teased.

"Turn around!"

I turned. I could hear him pulling on his pants and connecting the tags. The sound of his feet slapping at the floor as he strode towards me kept me from being startled when he whirled me around to face him. "Why are you here?" he demanded.

My legs were suddenly feeling wobbly. With his touch, I was reminded too vividly of his great strength. Would he beat me? Would he forget his promise and become an Isandor?

"Please, could I sit down?"

"No, you're not staying here. I told you I don't want you in the casino."

I sighed. He was gruff with irritation, but he wasn't angry.

He was holding me away from him. Instinctively, I attempted to lean inwards against his long, lean body. As if I were a sheet being hung in the breeze, he flicked me away from him yet held me with hands that clinched pinchingly against the skin of my inner arms.

"Answer me," he ordered. "Why are you here?"

Gray eyes. His eyes should be gray, I thought. Then, I shuddered and looked down at the floor, wondering why I would have such strange thoughts. With a body like Tren's, what difference did it make in the color of his eyes? I sighed. "There's a man named Blair who owns landoors," I said. "He's kind of a friend."

Tren's eyebrows went up. "A male friend?"

I nodded. "He said I could talk to his landoors only if you gave your permission."

"Is this supposed to make sense?"

Tren was no longer irritated. His eyes were amused. I looked up into them, admiring their greenish tint. "Please, please say that I may," I pleaded.

Tren was shaking his head at me, but he was smiling. His eyes were resting on my hat, noting the fine strands of hair that poked out at the sides. One of his hands released me and moved up to slide the hat off. My hair dropped down, falling in curls around my shoulders and back.

The woman, who I'd thought was drifting off into sleep, suddenly sat up. "It's a girl!" she cried out, her eyes bulging like day-old fish eyes. I don't think Tren saw the similarity. His attention was on her bone-white breasts that overflowed and jutted out into the room. Tren's bed partner had a lot more conical mass than the green lady.

I tossed my head and felt the hair springing out in its full volume. Even that did not take Tren's eyes away from the woman. They were staring at each other like I wasn't standing there between them.

Recklessly, my hand reached up and began to stroke the fine brown hairs on Tren's naked chest. I could feel the ripples of his muscles as he jerked away.

"Stop that, Skeva," he ordered sharply. His hand gripped mine so firmly it hurt, but his eyes were back on me. "Cover yourself, Malla, and don't speak until you are spoken to," he ordered the nude.

"Crimson Black is going to be killed if you don't come to tell Blair that I may tame him."

"Tame who? Crimson Black? Is that the name of a landoor?" Tren's eyes were once more where I wanted them. I smiled up into his face. I had been told that my smile was beautiful. I hoped that Tren would find it so.

Tren had not let go of my hand. I enjoyed holding his hand. I liked the feel of it — strong and big but not callused and rough. I wanted to rub my face against it, but I knew he would not allow me to, and the woman might protest and steal his attention once more.

"Yes," I replied. "But Crimson Black is really called High Mountain Peak."

"So you came to the casino to drag me to your friend's house to give permission so you can talk to a landoor?" Tren asked, shaking his head. "Skeva, did it ever occur to you that I might be busy?"

"I saw that you were busy," I told him. "I will wait outside while you finish if you would like." I sheathed my eyes slowly and then looked up at him with what I hoped was an innocent look of appeal. I hoped he could not feel the beat of my heart, which was pounding away like a Garon's tom-tom, as I waited for his reply.

"No, that won't be necessary," Tren said. "I have no intention of letting you out of my sight, not in the casino."

He let go of me and turned to finish dressing. My eyes met Malla's. She was beginning to pout. Tren was too busy putting his shoes and socks on to notice. Malla's mouth was red from artificial color, and what she did to her lips when she pouted made them even redder. She shot a glance at Tren and saw that he had not noticed.

Holding her sheet up under her chin to cover herself, she risked his anger by flashing me a gesture of promised violence. I decided that she had an ugly nose.

Tren finished fastening his shoes. He seemed unaware of what a viper he was bedding. I wished that I dared enlighten him.

Once more, Tren reached out and gripped my arm. He shoved my hat back on my head and tried to stick my hair into it. I shook my head.

"Please?" I asked.

He watched me as I twisted the hair into a cord and poked it all at once into the hat. Then, I pulled the cap down over my head, covering my ears.

"Amazing," he said. Once more, he grabbed me and turned me to face the door. "All right, pest. Let's go."

I was happy to oblige, but as we approached the door, he stopped and turned back to the woman.

"Malla, you hold onto those thoughts we were sharing before Skeva interrupted. They're luscious thoughts. I shall go save a landoor's life, and then I'll be back, and we will continue."

I raised my chin and smiled insolently at Malla. "Thank you, Tren, for caring. You're so wonderful," I told him.

Malla glared. "I'm supposed to wait while you go off with that little spit in the wind?" She sounded cranky and spoiled to me. How could Tren stand her?

"Watch your mouth, woman. And you'll wait just as long as I tell you to if you know what's good for you."

Tren pushed me out the door and slammed it behind us.

"I'm sorry, Tren. I did not mean to cause you problems with your wife."

He laughed, and the tension was gone. The grip on my arm eased. "You know she's not my wife, Skeva. I don't believe in tying myself to one woman."

Was he warning me? Why would I care? I didn't want to be tied to a male.

There were stares everywhere as we descended. The place grew silent. The males looked like baby birds wanting to be fed with their mouths all ajar. Tren ignored them, and I scurried to keep up with him. I looked for the green woman, but I didn't see her. I wondered if Gipa had taken her up on her offer.

The man who'd twisted my shirt around my neck chose that moment to make a rude noise. "Well, look at that! Tren does like little boys."

The males tried to shut him up. One tried to pull him away from the bar, but Bebor wasn't budging. The bartender shook his head warningly and handed the man another drink.

I thought Tren was going to ignore it. He kept walking on as if he hadn't heard Bebor, but then he stopped, turned around, jerked me almost off my feet, and said, "Yeah, I do. You got a problem with it?"

Bebor looked up and met Tren's eyes. He seemed to sober suddenly. He looked around, noticing that all his pals were sliding away. Then, he looked back up into Tren's eyes and shivered. "Nah, no problem," he grunted, shaking his head and drinking down the whole glass of liquid in one gulp.

Tren nodded, satisfied. Without glancing down at me, he turned and marched out into the sunlight. I jogged to keep up with the hand that was painfully gripping my arm, but I said nothing until the giant doorkeeper was back inside, and the gate had closed behind us.

"I'm sorry" I started to say.

Tren cut me off. "I don't want to hear that again."

We walked in silence. It lasted maybe a block, and then I volunteered my opinion about the casino. "Tren, you know it could be a nice place, but it needs more lights. I like the carpet, though, but not the walls. And the people who go there aren't very . . . "

"My customers don't want lights, Skeva."

"Why? You can't see if a place is clean if you don't have lights. Wouldn't they like it better if they could see what they were doing?"

"Do you always ask this many questions?"

I shrugged. "If permitted."

"They don't like lights because they don't want to be seen."

"Why? Why don't they want…?"

"Because most of them are what you'd call *trouble*."

"Why are they in your place, then?"

"Didn't Blair tell you I'm one of them?"

"He said something about your spitting funny or killing people who spit funny, but I told him I think you're nice because you didn't force me."

"I still might, just to shut you up."

I stopped abruptly and stared at Tren. "I'll be quiet if you want me to."

Tren stared at me a moment, and then he burst out laughing. "You shift like the winds."

He was laughing at me. It brought the truth back to me sharply. Tren owned me and could do with me whatever he wanted. Why had I thought he was different? Why had I believed that he cared? There were many ways to be cruel, some of them just as painful as Isandor's.

Tren lifted up my chin. "Skeva, keep talking. You amuse me."

I froze. It was like a shadow of a memory, so nebulous that the wisps of it floated off before I could reach out.

Tren was watching me. His eyes no longer laughed. "Your husband used to say that to you, didn't he?"

"I don't know."

Tren's hand reached out and almost touched my cheek before he dropped it and turned away to look out at the street around us. "You will know soon. I sent a message over the telo already. We should hear something from the Shapechanger in a tenTide."

I nodded, but I'd be just as happy if I never heard from them. I knew nothing of the Shapechanger except that everyone feared them.

I was silent until we approached the farm, and I could see the landoors. Tren didn't know much about them. He didn't act really excited about them, either. I told him all about Crimson Black and how Blair had finally come to allow me to try to gentle the stallion. Tren nodded a lot, but mainly, he just watched my eyes.

Blair came up to us the moment we walked up the path and stopped at the fence. He nodded to Tren politely, but Blair looked really uneasy. I wanted to tell him to relax, but Tren seemed different suddenly. Tren was swaggering and acting tough and dangerous. He didn't act at all like he did when it was just the two of us. Blair kept looking from Tren to me and back again. I could see he was wondering how good an idea this was.

"Skeva says that you are a friend," Tren said.

"Kind of a friend," I corrected him. I wasn't sure how Blair would feel about my calling him that. I was only a slave.

Blair started to stutter. "Skeva? Uh, uh . . . yeah, she's a good kid. I wish her well."

"How well?" The way Tren said it insinuated that Blair had foul intentions.

"Tren!" I protested.

"Skeva, shut up."

Blair didn't like the way Tren had addressed me. He stood up straighter then, and his eyes narrowed. "Look, the kid had a rough time with Isandor. I hope you are planning on treating her better."

I was worried. The silence between them wasn't a good thing. The two of them were like stallions getting ready to rear up and tear each other apart.

"Tren," I begged, almost in a whisper. I touched his arm, wanting to remind him of why we were there.

He jerked my hand away and then reached out and tore the hat off my head. Of course, my hair fell down, falling every which way into my face. Angrily, I grabbed the cap from Tren's fingers and began stuffing it back in. I wished that I could braid it as I did in the household, but a braid always showed through my hat.

The mood between the two men had lightened. They watched me, struggling to cram too much hair into the hat, and they smiled. Tren looked up and caught the look on Blair's face, and he nodded at him. "I'm returning her to the Shapechanger."

Blair looked surprised. "Is that wise?"

"It's wiser than risking one of them discovering her here."

Blair raised up his leg and supported his boot on the bottom rail of the fence. His hand brushed off a speck of dirt on the shiny black of them. "I've always thought that bringing yourself to Shapechanger's attention could complicate life considerably, sometimes even dangerously."

Tren looked over at me. I'd finished putting my disguise back together and was listening but at a distance.

He smiled. "I know what you mean, Blair. I'm already finding that a Shapechanger complicates your life — as too dangerous?" He shrugged. Both men smiled that superior sneer men get when they are mocking a girl.

I was glad that they were relaxing with each other, but I didn't see why I had to be the joke that bound their friendship.

Tren grew more serious. "Skeva says that you need to talk to me about High Mountain Range?"

"High Mountain Peak," Blair corrected. "He's a nightmare landoor. The girl seems to think she can gentle him, but I don't know."

"Let her pleasure herself as she wants, as long as she's not injured, and I guess you know she is not to be touched by anyone. Understand?"

"Understood."

I sighed loudly. Men could be so ridiculous in their worry. No one was going to lay hands on me while Tren owned me, and as to getting hurt, now that Isandor was gone, my odds of having broken bones were considerably lessened.

"Tren, I'm a really good rider. Could I just show you?"

Blair spoke first. He seemed angry. "I told you not to bring up that ridiculousness. Girls do not ride."

Tren was watching me. His eyes narrowed, and he seemed to speculate. "You're good, huh? How do you know?" he challenged me.

"I don't know how I know, but I know I've ridden lots."

"All right. Show us," Tren said.

"You want her to ride a landoor? That's a sport for a man, not a girl."

Tren shrugged. "Let her try it. If she falls off, she won't keep nagging you about it. If she's good, what's the harm?"

"How good a rider?" Blair asked me, looking worried.

"Good enough to ride Showboy," I said, cocky as a yearling colt.

Blair shook his head. "This is on you, Tren, not me. If she breaks an arm or a leg falling off, you're the one who has to set it!"

"It's a deal. What do you wager she can ride as good as one of your grooms?"

"Gamble with a gambler? I'm no fool. Saddle Showboy," Blair called to one of the grooms.

When they brought the gelding out, I checked the girth. It was far too loose. The grooms had tested me. I tightened it and asked for a leg up. A groom obliged when Blair ordered him to.

Showboy was every bit as good as I'd known he would be. His walk started out nervous, bobbing his head up and down, prancing and dancing about. I put my hand down on his neck and talked to him. One of the grooms made a sudden noise, and Showboy threw up his front feet into a half-rear.

"Easy, boy," I cooed. Again, he calmed. Once more around at a walk, and then I let him ease into a sitting trot. He was sweet music, fluid, and as lovely as a melody. I moved on into a canter. Showboy cantered like a dream. I knew they'd been working him on the elements of simple dressage. I moved back into my collected sitting trot and did a half-pass. Smooth as chocolate pudding!

They had a jump field set up, and I figured I'd go for broke. Showboy was eager. He flowed in a perfect rhythm. I matched the jumps, stride-by-stride extending and collecting so that each jump was on time and precise. It had been a long time since I'd ridden, but it was like I'd never stopped. The instincts were still all there.

When I brought Showboy over to the side, I couldn't help glowing. I was sure I'd made my point.

Blair was stunned. "I don't believe it. A girl! A girl just took Showboy over the best course he's done all training season."

Tren laughed. "Too bad you didn't wager that bet. I'd have won, hands down. I shall leave you two now. Blair, Skeva may ride whenever she wants, as long as she has your permission, of course. Just see that she's protected from your crew. I wouldn't want there to be an accounting over it when the Shapechanger arrives.

"Oh, and Skeva may talk all she wants to that landoor she's so fervent about."

"Wait," I cried out. I jumped off Showboy and tossed the reins at Blair. Then I threw my arms around Tren. "Thank you, thank you!" I said.

Tren pushed me away. It wasn't rough, but it was firm. "Skeva," he said, frowning down at me, "if you want to thank me, don't touch me."

"Why? You afraid of me because you say I'm Shapechanger?"

"I think you know better than that."

"You mean, you're afraid of the Shapechanger. They're not going to care that I thanked you!"

"Skeva, go back to your landoors."

"But . "

"Now, Skeva."

I obeyed. I took Showboy's reins, waiting to see what Blair wanted me to do with the landoor. Yet, I couldn't help looking back at Tren. He had turned away from the stable and was heading back to his casino. He was an incredible man, kind and gentle, despite his constant act of being tough. He was handsome, too. I shivered, remembering the way he'd looked when I'd interrupted his sport. What would it be like to share his bed?

It was then I decided that I would take him. I didn't care what some supposed Altarian husband said. If I had Shapechanger Power, like Tren had said, I would use it. It was Tren I wanted.

I rode Showboy once more over the course for Blair. Then, he let me ride two others. I knew that tomorrow I'd be sore, but I didn't care.

Frieda's god, Barquel, must be sleeping. He'd let too many good things come my way. Isandor was gone, and Tren owned me. And Tren was a whole lot better than Isandor. He had promised never to beat me. He had said that I could spend my days with the landoors. And now, I could not only ride, but I could train Crimson Black. What could make life more perfect?

Perhaps that's how the religious got religious. Just when I laughed in his face, Barquel sprang another one on me.

Shaarvan

Two entire planets I have searched with a hundred men and Shapechanger. We have spent plastic like it was water, and for nothing — no hint of Shaara's whereabouts, no rumors, no trails.

I have toured through tents with lines of girls, sat through shows and sales, visited dealers and slavers, talked and questioned, and passed offers of rewards for information at each one of them. The whole girl business nauseates me now. Each half-naked girl I see on the stage in a line-up or being beaten by a slaver takes on the features of Shaara. And I am enraged and repelled by the horror of it.

Where are you, Shaara? You must be fully Shapechanger by now. Why have you not escaped or contacted someone to help you? Why haven't you revealed your nature? How can it be that you are still hidden away unless you are dead, as my father believes? But you are my bonded mate. I would be aware if you had Passed over. I would feel the broken bond between us. Wouldn't I?

Tomorrow, we depart for Casam. I have little hope that you will be there. The Casish are friendly folks who like the Shapechanger. One of them would have told us if a gray-eyed woman was someone's captive. But it is on our way to Melo. We will check it out and leave our reward bulletins.

May the Somber Tree watch over you, my darling. May the Saberey wake your soul. May you come back to me, whole and well.

Skeva

I had thought Isandor was out of the picture, but when I got home, he was lying in wait.

"Took you long enough to get here. Where have you been?"

"With Tren."

Isandor's hand slapped my face. "You lie. You reek of landoor. You've been with your lover, Blair." Isandor reached behind him and pulled out the pain stick.

I saw it, and I knew what he planned to do, but I couldn't believe he'd go up against Tren. "You don't own me anymore," I cried out. "Tren owns me now."

The pain stick tapped me on the stomach. I screamed and doubled over.

"I'll always come back to play with you, Sleena, always."

The smirk on his face should have warned me how dangerous he was, but I was angry. "Leave me alone. You are not my master."

Again, the stick reached out and found my skin. I ran to the door, but Isandor barred the exit with his body. I could only sprint towards my room. It was where he wanted me to go. He drove me there with the stick, slashing at my bottom and my legs. In the room that we had shared for so long, Isandor did not bother to bolt the lock. Frieda and Flar were gone, sacrificing to the Sky Demon. Isandor knew that no one would interfere.

He threw me on the bed and held the stick against my leg. It was on full power. "Thought you were free of me, did you? I bought you, girl, and you are mine. And, although you are as cold as a winter storm, I know you feel this. Feel me, girl, feel me!"

The pain stick kept jabbing at my body. Every muscle ached. My world was nothing but agony. I screamed and screamed, but that did not stop the torment. Blackness found me and embraced me in its arms. I ran to it.

"Skeva, Skeva," a voice kept calling.

"No, I am still Sleena," I whispered sadly.

"Skeva, are you all right?"

I didn't open my eyes, but I answered the voice. "No. Isandor is still with me. I want the knife. I can't endure this."

"It's over, Skeva. Isandor will never hurt you again."

Still, I wouldn't open my eyes. I knew it was Tren I was talking to, but he was too late. I was never going to open my eyes again. I was too tired and too sick of being hurt.

"No," I told him tonelessly. "Isandor will always come back. He told me so."

Tren's hands lifted my body towards him. He was clutching me to him, drawing me up against his beating heart. "Listen to me, Skeva," he demanded. "Isandor *can't* hurt you anymore, Skeva. I promise you."

I listened to Tren's heart. It was a soothing sound. I matched my breathing to his. I ached, but the rhythm of his body helped to take the pain. Tren smelled like smoky wooden casks drenched in alcohol. I breathed it in. It was a pleasant smell. It blended well with the warm muskiness of his masculine body.

Had he asked a question? I didn't remember. I suppose I had to respond. I had trusted him once, but he had let me down. I must not get used to his arms holding me. I sighed heavily. "I don't believe you," I said. "Bring me the knife. I cannot endure more."

Tren tightened his hold for a moment. Then, he pushed me away and shook me. "Stop it, Skeva. Listen to me."

I had been listening to him. His heartbeat had been the song that stilled the pain.

"I will listen if you bring me the knife," I told him.

Once more, he shook me, not violently as Isandor would have done, but gently, as if he merely wanted to wake me. I didn't protest it. I ignored it. It didn't matter what he did. I would leave this Plane. There must be other Planes of existence that would not rob me of joy. The knife would show me the way. A single cut. How long would it take? Would it be like sleeping without dreams? Or would it . . .

"Spit on Barquel! I order you, Skeva. Open up your eyes and look at me. Do it!"

He was shaking me again, more fiercely this time. I reacted to his violence. "Beat me," I said. "I don't care. Just bring me the knife."

A wave of his anger hit me. I cringed, knowing that a fist might follow. But Tren only sighed and sat down on the bed beside me. He drew me closer. Once more, I heard the beating of his heart. One of Tren's hands was gripping my arm. His hold on me was overly tight. It hurt, but I said nothing. I breathed in his scent and matched the rhythm of my body to his.

He could not possibly have read my thoughts about his overly tight hold, but he let go. The hand moved to touch my face. He caressed my cheek and jawline. If I opened my eyes, I would see him. He would be looking into my eyes. Was it worth it? Did I care enough to wake and take him?

"I know it hurts," he said softly. His lips touched my forehead. It was the lightest kiss, but something stirred inside me.

"I am sorry I was too late to help you. I will take better care of you from now on. I promise you that, Skeva. No one will ever hurt you again. Isandor will never touch you, never again, my little one. He is dead. He can never hurt you now."

That got my attention. I opened my eyes and looked at Tren. "You're telling me the truth? Isandor is dead? How could that be? He was here."

Tren kissed my forehead. An electric current rode through my body. I wanted to respond to it, but this new information was short-circuiting my hunger.

"He is dead, Skeva. I promise he's dead. I killed him."

I sat up then, pulling away from Tren's arms slightly so I could look around. There was nobody on the floor. "You really killed Isandor?" I said, staring at him. I looked fully into his eyes, probing for the truth. He was not lying. I could tell that.

He picked up a strand of my hair and kissed it. "I told you I was a bad guy," he said, and his teeth flashed a gorgeous smile.

I threw my arms around his neck and hugged him. "Thank you, thank you," I cried, and I kissed his face, moving towards his lips.

He pushed me away. "Skeva, stop it! You endanger us both." He stood up and moved away from me.

His fear confused me. "I was thanking you," I told him, reaching out for his hand.

He cringed away from me as if I were loathsome. "I don't know where you're from originally, Skeva, but Shapechanger do not allow their women to hug other men."

A moment before, he had been kissing me. Why did he run from me now? "I don't see the harm in it," I pouted, stung by his rejection.

Tren stood up. "I have to go now, Skeva. You will be OK. Sleep. There will be no more pain for you. I will not let you be harmed again."

He was fleeing from me. The same look was in his eyes as in the eyes of the buyers who'd backed away from me at the slaver's market.

"Please don't go, Tren. I am afraid," I told him. I hated to say it, but the words came bubbling out, and they must have been true because they didn't make me sick.

He laughed. "You? Afraid! You have more courage than a troop of guards! Now close your eyes, little one. I'm your master, remember? There now, keep them closed until morning."

"Tren?"

"Eyes closed."

I obeyed, but I had to know. "Tren, how did you know to come?"

"I had Isandor watched. When he got within a radius of where you were, I came."

I missed Tren's arms about me. I missed the beat of his heart, but I sighed happily. It was nice to have someone who cared. "Thank you, Tren," I said.

"You already thanked me. Remember?"

"Where's his body?

"It's gone. You won't have to see it."

"I'm sorry I keep bothering you."

"Good night, Skeva."

I listened to the sound of his feet going down the stairs. *I will make you love me, Tren,* I vowed. *I will make you forget your fear. And, by Barquel, I will force you to claim me!*

The smell of Tren's body clung faintly to the bedding. I pulled the top blanket off the bed and curled up around it, holding it to my nose. Then I sighed contentedly and slept.

Chapter Six

Trevor

I am concerned about my son, Shaarvan. He has not rested since he left the accident ward on Westla. I have spies in the crew who report to me at regular intervals, a common practice among traders who own many ships. Each new account they send me fuels my apprehension. My oldest son is barely eating, and he sleeps only the minimum of his body's needs. He has not taken a girl, either, which among the Shapechangers is unwise. I suppose he is using the machine, but it is unsatisfactory for long periods.

Strangely, Teea seems less concerned with his decline than I. She has been the best of mothers to Shaarvan, and I find her lack of worry difficult to understand. When queried, which I often do with my young wife, she looked sad and said that perhaps I should be more concerned about Shaara's well-being than that of our son.

Of course, I grieve for Shaara. She was a delightful woman — full of spirit and good cheer. She was pleasing to look at and had proved herself to be a reliable breeder. But Shaara is gone, and I believe that she is dead. Teea should recall the woman's argumentative nature, her constant questions, and her rebellious temperament, which all indubitably took her life.

I am extremely disappointed — no, dismayed — by Shaara's loss, yet sorrow must end, and life must continue. Shaarvan must let her go. He must choose another. I do not comprehend why Teea does not see this. I understood even less when my words to that effect brought her tears of anguish.

Females are often moody and ridden by emotion. I shall allow my wife to mourn in her own fashion, and then I shall approach her again. There is a matter that I wish to discuss with her. When she is calm, I shall tell her, again, how sorrow must end and life must continue. You see, it seems that I am dying, as are all the Elders in Altar. I hate to trouble my beloved Teea with such a thing. It will surely cause her to cry again, but I must prepare her for what is to come. She must understand about her Second. He will take my place. It is our way.

Skeva

The next days were blissful. I did my usual chores for Flar and Frieda, and then I headed over to help Blair. Working with the landoors was everything I'd ever wanted. I loved the ripple of muscles beneath my thighs, the challenge of communicating my desires to these noble animals, and the joy of our empathy. I could feel them responding to my every move. Training them was the striving for a goal that I had lacked before. And, when my body was worn out with fatigue and numb with happiness, there was Crimson Black, whom I loved.

For hours, I sat by his stall and told him things. He no longer trumpeted or blew warnings at me. His long black neck would stretch out and down to me, and he would sniff at my clothes and my skin, probing for information about this strange creature that had become a part of his life. I did not attempt to pet him, although the sleekness of his neck and the warm breath blowing at my face urged me to. I kept my promise. But, as the days went by, and Crimson grew less and less afraid, it grew harder.

Only the nights troubled me. I dreamed of Isandor. Sometimes, Tren was in my nightmares, and his pipe weapon shot Blair and then

Frieda and Flar. Other times, a blank-faced Shapechanger tortured me, sometimes with Isandor, sometimes on his own. Once, I woke up Flar. He came running into my room to defend me and found me alone in my bed. I had no memory of screaming, only of the torment of my dreams.

The nights were often long. The dark stretched out like a coiled rope, waiting to drag me into reruns of horror. I wished I could sleep with Crimson, but I had given my word to Blair. I stayed in my room, and often, unable to sleep, I sat at my window watching the stars perform their dance.

A sixTide sped by, a period in which my life flowed evenly and happily — except for the nights. But, at last, even Barquel seemed appeased, or maybe he had moved on to fret others. Flar and Freida were now in the Golden Chair, and the meals that Flar prepared were scorched and lumpy. I often left the table dissatisfied by the taste of the meal, but I ate the food anyway, knowing that to train the landoors, I needed the strength it gave me.

Flar and Frieda both warned me to be careful of the Wheel, which was slowly rolling in the sky's path. The Wheel creates times of change, Freida told me, and had already been at work in my life, even though, it was only the beginning of its influence. Frieda said that when change occurred at the beginning of the cycle, the turmoil through its reign was magnified four-fold.

But how could I be careful? If the Wheel was in the heavens determining my fate, how could caution influence it to halt the changes that were in store for me? I puzzled over it and finally asked my friends to explain.

"The changes are not what we caution you of, Skeva," Flar told me. Frieda nodded. Her eyes grew bright with religious fervor. "All time flows towards change. It is the waterfall that bridges life's flow. The turbulence is necessary. It leads to the mighty chasm of the fall where change occurs. For some, the river of life in this passage is calm and placid, and the fall is only a short plunge. For others, like you, the falls come between rough and rushing rapids. Then, the change is from great heights, and the fall is dangerously turbulent.

"Do not fight the changes, Skeva. Ride them through the falls with peace and the joyfulness that there is life so that your flow continues," Flar instructed me.

"My poet husband! You have still not explained what she needs the caution for." Frieda smiled at him with great fondness in her eyes. I was jealous of what they shared.

"I am coming to that, my love." Flar blew a kiss to her, and I had to smile. They had been like new lovers since the Sky Demon's sacrifice. Perhaps there was merit in the demands of their god.

"Skeva, in the streets as the great Wheel turns, there will be the turbulence of the waterfalls. The drinking of alcoholic beverages and debauchery will be prevalent. That is what we warn you about. Sick souls are churned to release their poisons. They will lie in wait for innocents. You must be leery of them."

I smiled. I would not worry about the fears of Flar and Frieda, but it was nice to have friends who were concerned. "Thank you," I told them. "Thank you for your words. I shall be wary."

As I hurried off towards the stable, I crammed my pockets full of sweets. The small fruits would hold me until I returned for the next meal Flar blundered through.

I trapped Blair that day. The time of change seemed a good environment for my request. "Blair, Crimson is not blowing at me or snorting anymore. Please, may I pet him?"

"He is still wild. What will I tell Tren if you lose a couple of fingers?"

"Crimson will not bite me."

Blair studied me. He had given up correcting me on my renaming of the stallion. "Skeva, you're like no girl I've ever seen. If there are others like you on your home planet, I could use them."

"You just like me because I work for free," I joked.

"Didn't Tren tell you? You're earning a wage. He demanded payment for your labor."

I laughed. "Good, maybe I can start paying him back for all the trouble I've caused him." I wished that Tren had told me. I wished that he would talk to me.

I turned to walk away, "Thanks for agreeing to let me pet Crimson. I promise not to lose any fingers." Blair didn't call me back, so I took it as permission.

As I walked away, I started thinking about Tren. I did that a lot. Since the night he killed Isandor, I had not seen him, yet he had sent his men to check on me almost daily. I knew their faces, but I didn't attempt to speak with them. I knew they would send Tren's orders to me if he had any.

I dreamed of Tren, sometimes, in dreams that were not horror driven. In those dreams, his hands plied my body, but he never went further. His lips did not crush me to him, and his eyes did not seek the sharing that I knew came with coupled souls. I lay there, every now and then, and tried to imagine joining with him. His body was all that I could long for. I remembered well the look of it, as he'd come from his bedding of Malla. The muscles in his hips, as he'd driven himself into her, often played on my mind, and inside me, there was a calling. I wished that my dreams would go further and linger a bit longer.

I reached the line of stalls where Crimson was and mentally kicked myself at my thoughts of Tren. Joining with Isandor had been a nightmare. Why would I long for it with Tren? I was better off the way I was, alone and safe.

Crimson greeted me with a low nicker. It was uncertain, but it was a start. I took my usual spot. And, then, I began to explain to Crimson about the Wheel of Change and how he, too, would have to be resigned that things could not continue as they were.

At first, Crimson Black was spooked each time I moved to touch him. I couldn't reach my fingers close to him without his jerking back. Still, he was curious about what I was up to. Each time, his inquisitive head came restlessly back to me, and he nickered, soft and low in a question.

It took me three days, but I did it. My hand touched him. Crimson stood there silently, quivering under my fingers. He was frozen like the statue landoor I'd seen when I'd visited Blair's house.

I'd been so entranced with the statue. I'd barely been an honorable guest. It had been carved of wood and was so lifelike it could have been Crimson who had posed for it. Gtlat, Blair's wife, had only laughed and said, "I see why Blair has taken to you. You are much alike. It is too bad he was not able to buy you. You could have polished that wood carving for me. I grow tired of doing so."

Gtlat and I had had little to say to each other. She had no love of landoors, so we shared no interests. It soon became apparent that she had honored the wishes of her husband, and I was only a clever slave she felt sorry for.

Blair and the others treated me so differently that I often forgot my place. I remembered little of Gtlat afterward, except for the lesson of who I was and my memory of the beautiful wooden, carved landoor.

Crimson grew restless with my musings. He had decided he liked the feel of my hand. He butted his head against me and made me scratch over his eyes and all around his ears.

Each day, I worked closer and closer to him, touching more of his beautiful coat caressing his strong muscles. One day, I ignored Blair's fears and entered Crimson's stall. The stallion was so used to me he just dropped his head for another rub. In days, I was brushing Crimson and cleaning his hooves. He glowed from the attention, and his nickers were heard throughout the ranch as he called out for me to rush through my chores and hurry back to him.

Blair only yelled at me once during that time, but it was already too late to stop me. He found me in Crimson's stall one day. I thought the poor man would have a seizure. His face grew red, but he couldn't holler at me. He didn't want the stallion to become frightened and trample me under his hooves. Blair's lips moved, and his hands waved for me to exit. I laughed and placed my head on Crimson's warm, solid chest to show Blair that the horse wasn't going to hurt me. Blair's fury blasted me. He flashed a sign that I knew at once, a warning of an intended beating.

I came out then, unsure of Blair. I had forgotten the Power he held over me. Had I angered him enough that he would truly beat me? Or worse, would he bar me from the ranch?

For the first time, as I retreated from Crimson's stall, Blair touched me. His hand circled my arm, and his grip pulled me out the rest of the way.

"Mother of Spit," he yelled. "You know fully well that you have no spitting business in that stallion's stall! I feel like tying you up in a bundle and having you delivered to Tren's casino. Let him worry about you for a while."

"Blair."

"Don't you start with those sad, little eyes at me, you Shapechanger witch! Go home. You may not return today. And when you come tomorrow, you will pay for your disobedience with a shovel. You will clean every landoor dropping from each and every stall before I let you near that crazy stallion again. You must learn that I will not be disobeyed. You understand me?"

The force of Blair's anger had not dimmed. I understood that part. Yet, he had not beaten me, and he had not forbidden me to come again.

I nodded humbly, waited a moment, and then looked up at him. "But Blair," I said, flashing him an impudent smile, "in order to clean the entire stable, I will have to go into Crimson's stall."

Blair roared, and I ran off as if the sons of Barquel were hot on my heels. It was not until I'd reached the lookout boulder that I realized how early in the day it was. What did people without landoors do with their spare time?

For a while, I sat on a boulder and watched the colts frolicking in the fields. Then, my restlessness drove me on. I walked toward the small section of commerce where I usually acquired our vegetables and cheeses for the table. I had no money to buy anything that day. During Golden Chair, a woman could neither cook nor purchase food. So, I merely meandered among the street stands, watching the crowds, taking note of the wares and produce. The streets were filled with noise and drunkenness. Several women offered to let me sip from their hand kegs, but I shook my head and walked on. I always wondered why people craved a liquid that interfered with their thinking processes. Some had so little brains already. The drink must make them as foolish as Isandor.

A fight was starting in the corner by the bakery. I watched at a distance, wondering why the Wheel demanded that people unused to alcohol should drink it. I supposed that there were some people who became frozen in their niches and needed help to change, but if they endangered their lives with city fights, would the change be worth it?

A drunken sot began to vomit all over a broken wagon. The disgusting odor made me nauseated. I turned away.

It was then that I realized that a man was following me. I felt his presence before I saw him. He was not drunk, nor did he seem to be a disciple of Barquel. What did he want with me? I thought about the things that Flar and Frieda had warned me of and what Blair had said about some men wanting boys for their bed play. For the first time, being alone made me uneasy.

I twisted and turned in the alleyways, attempting to lose him. I passed a glass window. The man's image stared back at me — tall, broad-shouldered, a weathered face with a craggy nose. Isandor had given me a very vivid picture of the cruelty of men. I did not want to find out what this one wanted.

I could not go back to the ranch. Blair would not allow it. I knew the house was empty. There was still no lock on the front door. The man could easily follow me up to my room. I had only one other choice — Tren would deal with this man. I headed for the casino.

As the huge black building came into sight, I darted a look backward. The man was still following. I broke into a run and heard him pounding the dirt behind me. Breathlessly, I reached the door and banged on it with more enthusiasm than the giant doorman liked. He glared at me, shook his finger, and then turned away, holding his nose.

"Stapen," I said, "I do not smell."

He roared with laughter, nodding his head emphatically. He was one of the men Tren sent to check on me. He knew where I spent my days. He had watched me ride many times before.

"What do you need, little ruffian? Have you tired of landoors?"

"I need to see Tren."

"I do not think he wants you here."

"But I have to see him!"

Stapen shook his head at me but allowed me to pass. I was relieved that Tren had not ordered my entrance barred.

The casino seemed darker than before and half-empty. Did the males not favor it some days? Were they celebrating Golden Chair out in the streets of the town? Perhaps they were still sleeping their night's carousing away. I wondered if Tren would be upstairs again. If so, I would wait until he was finished. I knew he would not be as amenable to interruptions if he were in the middle of riding Malla.

The man at the bar was polishing a bottle. He called out, "Hey, Tren, your boy is here," when he saw me.

I heard a low moan from under the counter. Apparently, Tren was working there. I gestured to the barman, and he pointed under the sink. I boosted myself up onto the counter and looked down. Tren was lying on the ground beneath a faucet. He had a metal tool in his hand and was twisting it back and forth.

"Skeva, what now?" Tren said, sitting up and bumping his head on a keg spigot.

I wished I had not bothered him. His mind was awash with irritation, frustration, and pain from his bump. He was about as happy to see me as he would have been to find a landoor on his pretty carpeting.

"Never mind," I said, turning sharply on my heel. "Forget it."

But, as I turned, I saw the same man who had followed me through the town. His weathered face had taken on an ugly expression. He was as annoyed with me as Tren was.

I admit I panicked. I should have known he wouldn't try anything in the casino, but I took a running leap and soared over the bar's short door. Tren was still standing there, holding his head where he'd knocked it. I rammed into him and said, "Get your pipe gun. There's a crazy man coming over here."

"Skeva, what are you talking about?" Tren's hands were busy prying my fingers away from his shirt. Why didn't he look up and see the stranger?

"That man has been following me," I said, pointing to the dangerous-looking brute that was still staring at me. "He chased me all over the city streets, and then he pursued me even into the casino. Please, get your pipe gun and tell him to leave."

"Skeva," Tren sighed and wiped his hands on a small white towel. "Goorda, give Nardar a drink. I think he needs one."

"But."

Tren shook his head at me. His hand gripped my arm, and he walked me to a table. "Sit down.

"Goorda, bring a juice and a Stellar." I watched with wide, frightened eyes as the crazy man was given a drink. I sank down into the chair. I felt so stupid. The man must be one of Tren's, but how was I supposed to have known that?

Tren was still shaking his head at me.

"I have not bothered you for a long time," I blurted out. "I wouldn't have bothered you today, but…"

"Shut up, Skeva." Tren took the drinks that Goorda put down on the table and handed me the juice. "Why were you walking the city streets?"

I listened for a moment to the sounds of the casino. It never closed. Off in the other room, I heard a man arguing over his cards. Goorda was preparing another round of drinks. The glasses tinkled as he slid them together on the tray.

"I'm sorry," I said. I looked down at the juice Tren had given me. I drank some, but I could hardly swallow with his angry eyes on me.

Tren sighed, tilted his glass, and gulped down half of it. "For the second time — why aren't you at the ranch?"

I didn't want to go into that. "It doesn't matter," I said, putting my glass down. "I'm sorry I bothered you." I stood up to leave.

"Take one step, Skeva, and I swear by Barquel's spit, I shall turn you over my knee, Shapechanger or not."

His voice was low and quiet, yet the way he said the words persuaded me not to argue. I sat down and took another sip from my glass.

"Answer me, Skeva. Why are you not at the ranch?"

I sighed. For all this time, I'd dreamed of Tren, and now that I was near him, I realized he scared me to death. I was so nervous under his continued observation I couldn't sit still. I sighed a second time. His words reminded me that he owned me, just like Isandor had. I knew that I'd better answer him, or he just might do what he threatened.

"Blair told me to leave because he found me in Crimson's stall. It was really stupid that he got mad, Tren because Crimson is not going to hurt me, not unless he crawls into my lap!"

I had said it all really fast so I could get it out before Tren told me to shut up, but he didn't try to stop me. He just listened. He sipped at his drink, put it down, and then folded his hands into a steeple, placing his lips on it and staring at me. "I see. So you decided it would be fun to walk through the alleys of the city during the Golden Chair?"

"I didn't have any problems until he," I turned and pointed at the man, "started following me."

"Skeva, I don't know your age. Your body is not that of a twelve-year-old, yet you act like one. Is it because of lost memories or because of the way you dress? Have you forgotten how to make the decisions of an adult?"

Why was Tren being so mean? I'd been taking care of myself for a halfPass, and I didn't need him insulting me. Had I really disturbed him so greatly? I glared.

Tren seemed unmoved. He finished his drink and said, "Goorda, I want you to put this one to work. He can clean every inch of your bar stools for a start. Then, the bottles need wiping down. Keep him busy so he doesn't find a second to get into trouble."

"Tren!"

"Lower your voice. You're a boy. Remember that. And get to work."

The work was no more disagreeable than cleaning the house, and it was much more interesting. I worked first on the curlicues of the barstools and saw designs in the wood that I'd never realized were there. As the polish made the legs glow, I took pride in what I was accomplishing. But, by the fifth chair, the pride was old, and I was imagining sprites and demons in the patterns on the wood. The seventh chair had a swirl of wood like a dragon breathing fire. The ninth had a perfect flower, with one leaf on the side of its stem. By the thirteenth stool, there were customers, and I began to listen to the conversations around me. The men didn't speak in Altarian, but my growth in Freinan had been great, and what words I didn't understand, I often could pick from their minds.

I finished the barstools and began cleaning the bottles stacked around the back of the counter. They were such beautiful shapes and colors.

"Goorda," I asked when Tren was over on the other side of the casino, "Why do the bottles differ so much? Why are they not all the same shape and size?"

Goorda looked around to see where Tren was before answering, "See this one here? It is from Salgo, and they make it with the bark of the *quimor* tree. It is such a light shade of green, it is almost like there is no color at all. This bottle is from a different planet. It houses a *sopwa* alcohol. They make it from a native plant. I once heard the name, but I have forgotten now. Each of these alcohols is in a different bottle because it is the design of the maker. The sopwa alcohol would go bad in a different shape. The *spila* over there, has to be kept in a blue bottle, or it becomes poisonous."

I gasped and regarded it cautiously. "How long does it take to become poisonous if it's in another bottle?"

Goorda admired the blueness while his hands caressed the bottle's shape. "It depends on the color of the bottle and who's drinking it. Me, I don't take chances. If I'm going to drink it, I'll drink it out of a blue bottle and in a blue glass."

"I wouldn't drink it at all! What if someone puts it in another bottle for a while, and then it's put back into a blue bottle. Will it still be poisonous, or does it revert back?"

"Spit and a half! I never thought about that. Heck, if I know." He looked suspiciously at the bottle and moved it back into its place against the wall.

"Goorda, why couldn't a robot do the things that Tren made me do?"

"Robots can't buff polish like a person can. They can only clean flat surfaces. If you leave all that paste in the ridges of the bar stool legs, and they get caked with it, they begin to look dingy. Then, it's even more work to polish them. You did a good job. I watched you. Maybe Tren will give you a regular job here. You're not old enough to work the nights, but you could clean and wax."

"I don't think Tren would let me. He's not too fond of me."

"Oh, that's his way, boy. If he didn't like you, he would have sold you to a dealer going out of town or killed you if you got under his hair."

"Sometimes I think he'd like to do both."

Goorda stared at me a moment and then smiled. "You're a strange kid. I see why he keeps you. But you need to appreciate what you got. At least you're not dead and rotting in a ditch."

Tren moved closer then, and I continued my polishing of the bottles. I had just returned a tall, skinny orange one to the wall counter when Tren ordered me to pour him a drink from it.

Goorda plopped down the appropriate glass, and I tried to pry up the cork. Tren took it from me and showed me how to release it. (I had been trying to pull it up, but it had to be pushed down before you pulled.) Tren passed the bottle back to me, and I poured the liquid into the glass. I tried to watch Tren's eyes and the liquid at the same time, unsure when to stop pouring. Tren nodded when it was time to stop, and then, without a word, he carried the drink to one of his customers.

I placed the cork back into the bottle and returned it. Goorda grinned at me and gave me a thumb-finger salute. It meant I had done well. I smiled back at him and pulled out the next bottle to clean.

The afternoon went quickly; I didn't realize when the place started filling up. Two guys were helping Goorda pour drinks and still not meeting the demands of the requests flying across the bar.

"Here," Goorda said. "Handle the keg. Use these goblets and pour to here. Got it?"

I nodded and began dispensing. I had trouble keeping up with the demands, but I think I poured as quickly as the men.

Once, Goorda passed by me. "Good job," he said, and he placed his heavy hand on my back for a moment. I flushed with the pleasure of his praise.

Then, as quickly as it had begun, the rush died out, and there were no voices yelling out for more. I plopped down on one of the inner bar stools, exhausted and thoroughly relieved that I hadn't messed up. Goorda shoved a plate in my hand. "Here, eat this while you have the chance. This space is a breather, not quitting time."

The bread had a hunk of cheese in the middle. It was delicious, or else I was suddenly so hungry I would have devoured anything.

Goorda slammed down a cracka juice and scurried off to wait on a customer.

"Kind of young, aren't you, kid?" one of the men who'd come in to work the rush asked.

I shrugged.

"I hope you find time to get a bath next time. You smell like you sleep in a barn."

He kept watching me and returned after he'd served the customer. "I've seen you before. Aren't you Tren's play toy?"

My face burned and I could just barely swallow the chunk of food in my mouth.

"Pleth, leave the kid alone," Goorda said, passing by to grab the orange bottle I'd polished.

Another rush soon followed, and I was back filling up goblets. The rush petered out faster than before, and again, I went back to my polishing.

"Hey, kid." I looked up and found Tren's eyes crinkled at the sides, laughing at me.

Carefully, I placed the bottle I had been polishing back onto the shelf and went towards him.

"Time to get you home."

"I like it here."

Tren clicked his fingers at me. I figured that meant something. I moved towards the small half-door through which the bartenders entered and left.

"I'll be back," Tren told Goorda. "Thanks for chaperoning."

"My pleasure. He's a good worker."

On the way back to the house, I got another lecture about the streets of the town during the Golden Chair. Tren was so busy telling me what not to do and why that he never mentioned whether I could come back and help at the casino. At the door, he almost pushed me in. His hand on my back felt completely different than Goorda's.

"Tren," I said, calling him back. He'd only taken a step away, so it wasn't a big deal, but his eyes were as cold as the night sky. I ignored them and continued. "Thank you for letting me stay at the casino. It was fun."

I swear he groaned. He shook his head at me and pointed into the house. "Go."

Teea

When Tevor told me he was dying, I could not help sobbing. How could he expect me to be clear and lucid and then listen to his plans for the future! I do not understand him at times, but now, I realize why he'd seemed so harsh with his mourning of Shaara.

"You may grieve only a short time for me, Teea," he commanded. "I shall allow you no longer than a twoTide for your tears. Then, you will get on with your life."

How dare he give orders concerning my feelings! If Trevor is truly going to die, then I shall grieve for him all the rest of my life. He had no right to order me to do otherwise.

I was surprised when Tevor allowed me the rebellion of my thoughts. It was not like him to overlook a chance to comment. Did he not know my mind now? It made me recall how infrequently Tevor had of late used his mind voice. Was that a sign of his decline?

Trevor had not yet seen our son Pathe, who is a doctor, but he promised me he would do so. I have always been told that Shapechangers know when their time has come. They can thus prepare their household for a smooth passage. But Trevor is too young to die. It is not fair.

And why would every one of the Elders all be taken at once? That does not seem logical to me. They are of differing ages. Nothing like this has ever happened before. I think that something is very wrong in Altar. I wish Shaarvan were here. He would not take this in stride. He would question it and probe it. He would never tolerate Tevor's casual acceptance. Yet, even if Shaarvan were here, Tevor would probably forbid me to tell my oldest son. And I suppose it would not be right for me to burden Shaarvan with more than he already carries. Yet . . .

I will talk to Pathe. He will contact Westla for me. Tevor's brother, Tem, must be told of this illness. (I refuse to accept Tevor's gloomy prognosis. I am certain Westla will have a drug that will solve the problem.) Perhaps Westla will also wish to investigate such a peculiar and unhappy circumstance as all the Elders plummeting in health within the space of a few Tides.

Oh, Tevor. You are a fool to think your command could ever stop me from loving you. I understand Shaara's snow now. If I had her Power, I would seek death, too. I will never accept the Second you order me to acknowledge.

Tren

She is an obnoxious little imp, yet she fascinates me beyond words — her quick temper, her daring, and her silly little antics . . .

All that morning, she toiled at the bar, working as hard as any hand I'd ever hired. Yet, if I'm correct about who she really is, she would never have sweated that hard. On Altar, it is probable that she was treated as a princess with her own personal robots and many guards surrounding her. I doubt she ever lifted a hand to clean a surface or polish a piece of wood. Yet, the kid enjoyed it! She fit in as happily as a saloon hopper.

I am sorry that Nardar scared her. I had told the man not to be obvious about his guarding of the "boy." It is clear he failed. But, perhaps the lesson of it has not all been to the bad, not if it has taught Skeva something. She needs to learn caution.

What a curious child she is, and yet, in the stray moments when my mind thinks back to her body lying on that bed in Isandor's room, I remember too clearly that she is no child. The lusciousness of her body still plagues my rides with Malla.

It is better not to think of Skeva's body — safer, anyway. It has only been a few Tides since I wired the Shapechanger Council on Altar. There is some kind of civil war on the planet, which may be delaying their response. I will try again. Surely, the girl has been missed.

I am more certain than ever that Skeva is a Shapechanger. Her eyes seem grayer than before, and more than once, I have felt the pull of her mind. She is untrained and probably not fully transitioned, but she is a Shapechanger. I must always be aware of that. I must never let those eyes of hers reel me in.

After I left her, on the walk back, I reminded myself again. I whispered to her, as if she were present, "Stay away from the casino, little Skeva. You do not understand how much danger you put us in." If only she had heard it. If only she would listen.

Skeva

The next day, I cleaned the stables. I had never seen so much manure, or at least never dealt with it all before. The cart was filled, time after time, and there were still more loads to make. My arms and shoulders ached, and still, I shoveled, load after load.

The other grooms laughed at me. They jeered at my misfortune. None of them were friends. They were all jealous of my relationship with Blair. Once, Tega, the idiot groom who had almost crippled a two-pass colt, pushed my loaded cart onto its side. I wanted to cry or to hit him. I did neither. I turned without a word and shoveled the piles of manure back into the barrel and then carted it off to the compost heap.

By the time I had done all the stalls, Ywequi, the sun, was in his highest position. I had no food with me, and my stomach growled, but I ignored it and went to sit by Crimson's stall. It was cool there in the shade, and the warm breath of him on my neck relaxed me. I must have fallen asleep. I woke to find both Tren and Blair standing there. They did not seem angry with me, but I rose up at once, nervous. As far as I knew, they were both still mad at me. Crimson bugled his distress at them. Angrily, he kicked at the stall door.

"Stop it, Crimson," I said over my shoulder. The stallion lowered his head and pushed his nose against my back, asking for pardon.

I ignored him and watched the two men. Tren came closer. His hand reached out towards Crimson. Crimson blew a protest, but he did not move. Tren's hand stroked the silky neck.

"She seems to have gentled the stallion well," he said to Blair.

"He's a demon stallion. You cannot trust him."

Tren looked at me a moment. I offered nothing. It would have been the wrong time to talk.

"You may go inside with him, Skeva. I shall watch. Do not stay if he is restless."

I smiled to myself and opened up the stall door. A soft nicker greeted me. Crimson's warm nose pressed up against me, begging for a scratch around his eyes. I scratched his whole head, and his neck grew limp with pleasure. My arms encircled him, and I hugged him. Crimson dropped his head over my back and shut his eyes.

Tren laughed softly. "Blair, it's a pity you won't bet with me. Your demon horse doesn't look very wild. He looks like a boy entering puberty who's fallen in love."

I stroked Crimson so he would not fear their presence. His eyes watched them, but he did not move, so complete was his trust in me.

"All right, come out now." It was Blair who had spoken. I gave Crimson one more pat and walked out into the sunshine.

Blair still wanted to argue over the dangers of my working with Crimson, but Tren dismissed it and gave permission for me to continue. "It does her good," he said. "And I can see no harm for you. Let her have her pet. It will keep her out of trouble."

"I warned you about walking about during the Golden Chair," Blair said, his eyes flaring at me briefly.

Why had Tren told him? I lowered my head and stared at the ground.

Still, it was a great day. I was free to enter Crimson's stall, brush him, and pet him all I wanted. And Tren had come in person to see that I was happy. What more could a person ask for? I hoped that Barquel was not watching.

The next day, I haltered Crimson and took him out. It was like trying to hold a cyclone. He whirled at every noise and every movement. I led him to the arena and let him run. I watched as he galloped and kicked at the air. When his kinks were all gone, I petted and baby-talked to him for hours. By the time I finally returned the stallion to his stall, my arms felt ready to fall off.

I had already worked the landoors in my care. I was so tired by then that I was heading home. I climbed over the gate rather than opening it. Blair didn't like my doing that, but I was too tired to work the heavy latches. As I jumped down, a giant of a man stepped in my way. He wasn't a groom or one of Tren's men, and I felt a strange, itchy kind of feeling at his presence.

His hair fell down loosely into his eyes, even when he brushed it back. It was the color of straw but fine. I liked his nose. It had a touch of arrogance. It blended nicely with the rest of his face.

I didn't dare meet the man's eyes. That wasn't allowed for a slave girl, but I knew somehow that the man couldn't be much older than I was. I was pretty sure he was young.

The itchy feeling was growing worse. There was something bothering me, scratching at my brain. I knew Blair was in yelling proximity — why was I so uneasy?

"You handled the landoor well, girl," the man said.

I looked up. He had called me "girl!" How had he known that? Something clicked in my brain. The man was a Shapechanger! That was what the eerie strangeness was.

All the stories I had heard about how Shapechanger changed into monsters who ate people and how they turned you into a robot person, obeying whatever they told you to do — all those bits and pieces flashed into my mind, and I remembered how it was said that a Shapechanger could steal your soul!

I lowered my eyes abruptly and hoped I had not waited too long. I wanted to run from him, but I doubted he would let me.

Shapechangers were lords. They must be served. I waited to see if this one would command me.

"What is your name, girl?"

There was Power in a name I had been told, but what Power could there be in mine? It kept changing. "Skeva, now, my lord."

I felt his surprise. "How did you know I was Shapechanger, Skeva?" he demanded roughly.

"I don't know, my lord."

"Are you perhaps Shapechanger?" he asked, coming closer. I wanted to back away from him. Would he let me? I remained still, ready to leap away, but frozen by my curiosity and my fear of him. Besides, Tren had told me I must find out the truth of my past. But why was the lord asking me if I were Shapechanger? Wouldn't he know?

"I don't know, my lord," I answered, but my eyes were once again studying his face.

"Why is that?"

A chinka lizard darted across the fence post. It stopped to sun itself. The iridescence of its scales shone like jewels in the sunshine. I pulled my eyes away from the chinka and answered the Shapechanger. "I have no memories of my past, my lord."

"I read in you that you tell the truth."

Of course, I did. I would not lie. My eyes flared at his insinuation.

He laughed. "Yes, you are Shapechanger. Come closer, girl."

I was already frightened, and he wanted me to come closer?

"You disobey Shapechanger command? You are foolish, girl. Have you no knowledge of what I can do to you for your defiance?"

I swallowed and fought my legs. They were ready to flee. "I respect you, my lord, but I cannot come closer."

Suddenly, he began to talk in another language. His words bound me. I felt my legs propelled towards him. His Power was like the undertow in an ocean. It pulled me forward.

"Look at my eyes," he commanded as his hand reached out and grabbed my upper arm, tugging me the rest of the way.

I would be lost if I did. My soul would be gone, and I would walk like the living dead. "No," I cried out, and I tried to free myself, but I couldn't move.

"I am Shapechanger," he said. "Obey."

As if my head were attached to a string he had pulled, my face looked up, and my eyes were his.

"Yes, it is in your eyes. Tell me your owner," he ordered.

I knew what he wanted. My lips parted, and I sought for a name, but I knew I couldn't please him. The blackness in my mind still barred me from my memory. "Tren," I said at last.

"No, you are not owned by Tren. He is not a Shapechanger. He is only a man."

The stranger studied me. His eyes were boring into mine. It hurt. I gasped as he withdrew. My legs buckled, and I sagged. He pulled me up against his chest. I sobbed once and then held my breath to regain my courage. The beat of his heart was foreign. It confused me. I struggled to draw away.

"Easy, girl. Be still. You are Shapechanger. I shall not hurt you. I shall find your history. If your husband lives, you will be returned to him. And, if he is dead and no one holds a claim on you, I shall take you and train you for my own. Beneath the dirt and the rags you wear, I am sure you are pleasing. No Shapechanger would have taken you if you weren't. Either way, little one, your blood will be honored."

His hand reached up to touch my face. With his touch, the spell was broken, and I was free. I whirled around to run. But his hand whipped out to catch me. The grip on my wrist was my prison.

"So, you have Power, little one," he said, holding me away from him so he could study my face. "Yet, you are too young to have achieved full transition. It does not make sense unless . . . Let me see your arms."

He pulled me closer against his body. One hand lashed me tightly to him. With the other, he rolled up my cuffs and examined both of my arms. A strange instrument flashed a black light along my arms, traveling slowly.

As he searched my skin, I could feel his hardness pressed against my bottom. It frightened me. I did not fancy being taken by a stranger again. I wanted to struggle against him, but Isandor had taught me that I could not win. I knew that my wrestling against the Shapechanger's hold would avail me nothing but his pleasure.

"You do not need to fear me in that way, girl," he paused to tell me. "I would never take you unless I knew your husband was dead. It is a code that we honor."

He turned off the light and stuck the machine back into his shirt. But, still, he did not let me go. His eyes continued to examine my arms.

A bear of a voice roared out. "Get your hands off of her!"

The Shapechanger did not react to the threat. His hold on me didn't loosen. Casually, he turned to face Blair. "I am here on Shapechanger business. Do not interfere with me, commoner. This girl is ours."

I watched the blood run from Blair's face as he backed away. His fear was pungent. He did not look me in the eye as he retreated. I wanted to cry out to him, but I did not. I knew that Blair could not protect me from a Shapechanger.

"Obey me now, girl," the stranger was ordering. "Perhaps I may soon be your owner."

He turned me to face him, but he didn't let go of my arm. His other hand cupped my chin, and his eyes penetrated into mine. His eyes flashed green — forest green, with pupils more triangular than round. His hand left my chin to trace a pattern on my cheek. The pattern burned like a brand against my skin. I yelped and sagged, sobbing from the pain his touch had brought me.

"You have a new bond on you. Who has bonded you besides your husband?" the Shapechanger demanded. Again, his hand jerked my chin up to force me to look into his eyes. His rage made the angles of his face change, widening it. Spots of fur were growing thickly at the sides of his jaw. The anger struck me like a badly dulled knife. I cowered and covered my head, sure that he would begin to beat me.

"Why do you hurt the girl?" a voice pierced my fear. It was Tren. Without any warning, I sprang away from the Shapechanger and ran to Tren. I would have thrown my arms around him, but his hands and arms were rigid, blocking me, holding me away.

"Skeva, no," Tren ordered.

I stopped and froze. Tren's eyes were watching me, narrowed in anger, but I knew the anger was not at me.

"I am Tren," he said to the Shapechanger, "I am the one who notified you of the girl."

"We of the blood, thank you. She is, indeed, one of ours."

"Why do you hurt her, then?"

The Shapechanger strode towards me. "Do not interfere in Shapechanger business, commoner." His words insulted, and there was warning in them, but Tren did not back away as Blair had done.

"I have been her protector, her temporary master. It is difficult not to feel concern for the girl's well-being."

"She will not be harmed." The Shapechanger's arm whipped out to grab me. He twirled me around towards him. I cried out and looked back at Tren. His eyes were like two round pieces of coal. His fury was great, but his hands, clenched at the sides in fists, did nothing.

The Shapechanger was equally angry. He pulled me back against his body, and his arm reached down over my shoulder to secure his hold.

"You are the one who has bonded the girl. I understand that now. Have you taken her?"

"Never," Tren said.

"That is good, commoner. It *may* save your life."

I struggled to pry away the arm that trapped me. The Shapechanger said nothing, but his grip tightened until I whimpered.

"Why is the girl bonded to you?" he demanded.

Tren's eyes were on me. I could not look at him. If Tren wouldn't help me…

"I do not understand," Tren said. "I thought she was bonded to her husband."

"There are levels of bonding. You have achieved the lowest. You have touched her soul. How did you do that to her? You are not Shapechanger." His arm across my chest was so tight I couldn't breathe. I couldn't speak either, and my fingers were prying at his hold on me, desperate for air.

Tren frowned. Did he know I couldn't breathe? Was I going to pass out from lack of air right in front of them?

Tren's eyes were examining me, but he said nothing more about about the Shapechanger's abuse. "I merely tested her to see if she reacted to the Shapechanger patterns. I meant no harm."

The Shapechanger looked down at me. He was studying me further. I stopped fighting him and went limp. Immediately, his hold loosened enough for me to breathe. I gasped and took in air.

He spoke after a moment. "There was little harm done from your bonding. Her husband will be able to remove it if he lives."

I felt it when the Shapechanger's eyes left me and traveled back to Tren. "How did you know the patterns?"

"I saw them done once on a young captive. I do not know the patterns. Whatever I did, it was an accident."

My heart was beating twice as fast as the Shapechanger's. The unmatched rhythm made me more aware of my fear.

Once more, the Shapechanger's eyes focused on me. "The girl has Power, and she projects it well. It took strong Power to bond her."

Again, his eyes studied Tren. "You have Power in you, or the patterns would not have worked. The Shapechanger would welcome you to our blood. The transition would not be painful."

Tren did not move. His face showed no emotion. "Thank you. I am honored, but I am content as I am."

The Shapechanger's eyes again came back to me. "If the girl's husband is dead, you will have no choice. She cannot be mated to one, not of the blood."

"I do not want her," Tren said.

I couldn't help but gasp. His words hurt me, even though I had known how he felt already.

The Shapechanger released his hold on me and pulled me around to face him. One hand still gripped my wrist, but his other hand brushed the hat off my head, and it fell to the ground. My hair cascaded down in its release.

Again, he grasped my chin and pulled it up, staring into my face. "I would imagine she is a treasure underneath the layers of dirt." His eyes raked my body, but my baggy clothes gave him no sight of what he was searching for.

"However, you misunderstand, commoner. It really does not matter what your wishes are. It is too late for regrets. Your claim is on the girl. She is yours unless her husband lives."

"You would force me to become Shapechanger?"

"If necessary, but you would find many benefits."

They had spoken in Freinan, but I had understood most of their words, or at least their thoughts. I knew that Tren did not want me and that in return for his care of me, they would force him to go through some kind of change. I was sorry I was always such a burden to him.

I raised my eyes to the Shapechanger. "You do not need to make Tren Shapechanger. I do not need an owner! I do fine without one."

The Shapechanger waited a moment to see what Tren would do. He did nothing but grin at me.

The Shapechanger tightened his grip and jerked me back against him. "Girls are not permitted to yell. Your words are a challenge that would automatically warrant a beating. If I were your master, I would make sure you knew your place."

I twisted my neck to glare up at him. "I have already been beaten daily. There is nothing left for you to threaten me with. And, if you think that taking away my air again will make me obedient, you are wrong. You can kill me, but I will die defiant."

"You are ignorant of what a Shapechanger can do, girl. You speak like a commoner."

"Perhaps I am, and you are wrong. But you said that Tren owns me, so if he does not wish me, then I am free!"

The Shapechanger raised up his hand to slap me. I knew before he moved that he would do so. I had seen it in his eyes. I lifted up my chin and challenged him.

Tren leaped towards the Shapechanger and clasped the hand. His eyes glared. "You said that she is bonded to me and that she is mine to do with as I please. I will not have her beaten again. She has had enough of that."

If Tren had allowed it, I would have leaped into his arms and kissed him a hundred times for saving me from the Shapechanger's beating. He had dared a Shapechanger for me. As it was, all I could do was adore him with my eyes.

The Shapechanger loosened his hold on me and then dropped even his grip on my wrist. Still, Tren and the Shapechanger were fastened eye to eye.

"Skeva, do you have another landoor to work?" Tren asked, his eyes not moving from the Shapechanger's.

"I'm finished, but if you wish me to ride another, I will."

"Do so."

The Shapechanger moved his gaze to me. I thought he would forbid me to leave, but he glanced once more at Tren and shrugged.

Just to make him angrier, I met his eyes fully, raised my chin, and with the haughtiest, saucy glance, I turned my back to him and walked away.

The male's eyes watched me, burning with his anger. I laughed as I walked away. I knew that Tren and he would have it out, but I was pretty sure now that Tren could hold his own.

My legs were shakier than I liked to admit. The Shapechanger had made me so furious I had forgotten my fear of him. But, as I went back to the stable, I thought over the things I'd said. I'd been a fool to challenge him.

I wondered what Tren would say to him with me gone. Would they speak of Isandor? Would he tell him of how I'd been beaten so frequently? Would the Shapechanger care? Perhaps he would think I deserved it. I shuddered with the thought.

Isandor still gave me nightmares. Although in the day, I knew he was dead and gone, at night, he haunted my sleep, still torturing me with his abuse. Sometimes, I woke up in the dark, hearing a noise, and I lay there cowering, waiting for the blows. I'd tremble for a long time before I'd wake up enough to remember that Isandor was dead.

Other times, it was just strange dreams that destroyed my peace. Flar and I would be talking, and Isandor would come in with the pain stick. Frieda would be talking about her religion, and Isandor would find out that I was listening. I woke so often with the sheets all twisted around me that I'd stopped using them.

I was glad to leave the Shapechanger and Tren behind. Even if their words weren't of Isandor, they would be of a future not here but far away. Perhaps they would discuss the husband I did not know or how the strange Shapechanger could claim me since Tren had no desire for me. I was quite content to avoid hearing their thoughts on what would become of me. Not hearing them might keep them from becoming real.

Basha, the gelding I had decided to ride, was full of sass. He'd gone too long without a workout. I was glad I'd saddled him up. He danced a jig across the paddock before I even mounted him. Then, his front hooves met the sky. He was crazy! I laughed with the thrill of it.

"Steady, Basha," I urged, but I didn't care. He was alive, and he took my mind off things I did not want to think about. I let him run some of his energy off, but he still wouldn't calm down. When I paused to let him catch his breath, he blew his nostrils out, the same sound as a whale clearing his spout. With a whale, it was only getting rid of the water. With a landoor, it was a warning of alarm. For a moment, I wondered how I knew about ocean animals, but it was just another loose piece of the puzzle floating around in my brain.

I worked Basha hard. Around and around the arena, we traveled in a slow jog, then a canter, and back and forth. I made him practice his flying lead changes until he was sweating and starting to settle. For ten more minutes, I drilled, and then I let him walk and relax. After that, it was time for jumping. Basha loved to jump. He knew what was coming. Once again, he nervously tossed his head up and down. I took a couple of low triples first. Basha was in even stride. I began the field.

Basha jumped over the first jump a bit too high, but his back rounded nicely, and he "gave" to me. We turned back around to take the high jump. It was almost as tall as I was, and there was a feeling of flying as we soared over it. Basha was a dream.

"Come here," ordered the Shapechanger in a voice that made Basha rear in alarm. The Shapechanger was angry again. What was his problem now?

I rode Basha towards him. The closer I got, the more rebellious Basha became. About ten feet away, he refused to go closer. His head tossing was pulling at my hands. I had been a fool not to wear gloves with him. I would have blisters in an hour.

The Shapechanger did not wait for me to come closer. "You will not ride the beasts over the obstacles."

"What!" Basha began to paw at the ground. He whirled around, trying to gallop away.

"I forbid it," the Shapechanger said. His eyes glowed a sickly green. His face held the residue of fur.

I glared my hate at him. "It's my job, Catman." I turned Basha's rump towards him and rode away.

"Skeva!" It was Tren's voice this time, just as angry as the Shapechanger's. I turned Basha so I could look at Tren.

"Get down," Tren ordered. His eyes were not smiling. They were livid. I dismounted.

"The Shapechanger's name is Targone. Say it."

"Targone."

"If you are rude again to a Shapechanger while you are under my ownership, I shall forbid you to ride —period."

My mouth flew open. I could read that Tren meant business. I wanted to argue, but I did not. I lowered my eyes and submitted. "I obey."

Tren continued. "Skeva, you may jump the low poles, but not the high one you went over last. Understood?"

"But Tren, it's part of my job. I . . . "

Tren flashed the *no argument sign*. I stopped and stared at him.

"She does remember it," said Targone. "Good, that means some of her conditioning is still there. It will make her retraining easier."

I glared at Targone, but I did not speak.

"You will obey Targone. He and I will *share* the responsibility for you until your husband comes for you."

"Why can't everything just stay the same, Tren? Why does *he* have to come here and change everything?"

"All things change, Skeva. Whatever happens now, your future is going to be vastly different from your recent past.

"Targone, where do you think she came from originally? Any ideas?"

Targone stared at me like he could see into me. "xxxxxxxxx xxxxx xxxxxxxx xxxxxxxxx? zzzz zzz zzzzzzzzzzz zzzzz zzzzz zzzzzz? yyyyy yyyyy yyyyy yyyy yy yyyy yyyy yyyyy yyyyy?" Tren asked.

I thought he'd gone crazy. Why was he babbling in meaningless syllables?

"I have tried her on the three most common languages for her body type and characteristics. She is not from any of those planets. I do not know where she is from. She should have had a *flaorth* implant. It was obviously removed. I checked her arms for it. If she had had that, it would have simplified finding her husband. The removal of the *flaorth* makes me even more suspicious about the story the slaver told her. Shapechanger do not sell Shapechanger, nor do we remove the identity marker."

"Skeva," Tren said, looking at me, "What do you remember about the slaver who first owned you? Did you ever hear his name?" Tren's eyes were gentle. He had forgotten his anger.

"Nothing. He was cruel-eyed, and taller than I. He was thin, and not very muscular, and he was Theinian. I never heard his name."

"Skeva," Targone said, "Come here and touch me. Perhaps I can see the slaver through your eyes."

I did not want to go near the Shapechanger again. I looked over at Tren.

He nodded and indicated that I should obey.

"Basha won't let me get nearer to the Shapechanger," I protested.

"I'll take the landoor. Obey Targone, Skeva."

Tren came towards Basha and reached for the reins. Basha was fine with him. It was only the Shapechanger he didn't like.

"Why are landoors afraid of you?" I asked Targone suspiciously as I walked towards him.

"They sense what we change into. Our Shapechange is most often a large cat that kills and eats landoor."

Targone was watching my eyes. I hoped he could read me fully. I was disgusted. Any creature who killed a landoor was not a friend of mine.

"You claim I'm Shapechanger, then why do the landoor not fear me?"

"Interesting question. I would guess because you have not Shapechanged. Come closer."

I walked towards him, but I stopped beyond his reach.

My face grew heated with embarrassment. He must have pulled that from my mind. I looked once more at Tren, questioning whether I really had to do this.

"Obey," Tren ordered again.

Spittin' men! Did they never stop issuing orders?

I stepped closer to Targone and put my hand on his arm. His arm felt different than Isandor's. His arm was sinewy and hard as if it were flexed rubber. I looked into his eyes. There was a flash of lust like I'd seen so often in Isandor's eyes. I almost withdrew my hand when I saw it.

"Think of the slaver, Skeva," he ordered.

I remembered the man and his pain stick and the way he had gloated over my submission. I felt a sudden wave of hate. He'd made me wear that awful outfit and painted my nipples. I would rip him apart with my sharp teeth, tearing his body to shreds. I would leave him lying there for the wild beasts to devour, and . . .

"No!" I stepped back. That wasn't my image. I whirled around and ran to Tren. I didn't care that I frightened Basha. I threw my arms around Tren's waist. "I will never touch him again. It was awful," I said, and I began to cry.

"Skeva, let go."

"No, I belong to you. Take me, please. Take me, so Targone will go away. I want to be yours."

Basha had had enough of all this noise and confusion. He pulled back once too often, and suddenly, he was free. He went galloping back to his stall.

Tren's hand cupped my chin and brought my eyes to his. "Taking you would wreck my life, Skeva. It is not that I do not want you. I'm a man. I would love to sweep you up and carry you to the nearest bed, but doing so would change everything."

"I promise I won't change your life, Tren. We can keep everything the same, only I'll service your needs. I'll obey you and do everything you want me to do."

Tren's hand touched my face with wonder. "Your skin is so soft. You are almost worth the price."

"Kiss me, please, Tren." If only I could get him to meet my lips, he'd be mine.

His eyes were pulled to my lips. I wet them and opened them just slightly. I could almost taste Tren. My hands went around his neck. He was bending to me, coming closer. I could feel his breath, warm and pleasant. I reached upwards with my lips.

"Stop." The command hung there in the air, shimmering like an electric wire.

Tren backed away from me. I'd lost him. A ripple of fury ran through me, followed by despair. It had been so close. I had almost won.

Targone was laughing. "You almost lost yourself to Shapechanger magic, my friend. She may be as small as a tenPass boy, but she's got Power I could feel clear over here."

I glared full force at Targone. I wished I had enough Power to shoot laser beams with my eyes. I would zap him like a fly hit by a flyswatter. Targone laughed. His eyes mocked me.

Tren disengaged himself from my hands and arms. "Skeva, you will not touch me again," he ordered sternly.

Once more, I shot a look of bitterness at Targone. It was all his fault.

"May I go unsaddle Basha?" I asked. There was no point in staying. The damage had been done. Why hadn't I waited until Targone wasn't around?

"Yes, go," Tren said so quickly it was as if he couldn't wait for me to leave.

One more quick dart of hatred at Targone, and off I ran. My tears would not be cried in front of them. I'd save them for Basha. He wouldn't mock me.

When I had cried my full and finished brushing Basha down, I nerved myself to go out and face them, but when I did, I found that both of them were gone. I guess I was glad, but I stubbed my toe, kicking a rock to pay Targone back for his interference.

Chapter Seven

Thenos

At last, I have received information concerning Shaara. It is not pleasant. I am outraged beyond words. It was Goria, the wife of Pathe, who caused my Shaara's disappearance. That my sometime lover would betray me wounds me gravely — but not as grievously as what I shall do to her. Goria will not live beyond my next taking of her. She is dirt. She will know my wrath in the most horridly spiteful manner. She will rue the day that she bribed Megloztar to sell my princess as a common slave.

I must return to Altar to settle the score with Goria, and it is time for the Elders to meet their end. It saddens me that I shall not have Shaara at my side when I take the throne of Altar, but I shall find her soon. She is strong like me. She will survive. Perhaps I may even turn her misadventures into an advantage.

As do all females, she will feel guilt at being raped, and she will need arms to comfort her. I shall speak softly to her and listen as she cries. I shall bear the bittersweetness of her tears and hold her in my lap. I shall restrain my hands from fondling her, not even to kiss her soft, warm brow. Being gentle with my Shaara will be my next goal, and she will be grateful. Then, I can seed her with my sons, and together we shall rule the galaxy.

When I find the owner who has held her all this time, and when Megloztar is caught, they will both feel the claws of the Saberey, and my teeth will know their blood. Perhaps I shall practice on Goria to perfect my skill. She who does not merit even speaking the name of the one I love shall end her days in agony.

But I shall not tell my princess these things. She will never know what I have done. I shall keep my Shaara forever innocent.

Skeva

That night, my nightmares were all of Isandor, but the Shapechanger was in them, urging Isandor to beat me. Tren was there, too, telling me I was wrecking his life, and Isandor laughed and hit me harder.

The blankets were such a mess. I had to remake the bed. I watched the sky for a while and located all the stars that had become my friends in the night. Then, I got up to go to the bathroom. I almost fell over the biggest cat I'd ever seen. It was lying across my doorway.

I stood frozen, looking at the cat's eyes watching me. They were glowing in the dark, like green stars. I knew it was Targone, and I knew he wouldn't hurt me, but the size of the beast and its fierce-looking teeth as it lay there, grinning at me, was frightening. I tried not to show my fear, but I wasn't quite brave enough to try to jump over the cat.

"Targone, if you will, please move. I need to go to the necessary room."

His mouth opened into an enormous yawn. The sight of so many sharp teeth made me cringe back. The cat roared softly. It was contemptuous of my fear.

"Move, or I step on your tail!" I said through gritted teeth.

This time, the growl was heated, but the cat moved. I ran past it.

When I returned, Targone was himself again. "I shall try to force Tren to become Shapechanger for you, Skeva. But the possibility still exists that you might yet end up becoming mine. It would behoove you to learn to guard your tongue."

I raised my chin and glared at him. "Perhaps Tren didn't know you planned to spend the night with me."

Targone nodded, and his eyes grew hard. "I see why Isandor beat you."

I gasped. That was a below-the-belt punch. I didn't feel like challenging him anymore. "Please, let me by," I said. My voice cracked, and the tears were stinging my eyes. I held my breath to hold them back.

"I'll move aside if you tell me why Isandor beat you."

"It's none of your business."

"But you will tell me because Tren ordered you to obey me."

It was my house, and Targone was standing there, threatening me in the middle of the night. I had had enough.

"Fine, don't move. I'll sleep with Crimson."

I turned to walk away. Targone swung me back to face him. His eyes glowed angrily. "Never turn your back on a Shapechanger, Skeva. It is an insult that will be severely punished. You have done it twice now. The next time, there will be a reckoning."

All the noise in the hall had awakened Flar. "What are you doing, Skeva, to make such a racket?" he demanded irritably as he climbed up the stairs. Then he saw Targone. "Skeva, you've been sold again?"

"No, Tren still owns me. Targone is a Shapechanger."

"A Shapechanger in my house! Oh, no!" Flar started backing up. He turned around and juggled off down the stairs, calling over his shoulder. "Carry on, my lord. I must go back to bed." His steps on the stairs were very quick for a man of his bulk. In another moment, we heard the door of his room slam.

I couldn't believe the way everyone acted. So, a Shapechanger turned into a cat. So he could read minds — big deal! The Shapechangers weren't demons or vampires! For a second, the image of a vampire with fangs for teeth flashed in my mind. Then it was gone. I shook my head. "Why do you have to make everyone fear you so?"

"They are smart to fear us, Skeva." Targone's grip on my hand loosened slightly, but he didn't free me.

"Why? Are you going to eat them?"

His eyes smiled, but there was a ring of truth when he spoke. "It is possible."

"That's disgusting!" I whirled around to return to my room, but Targone didn't let go of me.

"Answer my question about Isandor. Why did he beat you?"

I tried to jerk my hand away. Targone only tightened it and reeled me in closer.

"Let me go, you cat!"

The grip tightened more. I gasped and buckled to my knees.

"Stop it! Leave me alone," I cried, but my eyes were down submissively.

"Obey me."

It was Isandor all over again, but Targone didn't need a pain stick. His brute strength was enough.

"All right." I gave in. "He beat me for arguing." My lie smelled like spoiled eggs. I gagged at the odor.

"Confess the lie. Quickly, or you will be sick."

"It's a lie," I said at once, and the nausea slipped away.

I could breathe without the horrible smell. I took three huge breaths, and then I stared at Targone. "How did you know?"

"I smelled your lie, same as you. Shapechanger cannot lie. It makes us sick to do so. Now, you were saying . . . "

"I'm tired, Targone. Can't we talk in the morning?"

"No. You would spend the rest of the night trying to find a way to avoid telling me the truth."

I tried to free my wrist again. "If I tell the truth, you'll let me go?"

"Yes."

"Isandor beat me because I was lousy in bed. Now, are you happy?"

My wrist was freed, and I turned to go. Targone was laughing. I turned back to him in annoyance. "What's so funny about that?"

"I cannot believe you accept what that fool said. Shapechanger women are never lousy in bed."

"I guess I'm the exception."

"I am sure your husband would not agree."

"You don't see him rushing forward to claim me, do you? If he's not dead, he probably dumped me."

"You do not understand . . ."

"No, I don't. I don't understand why a Shapechanger feels he has to come to sleep on my doorstep, harass me on the way to and from the bathroom, and mock me when I obey him. Good night!"

"Skeva."

I stopped, wishing again that Tren had not ordered me to obey Targone. He was such a jerk!

"Skeva, if I were sleeping on your side of this door, I would prove to you how wrong Isandor was."

"Good night!" I said between clenched teeth and stomped off to bed.

Shaarvan

Shaara, my sweet, gentle Shaara — they have found you. My heart is joyful. My thankfulness is unbounded. The ship rushes towards you at top speed at this very moment. Freinana, you are on Freinana. How could we not have sought you there? How could I *not* have been instantly drawn to the planet that held you in its keeping? Shouldn't I have felt your pull? Forgive me for my failure, my lateness in coming for you. I shall not fail you again, my wife. Will you ever again trust me?

Do you still feel the rhythm of our shared heartbeat, my love? Mine is dancing within my body. It is singing all the Shapechanger chants of marriage, one by one, and then repeating them. It is ascending with the Soaring Eagle, riding across the currents, dipping and plunging its happiness on the wind. I am breathless with the incredible wonder of your finding, my little one. I cannot stop blessing the stars and the Somber Tree that you have been located alive when I had almost given up every thought of ever finding you.

Do not misunderstand. I would not have stopped looking. I would have spent my life in search of you, but it would have grown methodical and lifeless, for I had begun to be numb in my disbelief. Can you comprehend, my wife?

I have read the reports of your discovery over and over. They say that you are mindwiped. That explains so much. I understand why you did not call to me or answer my silent probes — all those nights I spent hoping that you might hear my thoughts across the stars.

Ah, Shaara, I shall bring your memories back. I shall hold you on my lap with gentle tenderness, my arms about you, my lips pressing against your brow, and I shall recite the Shapechanger stories once again. I shall instruct you of your history and that of the Trendacons, your family. I shall reacquaint you with your son, who sleeps in Westla, waiting for his parents and the love we bring him. I shall divulge my thoughts, my dreams, and the depth of my feelings for you. I shall be unendingly patient with you, my wife. And I shall give you ample time to get to know me once again.

My sweet, delightful Shaara, could there ever be so wondrous a miracle as finding you?

Skeva

When I got up the next day, Targone was gone. It was nice not to have him needling me.

Flar and Frieda were as leery of me as they had been when I first arrived. Neither one mentioned my visitor of the night, but they wouldn't look me in the eye, and they were cold as the icy winds of winter. I did my chores, baked two loaves of bread, and was out in the stable by the quarter sun.

The landoor were lethargic and sluggish. They refused to concentrate on my leg commands and were stubbornly disobedient. I worked them through their paces anyway, but I rushed to Crimson Black. It was the day I'd dreamed of. Crimson Black was ready for his first ride. Blair was nowhere around, and I felt almost guilty for saddling Crimson without reminding Blair of the importance of the day, but he should have remembered.

The ride turned out to be anticlimactic. Crimson had already been taught my voice command on the lunge line and on the long reins. He traveled his paces with me on him, like a steady, older landoor.

Blair came out when I was just cooling Crimson down. "What are you doing up on him?"

"He was ready, Blair. I told you. And he was a perfect gentleman."

"Where in spit do you get these expressions, girl?" He shook his head as if puzzled. "Perfect gentleman. A gentleman is not perfect. That's the spitball reflection of a fool."

I ignored Blair's dissection of my sentence. "Isn't he wonderful!"

"Who? High Mountain Peak?"

"Yes!"

"You have done wonders. Too bad you can't show him. I'll have to get Raja to get him ready."

"Ready? Why can't I show him?" I stroked Crimson's lustrous mane, threading my fingers through its incredible length.

"Skeva, I know you try to look like a boy, but you're not. There's no way, with that little heart-shaped face, you could masquerade at a show. You only get away with it here because of your dirty face and the bulky, oversized clothing you wear. Cleaned up and in proper clothing, you would fool no one."

"Then I'll show as a girl. Does it say in the rules that girls are excluded?"

"I don't know, Skeva, and I don't care. I won't have a girl represent me. I'd be laughed off the show circuit. You've been good for High Mountain Peak, but you're going to have to let him go."

Barquel must be up in the heavens laughing. For every sweet, he continued to send down sour. As quickly as that, I was robbed of my only delight.

I was moping around, a Tide later, watching Raja work Crimson Black, and feeling like crying as I watched Crimson cavort and shy at every imagined weed instead of buckling down like he should when Tren came up to stand beside me.

"Why the sad face?" he asked.

I smiled up at him and thought again how beautiful his smile was. I liked the way his green eyes always watched me, pretending not to, but stealing looks all the same. I had not seen Tren since Targone had arrived. With his presence, my heart thumped so loudly that I wondered if he could hear it.

I sighed. He was the other untouchable in my life. I wondered if anyone ever got what he or she most wanted. Was everyone always shorted just when they had it almost in their grasp? Or was it just me?

I looked back at Crimson. "Raja gets to show Crimson Black, so *he* gets to ride him from now on. Blair won't let me show the stallion just because I'm a girl."

"Things change, Skeva. I'm sorry."

"Boy, do they change! I can't even sleep at night because Targone's always around."

"What do you mean, he's always around? I don't see him."

"He's with me every night."

"Skeva, repeat that."

"He's with me every night."

"In your bed?"

That pulled my eyes away from Crimson. "Tren!" I sighed and rolled my eyes. "Targone sleeps at my door."

"On the floor?"

"He's a cat."

"I see," Tren said, and he was smiling again. "So you do see a lot of him."

I had an idea. I crossed my fingers and asked Barquel to help me just once. "Targone reminds me of Isandor. Every time I try to go to the necessary, he's there putting his hands on me."

"As a cat?"

"No, as a man."

"I do not believe Targone would touch you without cause."

I didn't answer. Now was the time to back away and let Tren worry about it.

I was silent a moment. Then, I put on the finishing touch. "I don't mind when he's a cat. It's when he's a man, he scares me."

Now, to change the subject. "Did you come to see me ride?"

Tren accepted the shift in the conversation. His eyes lifted to stare off towards the mountains. "Actually, Skeva, I came to see if you'd like to go swim in the lake."

"In the lake with you?" I smiled. Perfect! "Yes," I said. "When?"

"Now."

"I have nothing to wear. Don't I need . . .?" The image was gone, but I knew there was something I was supposed to wear.

"You need nothing. We will swim nude." Tren's eyes mocked me. "Are you still game, Skeva?"

Wow! Now, who was playing with fire? I nodded.

"Let's go."

When the bubblecar arrived, Tren took my hand and led me towards it. The vehicle was gorgeous, all Plexiglas and black chrome. The pilot surprised me when he got out and walked away. Tren knew how to fly a bubble car?

Tren was smiling down at me as he opened up the door. It was almost like he'd read my thoughts. He put his hands on my waist to lift me up. I was pretty sure that they lingered longer than necessary, but of course, I didn't say anything. Then, Tren walked around to the other side and sat down in the pilot's chair. I was staring all around the bubble car, trying to drink it in. Tren smiled again and then placed the belt across my body, securing it. He tugged at it to check it. His hand brushed against my breast. I froze. Tren's eyes met mine. He no longer acted the least bit shy of me. What had changed?

The bubble car lifted up gracefully. I was not surprised. I was beginning to believe that Tren was good at everything. I admired the white leather seats and the bar in the front panel. The whole car was tastefully elegant.

"Are you rich, Tren?" I asked as my hand traveled over the smooth feel of the soft leather.

"Yes." He smiled over at me and removed the bottle from my hands that I was studying. He placed it back in the bar and closed the bar door.

"How did you get to be so rich?"

"First, I killed someone. Does that shock you?"

I nodded. "Why did you kill him?"

Tren reached inside an ice kit. He pulled out a bottle of cracka juice and handed it to me, then took one for himself and shut the ice kit.

"The day is far too lovely to get into old, ugly history. I told you once that I am not a nice man, Skeva. You'd have to accept that if…"

"It doesn't matter, Tren. It's in the past."

Tren drank from his bottle. One of his gulps almost emptied it. I sipped at mine. I wasn't about to gulp it quickly. Cracka juice was too much of a treat.

He watched me for a moment. "I still kill people, Skeva. Why do you think so many people fear me?"

"You mean you kill bad people like Isandor?"

"I kill when it is convenient for me."

I looked down. He was making me uneasy. I wished Tren were easier to read.

"You would never be allowed to discuss that with me or any other part of my business," he warned. "It is what I do and who I am."

"I would obey, Tren," I assured him, but I was wondering why Tren was telling me all this. Was he trying to scare me away? Could he really be that cold and ugly inside if I loved him? With me, he was always kind — at least, as kind as a male ever was. Could a man be kind to one person and vicious to others?

"Look down there, Skeva," he ordered. "There's the lake."

"It's huge!" I cried out. "It has all those branches that wind everywhere and keep making new lakes!"

Tren laughed. "You do amuse me, girl. Any other female would have said that it was a beautiful lake. Why do you never call things beautiful?"

"I don't know." I tried for a moment to think about it, but the same void of memory was my only answer.

Tren veered down on the south side between two smaller branches of the lake. His landing was smooth and unhurried.

"Stay put," Tren ordered me, and he came around to help me down. I had unlocked the belt, so there was no need for him to do it. His eyes mocked me when he saw what I had done. Then his strong arms lifted me up and out, sliding me down his body until I stood up. Even then, he didn't drop his hands immediately, and my heart began to race.

I studied his eyes. Why had he invited me here? I had thought he was afraid of me — or of my Shapechanger heritage. Yet . . .

I took the hand he offered me, and we walked down to the water.

"May I take off my shoes?"

"You will take everything off, Skeva." Tren turned and faced me, his eyes watching me intently.

"Couldn't I just leave on…?" I started to ask.

"Everything, Skeva." His arms crossed, and he stood leaning against an old dead tree trunk.

My face turned red, but I knew he'd seen my body once before. It shouldn't bother me. I unbuttoned my shirt, slipped it off, and placed it on a boulder. Tren's eyes roamed my body. Then, when I began to unroll the strips of sheeting I wound around my breasts, he began to chuckle.

"So that's why you look like a boy," he said. "I thought I remembered you having more on top."

I turned away from him as the last of the binding fell away. I felt shy and exposed. I didn't know where to look. I removed my pants and laid them on top of the pile.

"Come here," Tren ordered. His voice sounded huskier than usual.

I swallowed hard. I had thought I wanted this, but now I was scared peeless. My legs trembled as I went towards him.

"For spit's sake, Skeva. Lift up your head," he said gently. "I have no intention of taking you."

My head came up, and I stared at him. "You don't? You're not going to . . ." Suddenly, I smiled.

Tren frowned down at me. "Why would you be so fearful of our joining, Skeva?" he demanded. "You must know I would not hurt you."

He came closer. One hand reached out and pulled me to him. I was trembling again. I could not meet his eyes. His hands reached out to touch my face. They were gentle, but they forced me even closer. "Why, Skeva?" he demanded once again.

"I have known only Isandor. I am not skilled. I fear you will find me lacking, too."

Tren chuckled softly, but the sound did not offend me. It sent chills up and down my spine. "I am not Isandor. I learned enough from my testing of you to know you would please me well. I told you once, Isandor was a fool."

Tren's eyes were full of desire. I thought he would kiss me, but instead, he ordered me into the lake.

I obeyed, but I wished he'd let me stay and watch him undress. Tren's body pleased me very much.

In a minute, Tren had joined me, and we laughed and splashed at each other like two children, but there was not a moment when I was unaware that we were *not* children. The water against my naked body was a freedom I had never felt, but it was also the caress I longed for from Tren. I did not understand how he could vow that he would not touch me when the tension between us was building higher each moment.

A bubble car zoomed over us and then landed beside ours. "Spit!" Tren cursed. "It must be your friend, Targone."

I sighed. I thought we would have to get out, but Tren ignored Targone's arrival. He dived under to pull at my feet. My head went under, and Tren let me go, swimming quickly out of my reach. I bobbed back up, laughing, and raced after him.

In another moment, Targone was on the sand at the water's edge. His eyes were glaring greenish-yellow darts.

"Come in and join us," Tren yelled out. "The water's great!"

I laughed and dove. Like a fish, I swam under the water, eyes open, seeing the huge boulders and the sandy depths of the lake bottom. When my air was gone, I surfaced. Targone was a length away from me.

"Go back to shore," Targone ordered me. I looked around for Tren.

Targone reached out and tugged me towards him. His hand brushed against my breast, and I recoiled.

"Leave me alone, Targone. Tren is my master, and he said I could"

Tren pulled me under. I broke the surface, gasping and coughing. I'd gotten a mouthful of lake water. Tren held me up while I tried to get my breath back.

"I warned you not to be rude to him," Tren reminded me sternly. His arm was wrapped around my waist. For a while, I was too busy gasping for breath to realize it, but when I did, I plotted. I was slippery as an eel, and with one twist, I turned to face him. Instantly, I was pushed backward. Tren was laughing. "If you're recovered enough to scheme, you don't need me holding you," he said. He was treading water, well away from me.

"Out, Skeva," ordered Targone once again. He was so angry he was almost spitting. I looked at Tren, pleading, but he shook his head at me and motioned with his head toward shore.

I swam back towards the place we'd entered — but climbing out naked with Targone there was harder than stripping in front of Tren.

Targone gave me no chance to climb out. His hand reached in and jerked me up. I ran towards my clothes and bundled them in front of me. Then I darted to the other side of the bubble car and put everything back on.

When I returned to Tren and Targone, they were dressed but in the middle of an argument. They were speaking in a language I didn't know. I tried to read the understanding in their minds, but it was harder than with Frieda and Flar. Both males had heavy guards on their thoughts. I sat on a fallen tree and waited.

"You should know better, Skeva," Targone scolded me. "Your husband may beat you for this."

"If he beats me, then he beats me," I said, with a pretense of far more courage than I really possessed. "It will be nothing new," I bragged.

"I would make it new," Targone growled. "There are ways to punish that you have not even heard of, girl."

I got off the tree and went to Tren. It was cowardly, but Targone reminded me too much of Isandor.

"You will not get the chance, Targone," Tren said. His hands, for a moment, held me. "I have made a decision. I will take Skeva as my wife and become Shapechanger if she does not already have a Shapechanger lord."

My mouth dropped open, and I looked up at Tren. "Thank you," I cried, throwing my arms around his neck.

Once again, Tren pushed me away. "Skeva, that does not mean I will not punish you for disobedience. Go back and sit on the log, now."

I was smiling broadly as I scurried back towards my perch. I made sure to give Targone a wide berth as I walked by him. He ignored me.

"You will give up everything for her?" Targone asked, eyeing Tren strangely.

"That will not be necessary," Tren assured him. "I believe I can manage both."

"Pity," Targone said, still watching Tren. "I was quite looking forward to taming the girl." He paused and turned to regard me. "Seeing her nakedness," he continued, "has made me realize how pleasing she is. I had imagined that she might be, but with all the boyish clothes you allow her to wear, it was difficult to be sure."

Targone's stare made me cringe. I started stirring up a city of ant-like insects with a stick. They were reddish gold and five-legged, but they crawled along in a perfect line, reminding me of insects I'd seen somewhere long ago. These had small, dainty pinchers and were larger than I remembered ants being. I wished I could drop some down Targone's back.

Targone stood up. "Shall we return?" he asked.

Tren came walking over to me. He held out his hand. "Come," he ordered me. "Targone is right. It is time to go."

I half expected there to be a fight about who would fly me back. I did not want to go with Targone. Perhaps the two of them had already argued it out, for Targone said nothing when Tren led me to his bubble car and lifted me up into it. I noticed that Tren did not buckle me in, though.

On the flight back, Tren was so quiet he made me nervous. I wondered if he was regretting agreeing to accept me. He had said that he would never take a bride.

"I am sorry that I caused you trouble with Targone," I told him.

He laughed. "Why? It wasn't your fault. I invited you."

"But I always bring you trouble. Does that make you angry with me?"

Tren's eyes were focused on the sky around us. He did not look at me. "I am not a woman, Skeva. I choose my fate."

He sounded annoyed. I dropped my eyes and stared down at my hands. I felt it when Tren's eyes followed my movement. He examined me for several minutes. When he spoke again, his voice was gentle. "Skeva, I know who and what you are. It is a foolish man who plays with a zorben wire and then becomes angry at the wire when it shocks him. I am not that reckless, but it is true that I play with danger."

I had put my hat back on when I dressed. Tren pulled it off. His hands swept through the long strands of wet hair. "You will wear your hair down, and I shall clothe you in dresses suitable for your position. Understand?"

Once more, his voice was fierce. Did I dare argue?

"I cannot ride in a dress," I hedged. I did not look up at Tren. I twisted my fingers and watched them turn white.

Tren's hand left my hair and stilled my hands. "You will be guarded heavily, much more so than now, and sometimes I will come to watch you ride. Perhaps I will even buy this Crimson Black that you love so."

"You would do that?" I looked up then, and I knew he saw the love in my eyes. He pulled his hand away as if I'd bitten him. His eyes scanned the horizon.

"This is foolishness. You may be owned by a Shapechanger, and I will be torn to shreds for my imaginings."

He was silent then, and I thought it best not to speak. Long minutes passed, and I stared down at the fields beneath us. We were flying over farms. The green of the crops and the occasional patches of purple sea seeds cheered me somewhat.

"Targone has a tracer on you," Tren said suddenly, breaking through the silence. He reached forward into the "cooler" and grabbed a juice for me and a drink for himself. He opened mine and then his and took a long gulp. "I don't know how or when he put it on you, Skeva, but you're marked. Targone can find you whenever he wants."

"Can't you take it off?"

For a moment, Tren stared at me as if thinking. Then he sighed and answered. "First of all, Skeva, I am not privy to the secrets of the Shapechanger, nor do I see a purpose in antagonizing Targone. The tracer does not harm you. Perhaps, knowing you, it's a good thing you have one."

"I don't like Targone knowing where I am. He frightens me."

"He will not harm you. I've said I will take you. That will keep Targone from using his Shapechanger Powers on you. And, of course, Targone would not interfere anyway until he knows for sure about your Shapechanger husband."

"If I ever had a husband, he is dead. Otherwise, he would have been here already."

"It has not been long enough to know. If he comes from any distance, he could still be on his way."

"I don't want him to come. Whoever he was, he is now a stranger. And, if all Shapechangers are like Targone, I don't want a Shapechanger husband."

"You do not want a husband at all," Tren said, laughing.

Thenos

Those fools of mine. I curse their stars. They are worms, fit for nothing greater than to grovel at my feet. They told me they tried to find my Shaara. I say they did not look. I gave them money and girls. Their hands had ready weapons. Yet, they feared to kill. Cowardly, they begged for my understanding. I have no understanding for peons. They all deserve to lie in the dust.

Peasants, dirtwalkers, I shall call them — such a lovely term. I came across it in my readings recently. I shall use the term when I rule. My first proclamation will be to separate the noble Shapechanger from the peons of the dirt, and I shall declare that to be their official name: dirt walkers!

My dirt walkers did not find Shaara. A commoner, one who, if the reports can be believed, had not even heard of the rich reward offered for Shaara's return, notified the Altarian Elders. Smart man. I shall not kill him, as I shall all the others involved. All those who came in contact with my little innocent will be removed at my leisure. I shall teach them the penalty for failing to recognize the gray eyes of Shaara's nobility. How could they not see her royal carriage? One look at her should have told them that she was a princess.

This day — which should have been victorious with the news of Shaara's discovery — has thrown me into the pit of devastation. I would weep if I were capable of it. I burn in wretchedness. Not even a new girl taken from the sleep chamber will appease this depression of mine. True, it will occupy my mind for a time, and I do so enjoy the almond smell of fear, but it is no replacement for the temporary destruction of my plans.

Shaara, my princess, too long has it been since I touched your delicate shoulder and branded you with my bonding. I can almost smile with the memory of how you trembled when the pain lanced through you. Your eyes feared me; they were great globes of terror, brimming with your woman's tears.

Your eyes are not like other girls that I have stolen from their barbarian planets. *They* are mere peons, dirt walkers. They do not have the depths of you, my little princess. They are shallow, grubby little creatures. Their panic does not send delicious tremors of delight throughout my body. There is no grayness in their eyes when they tremble before me. It is you that I see each time I plunge myself within them. Why are you not here with me?

Drat Shaarvan! His ship is closer than mine to the planet Freinana. I curse my dirt walkers for not looking there — stupid peons! They are worthless slugs! It would do me no good to rush to my Shaara now. Shaarvan would already have stolen her from her Freinan master. At least, I can count on my brother to revenge the sacrilege — although, sadly, he does not have the skill that I have in administering appropriate punishment, or the taste for it. What a shame to let such a dirtwalker off so easily. I would have made him rue the day he ignored Shaara's lovely eyes. I would have made him atone . . .

Let Shaarvan have his reunion with his wife. It will be his last. My day is almost here. Soon, the innocent princess will be mine, and she will adore me. Perhaps I worry needlessly. Undoubtedly, Shaara will come to me when she sees me atop the throne of Altar.

Skeva

When the bubble car landed, Targone was already there. He insisted on escorting me home. I didn't want to go with him, but Tren ordered it. Tren was already beginning to sound too much like a husband.

"Targone," I probed as we walked, "Where did you put the tracer?"

"Shapechanger women do not talk all the time," he grunted at me.

"I only asked you one question."

"It was one too many," he said.

I walked into the house without another word, but as Targone turned to leave, I called out. "Where are you going now?" Not that I wanted to go with him. I just wanted to know if he was going to be prowling around the house all night.

Targone turned back and looked at me. His eyes met mine. There was just the hint of a smile in them. "That was two too many questions," he said, holding up two of his fingers like I couldn't get the meaning otherwise.

What a jerk! I turned my back on him and stomped away.

"Skeva," I heard him call behind me. His tone was not one I dared ignore.

"What?" I said, turning around to glare at him.

"Come here," he ordered. It wasn't the words that issued from his mouth but the way he said them that sent shivers of fear up my spine. If only Tren had not ordered me to obey. Even so, I was still tempted to take the stairs two at a time, in a gallop upwards. Whatever Targone wanted, I had a feeling I wasn't going to like it. Dutifully, I returned to him, keeping my eyes meekly on the ground.

"I warned you about turning your back on a Shapechanger male," Targone said.

My body was attempting to respond to the threat in his voice. It was telling me to run, but my legs were frozen.

"I told you the next time you turned your back, there would be punishment." The way he said "punishment" made all the little hairs on my arm stand at attention, but I still couldn't move my legs. "I shall not beat you since you belong to another," he said, "but I shall punish you. Tomorrow, you may not ride the landoors."

I gasped. My legs might be frozen, but my mouth wasn't. "You can't do that," I blurted out. "Tren told me I could ride."

"Hold your tongue, girl. I shall speak to Tren and to the man called Blair. You will not ride tomorrow."

Targone waved his hand over my head, and I was free to move again, but his hand also issued the silence command, so I could not argue.

"You must learn to be Shapechanger again," Targone said, and he turned and walked out of the house.

I was furious. It was getting dark, and I knew I shouldn't go out, but I had to talk to Tren before Targone did. I waited a short period so I would not run into the catman outside, and then I set off running. The casino was all lit up. Even from the outside, it was loud, filled with laughter, music, and men talking.

The man at the door, a different giant than the one I'd met before, tried to bar me from entering, but I pushed past him and ran through the crowd. There were men everywhere, dangerous-looking men who made rude, kissing noises at me. Many of them had no shirts on, and their pants were daringly low slung. Several of them looked drunk.

I saw a girl with bangles drooping from her breasts and a bottom that was only a triangular patch. She was in a box in the center, crooning a song while she stroked herself, lifting each one of her breasts and massaging it like it hurt.

"Well, look at this," said a jeering ape-man of a male. "Is it a boy or a girl? It smells like a landoor."

A second man grabbed me and lifted me up high in the air for everyone to see.

"Put me down!" I yelled at him, attempting to kick him in any place I could reach. The man dangled me away from his body and then abruptly turned me upside down.

"Stop it, you spithead!" I screeched.

"Oh, my!" he said, jeering at my protests. "Did you hear that? Scary little bugger, isn't he?"

"You sure got yourself a live one," said another man.

"Must be a stable hand. What's the runt doing here?" asked the ape-man holding me.

I was holding onto my cap with my hand, praying that it wouldn't get jerked off. It was bad enough in the casino when they all thought I was a boy.

There was a whole crowd gathering around to watch. I was upside down, but I could see their laughing mouths and hear the things they were saying. The gorilla on the right kept telling my captor that they should all "see what's underneath my dirty wrappings." I thought that was a lousy idea, but I was too busy to argue. I was pretty occupied trying to make contact with my fist while at the same time holding the hat in place.

Several others started agreeing with the loudmouth. One man just thought they ought to throw me into a keg and hold me under. I had decided that I really didn't like Tren's casino much, and I was starting to get nauseatingly dizzy, swinging back and forth upside down. I wondered how many of them I'd spray when I vomited, which was getting likelier by the second.

"I wouldn't do that if I were you," a deep voice bellowed out. "That's Tren's waif."

The words were magic. I was lowered to the ground, propped upright, and given a push forward. The men opened up a path to let me through. I glared back at them and tried to walk in a straight line.

I wasn't feeling really great, but I hurried on. I headed upstairs, where I figured Tren would probably be. I hoped he wouldn't be busy with Malla again.

"Spit in the Wind, Skeva." It was Tren's voice blasting at me. I turned around, and there he was. I almost choked on my swallow. Tren was absolutely stylish! His shirt was ironed, with little frilly things dangling down all over. He had a half-jacket over that, with white leather embossed in a beaded abstract design.

I admired the way he looked for only a moment. My eyes quickly fastened on the body, drooling over him. Malla was sitting on the arm of his chair, dangling like a limp sausage, except there was a lot more of her. Her breasts were barely covered by the thin strip of material she probably called a blouse, and on her bottom was a pair of pants just like the ones I'd had to wear for the Slaver when he sold me. Malla's pants were even tighter.

I glared at her, but she only laughed. "Oh, Tren, it's your little boy-girl," she said, rubbing his chest like it needed polishing.

She wrinkled up her nose and jeered some more. "Doesn't he/she ever bathe? I can smell the landoor from here."

I wished I had the kitchen knife in my hand right then. I'd like to see how great Malla looked with a shaved head!

Tren sighed. Even with a frown on his face, he was not bad to look at. I admired the elegance of his shirt and the way the muscles bulged underneath as he disengaged Malla from his arm. As I walked closer, his hand was pushing her up and off of him. "Go play with the others, Malla," he ordered her.

I was feeling cocky until I saw the way his hand patted her rounded bottom as she slipped away. I glared at Tren. I had a lot of puzzles to solve about him. Malla was one of the more unpleasant ones.

Tren's finger was motioning me to come closer, but he didn't wait for my approach before he began his inquisition. "What are you doing here?"

"I need to talk," I told him. I obeyed his order to come closer, but I made sure that I stopped beyond his reach. So far, Tren hadn't been punitive in his disciplining, but he wasn't what I'd call predictable.

"Is this about landoors?" he growled at me.

I had his full attention, but with the look in his eyes, I wished I didn't.

"Kind of," I answered, watching his eyes for warning.

Tren sighed again. His hand, for a moment, covered his forehead like he was getting a bad headache. "I don't suppose you came over here chaperoned by Targone?" I shook my head, but the sarcasm in Tren's voice was dripping. I knew he wasn't expecting any other response.

"Figures." He reached down for his glass, lifted it, and poured the rest of the drink down his throat. Then, he stood up and came towards me. His size and the look in his eyes made me take another step back. He thrust out his hand, grabbed at my arm, and yanked me close. "I'll walk you home," he said. It wasn't an offer.

The grip he had on my arm was so tight it hurt. I doubt he was even aware. He didn't loosen his grip. I saw his eyes circling the room, checking to make sure everything was calm. He called out to the bartender to watch over the place. Then, Tren's eyes came back to mine. "You can tell me your big problem on the way back, Skeva."

He swung his arm around my shoulder. It wasn't a gentle, romantic touch. It was more like a warning that if I resisted, he would keep walking and drag me along. Before I'd had a chance to say anything more, we were heading towards the exit.

"Hey, Tren," someone called out. "What are you doing . . . babysitting?" Laughter broke out all around us.

I glared. I resented everyone thinking I was about twelve, but it was the only thing that allowed me my freedom. Most of the time, it was an even trade. Right now was not one of those times. I knew a twelve-year-old boy couldn't compete with Malla.

"Come on, Skeva," Tren ordered, ignoring the men's jeers.

I kept thinking about Malla as we walked towards the door, probably because she ran up and gave Tren a big smooch right in front of me. She and I exchanged hate glares. She knew I wasn't a boy, and she'd probably figured out that I wasn't twelve years old, either.

Tren ordered Malla to stay in the casino, and she walked off, pouting. I didn't like the way the man who'd offered to become Shapechanger for me watched Malla's bottom sashaying around.

When we reached the curb outside, I stopped, planting my feet so Tren would have to drag me along if he was stubbornly insistent. Luckily, his eyes were only amused, and he waited to hear what I had to say. I wished I had the courage to massage his chest like Malla had, but I kept my hands down and told Tren how the slaver had made me wear one of those costumes like the girls in the casino were wearing. "I could put it on if you want me to," I offered. "I mean, when I come to the casino."

Tren didn't seem pleased by the idea. In fact, he looked mad. His eyes sparked, and he grabbed my chin and held it still. "You are to throw that costume away," he blared at me. "That's an order. I don't want you wearing clothes like that, and I don't want you coming to the casino."

"But . . . " was all I could get out before he was squeezing my jaw to let me know to shut up.

"And you are never to go out in the dark alone again. Understand?"

I nodded cautiously. When he let go of me, I told him what I thought about his orders. "I'm not a child, Tren. I don't need to be sheltered. Malla wears costumes like that. If you want a woman like her at your side, why can't it be me?" I demanded angrily.

Tren's eyes flared and then softened. "Because you are not her, Skeva."

"That's not fair. I could be. I will be if you wish it." It should have embarrassed me to plead, but I needed him to know that I could be whatever he desired. I wanted Malla gone.

He cursed something about Barquel. "Skeva, I don't want you coming to the casino. But, if you do come because of something you deem is an emergency, you are to come only like this, smelling like a landoor."

His words took all the fight out of my spine. "You know, I bathed today. I still smell?"

"Like a landoor," he said, smiling.

"Is that why you won't . . . ?"

He cut me off abruptly and grabbed my hand to pull me forward. "Skeva, why did you come tonight?"

I was sorry the discussion had moved away from Malla, but I did need to discuss Targone's form of discipline. "Because of Targone," I told him.

"I thought you said it was about landoors," Tren laughed.

"It is. He said I couldn't ride tomorrow, *all day*."

Tren halted in the middle of Stred Street. It wasn't the safest place for a conversation. "You came to the casino in the dark, risking your life, because Targone said you couldn't ride tomorrow?"

I moved us along and explained. "He has no right to order me not to ride!"

Tren shoved me up against the concrete wall that separated a wealthy merchant's housing tract from the rest of the street. He held me there against the cold dampness of the wall and glared. I didn't fight him.

"Do you have any idea how close I am to ordering you to shovel manure like Blair did?" he threatened.

I thought Tren was really being unfair, but I sanely kept quiet.

Tren backed up two steps and stood there staring at me. Then, without a word, he turned and started walking again, still heading for my house. I had to jog to catch up.

"Why are you so angry?" I asked when I was beside him again.

He ignored my question. "What did you do to cause Targone to take away your riding privileges?"

"He says I turned my back to him."

"Did you?"

"Only kind of. He was leaving, and I turned and walked away."

"Then what he says goes."

"Tren, that's not fair." I stopped and tried to decide how best to argue my case.

"Keep walking, Skeva," Tren ordered as he grabbed my hand and pulled me forward. "I have a casino to run."

"Yeah, and a woman to go mount," I blurted out before I gave myself a chance to think about how safe it was to rile Tren further.

"Skeva!" This time, it was Tren who halted. "I never promised to make any changes."

"I never said you did. I offered myself, and you refused me, probably because I smell like landoor."

I could feel the heat of anger rising up in him. If he'd been a pot on the stove, he would have boiled over.

"Keep walking, Skeva," he growled. "I have no more patience."

I thought it best to keep quiet the rest of the way. Getting scolded is no fun. When we reached the house, I started to just walk in, but I stopped in the doorway and turned around to face him.

"Tren."

"Yes." He said it like he was bored with the whole situation — and especially me.

"I'm sorry I always bother you. I know I shouldn't, and you are always so kind, and . . ."

"Skeva shut up," he said. His hand reached out and grabbed my wrist. Then he pulled me close and kissed me. The kiss wasn't long enough. Tren was pushing me away before I could focus on enjoying his lips or securing him.

"Not a word, Skeva," he said as he pushed me away from him. "I already regret doing that. Just get up to your room and go to bed."

I walked up the stairs in slow motion. When I reached the top, I was relieved not to find Targone. I got into my bed and lay there thinking. It was a long time before I could shut my eyes.

Thenos

I have successfully dealt with the entire group of Elders, except my father. The rest of them are dead. Drugs, correctly administered, are such a useful tool for the ambitious. Not even their wives suspected that their husbands' lives were shortened by the hand of any but the fates. Ignorance should be abolished in the realm of the

Shapechanger. To go forward, we must understand the wisdom of the Old Ones. After I have been crowned king, I shall make it so. Long live the reign of Thenos.

Why have I saved my father? He has pestered my life for too long. His tirades over morals and productive service to the greater good have bored me. I would not be loath to bid him goodbye, but it is the thought of my mother's tears that prevents me. Her eyes are too much like my Shaara's. I never noticed that until her eyes flooded at parting with Gemder, her friend's husband. She wept in great heaving sobs of grief, and I was embarrassed to see it. I went over to "comfort her" (to quiet her down), and I saw the resemblance.

I had planned to give the final dose to Trevor that day, but I slipped it back into my pocket and viewed my mother with eyes unsullied by the past. My mother is a beautiful woman. She does not have Shaara's diminutive stature, but her hair is full (not possessing, of course, Shaara's exquisite golden streaks). Her eyes are huge and gray (although slightly blue, unfortunately).

I shall leave Mother with her depleted Shapechanger husband. My father is weak. He will die in perhaps a fortyTide. It will suffice for my plans.

Goria

At last! I saw Thenos at the Passing Ceremony of Elder Truble! Thenos took me aside, away from my husband. (How hilarious that such is allowed because Thenos is my brother. It is almost too bad I cannot tell my husband how my *brother* rides my body. I wish Thenos did not demand our meetings to be held in secret. I should delight in being free from Pathe. Pathe would never punish me for it. He is too spineless.)

Thenos is even more handsome than the first time I saw him. I think he grows to look more like Shaarvan each day. He has been working out, and his muscles are greater by far than when he last took me in his arms. I yearn to test the width of each bulge with the stretch of my fingers. Will his chest promise such thrills as well?

Also, there is an element of Power about him. Thenos walks about as if he were king. I like his confidence and the way he surveys Altar with eyes full of greed. He and I are much alike.

Thenos has asked me to meet him. Of course, I will. How could there be any doubt? I would willingly run away with him. All he would have to do is beckon with those Shapechanger eyes of his, and I would grovel at his feet. What Power he has. How luscious it feels!

Hopefully, Thenos has given up his search for Shaara. It has not been easy for me to be patient with his prolonged lust for the girl. I am glad for what I did. Wherever Shaara is, she is a slave by now, groveling at the foot of some ignorant commoner. She will never bother me again.

Frankly, I do not understand why Thenos has been so obstinate in his pursuit of her — but males are like that. The unattainable is so much more attractive to them. Happily, though, they eagerly ride what is freely given. Perhaps I should be more difficult in this meeting. Maybe I should make Thenos beg me for my favors.

Chapter Eight

Skeva

The next day, I groomed the horses until they were all immaculate. Then, I still had half the day left with nothing to do. I visited Crimson Black and sat in his stall talking to him.

"Hey, Skeva. That Shapechanger wants to talk to you," said one of the grooms. I smiled my thanks.

I kissed Crimson goodbye and went out to see what Targone wanted. He was looking at me strangely as if I had somehow changed since he'd last seen me.

"What?" I said. I knew it was rude, but right now, I wasn't feeling really friendly.

Unbelievably, he ignored it. "Tren got a message from Altar. Your name is Shaara — Shaara of Shaarvan. Your husband is on his way here."

"No!" I cried out. "I won't go with him. You can't make me."

Targone's eyes held a glint like he knew something I didn't. "I shall not be the one who makes you do anything, Shaara. It is Shaarvan who will bend you to his will."

"What about Tren?"

"I am sure he will be suitably rewarded. Your family is high in the rank of the Shapechanger. They are as rich as the whole planet of Freinana."

"Why was I sold, then?"

"You were stolen. It is a good thing I found the slaver. I imagine your husband will want to 'talk' to him, among other things."

I stamped my foot. "I wish Shapechanger lied. I wish you were telling me the biggest, filthiest lie in all the galaxy." My tears had begun to fall. I took off running. Targone fell in beside me.

"What are you doing?" I yelled at him. "Leave me alone."

"I cannot. You must be guarded night and day, as is fitting the wife of one of the elite."

I ran faster. I thought at first I could outrun him, but Targone kept up with me easily. When I was panting and blowing, he did not even seem winded. I had to stop. I plopped down on a boulder and tried to calm my racing heart.

"Keep walking, Shaara, or you will cramp."

I knew he was right. I stood up and walked. I knew where I was going. I must go to Tren. Targone's hand grabbed my wrist.

"No, Shaara. You will not go to Tren. I shall not permit it, and he does not wish it."

I glared at Targone. Then, it registered, just exactly what he'd said. "Tren doesn't *want* to see me?"

Targone shook his head. I turned away. I felt like screaming or throwing something. "Why? Why did this have to happen? Why did Tren have to send that message? Why couldn't he just have let me stay here where I'm happy?"

"Tren had to send that message, Shaara. And you would have been found, anyway. The Shapechanger have been searching for you, planet by planet."

"Maybe. But maybe they never would have found me. Maybe I could have stayed here and lived with Tren, and . . ."

Targone was shaking his head.

"Have you no compassion, Targone? This is wrong. I don't even know the man you say is my husband. I don't want him. I want Tren."

Targone's eyes were firm. "A Shapechanger mates for life."

"But I don't want him!"

Targone grabbed my arms, although I hadn't moved. "Listen to me," he said. "You have grown hard-headed because you have been allowed to run free. I do not know if your husband can bring back your memories. He is a Warlord, which means he has far more Power than I do, but whether you get your memory back or not, you had better think about whether you want to see Tren torn limb to limb. Your husband could do that."

I gasped and pulled away. "Tren saved my life. He rescued me from Isandor. He notified the Shapechanger."

Targone's eyes narrowed. "He also kissed you."

I sprang up. "You were spying on us!"

"No," he said, shaking his head. "I was guarding you, as I have done since I arrived."

"But Tren didn't know about *what's his name,* " I argued.

"Shaarvan."

"Tren didn't know that Shaarvan was alive." The name felt strange on my tongue. Why didn't it sound familiar if Shaarvan were really my husband?

"I know that, Shaara. Tren would be dead if he had kissed you, believing otherwise."

Did that mean that Targone would have . . . ? I swallowed hard. "Then nobody needs to know. Please, Targone."

He was silent. His eyes were not as fierce as sometimes, but they were unbending. I knew he would tell my husband everything.

I sighed. "Tren won't even say goodbye to me?"

"He will come when Shaarvan is here. He told me so."

I closed my eyes, trying not to see the image of Tren being ripped apart by a tiger the size of Targone. "But that's when he *must not* come."

"You think like a female," Targone scoffed.

"Targone, please. I don't understand."

He studied me for a moment. "Shaara, can you see Tren hiding in fear?"

I pictured Tren in the casino, where his word was law, standing up to Blair's anger, challenging even Targone, a Shapechanger. "No," I said, shaking my head.

"To confront danger is always better."

"Doesn't it make better sense to stay out of someone's way until his anger is calm — especially if that someone can turn into a cat and tear him apart?"

"For a girl," Targone said. "It is not a man's or a Shapechanger's way. And, if you remember, I did warn you about the danger. You ignored it and continued to stalk Tren."

I looked up to see if Targone was gloating, but he wasn't. He had turned away and was kicking a rock. "Shaara," he said, "I do not know what kind of person your husband is, but no Shapechanger male will accept the things you do."

I stamped my foot. "I will not be boxed in again by some man's will. I would rather face death."

Targone shook his head and studied me. "Shaara, look at your arms. Really look. What do you see?"

I had no idea what he was talking about. I rolled up my sleeves and examined my arms. They were the same as always. I turned my puzzled eyes to him.

"Do you see the three faint scratches along the length of them? It is the same on each of your arms. That is called the Shapechanger brand, and only the Old Ones do it."

"You mean my husband is old?"

"No." Targone chuckled. "The *Old Ones* refers to the pure-blooded families of the original Shapechanger. They practiced powerful magic. The scratches you bear are part of that magic."

"What are you trying to tell me, Targone?"

"Your husband made those scratches. As a Saberey cat, he clawed into your skin and tore ridges along your arms. The poison of his claws brought you into the family. That is why your Power is so great, but the pain of the scratches and the festering is said to drive the weak to their death."

"Targone, you're saying he's someone I should fear?"

"A husband who would do that to his wife is not a Shapechanger I would want to challenge." Targone picked up another rock and tossed it.

He noticed, then, that it was growing dark. "Come, you must go home," he ordered.

We walked along the trail together. The silence, with each of us in our own thoughts, was almost comfortable, like being with a friend. Targone, the one I'd hated for his domineering attitude, a friend? At that moment, thinking of what he'd told me about the violence of my husband, I decided I did need his friendship desperately.

"When will he come, Targone?"

"I do not know. The sending did not mention his planet of departure."

Targone had stopped to wait for me to continue walking. His eyes studied me. I knew he read my fear.

"Targone, please. . . would you teach me about being Shapechanger? Before my husband arrives?"

I could read nothing from him. His expression was guarded, but he nodded slowly. He searched my eyes, tapping my thoughts. "Yes, I shall try to teach you, Shaara. I think it would be very wise of you to learn."

His words would have made me angry, except that I could see the worry in his eyes. I think he also was concerned about what Shaarvan would do to me when he arrived.

The next day, lessons on how to be a Shapechanger's wife began.

"Keep my eyes down at all times?" I repeated. "How can I see anything? I'd bump into things. How can I read expressions on people's faces?" I protested.

Targone ignored me and continued, "A girl may not initiate a conversation with a male."

"That's the same rule as on this planet," I reminded him. "But how does a girl ask questions? How does she learn anything? What happens if the man never speaks? Is she supposed to go through life mute?"

Targone laughed. He jumped onto the top of a big, gray boulder, folded his long, lean legs under him, and stared down at me. He was shaking his head and laughing. "Shaara," he said. "I suspect your husband may have to remove your tongue to keep you silent."

"Would he do that?" I had been tossing rocks at an old dead tree stump. I turned around to stare at Targone. I couldn't tell if he was joking or not. "Is that ever done?" I asked him. I moved over to stand beside him. I felt like reaching up and jerking him down off the boulder. He was still laughing and did not answer my question.

Every day that passed, I was becoming more and more frightened about my mystery husband. Targone wasn't making it any easier with his stories of Shapechanger disciplining. The day before, he had told me about a Shapechanger who had killed a girl because she argued in front of clients. The way Targone told the story, I was one neck squeeze away from death. Maybe it would just be safer if I disappeared before the infamous Shaarvan from Altar arrived. But how could I run away with a tracer on me?

"Targone, what does a tracer look like?"

"You cannot see it," he said. He'd stopped laughing, but his eyes knew what I was thinking. He had that superior, cocky grin he got when he was reminding me how Powerless I was next to a Shapechanger.

"Where did you put it?"

He looked up at the sky, as if examining one of the white puffy clouds hanging overhead. "A girl may not carry anything in public," he drilled me, continuing the lesson as if I'd said nothing. I knew what that meant. Targone wasn't going to discuss the tracer. He always ignored what he did not wish to answer. I sighed and stopped thinking for a moment about running away. I played back Targone's words.

"You mean I can't carry a saddle? I have to get someone else to saddle up for me?"

"A girl may not be unaccompanied in public," he recited.

It wasn't fair. I had worked so hard to be allowed to ride the landoor. I had lived through the abuse of Isandor. I had made friends and settled in. Life wasn't perfect, but it was a spit and a half better than what Targone was telling me about.

I didn't want to be married to a Shapechanger. I didn't want laws and restrictions about what I could carry or say or do.

"Targone, I can't take any more of this," I cried out. "Isn't there anything good you can tell me?"

Targone started to laugh. I saw it in his face, but then he reconsidered. He climbed down off the boulder and walked towards me. "Shaara, it will not be that bad. You will adapt. Shapechangers are good husbands. We are fair to our women."

"But maybe I won't be able to adapt, Targone. Maybe Shaarvan will kill me, like the Shapechanger who killed that girl.

Maybe ." I couldn't continue. My tears had sprung. I slid down to the soft, dry dirt and gave in to them.

"Stop it, Shaara."

I knew Targone wanted to pick me up and hold me. I felt it in his mind, but he held his hands tightly clenched at his sides. "You will adapt, Skeva," he whispered. Despite his will, his hand reached out and touched my hair. I pretended not to notice. "You are intelligent and young. You are very pleasing to the eye. I am sure your husband will give you time."

Give me time — time to become his perfect slave girl! As quickly as they had started, my tears were gone, and I was suddenly full of rage. "I need to go talk to Crimson Black," I said. I rose up and dusted myself off. I knew Targone felt the strength of my emotion. He was already shaking his head.

I sprinted back to the stable and tried to ignore the sound of Targone's words as he jogged along beside me: "Little Shaara, your anger will bring you harm. You are so much safer with the tears."

Tren

She doesn't know, but I sometimes go to watch her ride. I have always done so. There is a tree out in the pasture, well-leafed and shady, and I climb it, as I did in my childhood days, and I sit in the fork where the branches form a natural platform. I can see her well, even without the hyper-glasses that make her face seem almost inches from mine.

Targone is aware of this. He joins me sometimes, and we talk, but today I am alone.

Skeva's — no, Shaara's — face, with its little heart shape and that stubborn chin, is serious as she rides. She concentrates with her whole body as she exercises the landoor. I couldn't say what her goal today is, but as usual, she is determined to obtain it. I have watched her repeat the same maneuver over and over until I wonder that the landoor does not kick up its heels and flee her persistence, but they never do. She has them convinced she is as strong as they are.

She stops to fix her hat. Stray strands of hair have begun to escape their hiding place. Her hair is wondrous. The curls are always tussled wildly about, but it suits her. It contradicts her small size and gentle nature. Seeing her lustrous hair, a man can only think of taking her to bed. Had Skeva ever let her hair down for the casino dwellers to see, I would have had to kill to protect her.

The hair is arranged suitably. She glances over in my direction. I double-check that I am well-hidden. I have thought, sometimes, that she sensed me here, but if she did, her concentration was so intense she never investigated or mentioned it. Targone says that she and I are not bonded tightly enough for that kind of awareness, but Targone always refers to other women. He has never understood that Skeva is special.

I am glad that he does not feel the way I do about her. One lovesick male hiding out in trees so he can catch sight of her is sufficient. I am not keen on being in love with another male's wife. I have never worried over morality, only in that she will never be mine. I am very used to getting what I want.

She is at the jumps now. I have never seen her fall, although Targone was very concerned that first day. I have watched her many times since then. She is a better rider than the male trainers that Blair employs. If we had married, I would have let Skeva ride in the shows Blair takes his horses to, and I believe she would have won.

Skeva has changed my mind about the abilities of a motivated female. There is very little that Skeva could not do if she set her mind to it. Are there others of her gender who share those attributes of spirit and determination? Would I find another Skeva if I looked? I do not believe it is possible.

When did I begin to love her? Was it that first time when I saw her with the kitchen knife and those sad gray eyes, so resolved to die with her pride intact? Or when I carried her up to her room and saw her valiant act of bravery, even though her teeth were gnawing her bottom lip in fright. I could barely stand to look at her body. The colors of Isandor's brutality had marked too vividly the life the girl had lived, but that chin of hers was still undaunted, like a banner carried into battle by a soldier who knows that all is lost.

I would have married you, Skeva, and dealt willingly with the daily problems you brought me. I would have changed my world for you, even become a Shapechanger. It would have been worth it. Your excitement as you talk about your landoors, your flashes of wit, your saucy arguments, and your passionate eyes urging me to bed you. We would have had many naked swims in the lake, Skeva, and I would have let you push Malla aside and take your place in my lap and in my bed, as you desired. It would have been no sacrifice, Skeva. Even in your rags and smelly clothes, I wanted you. You will never know how you strained my self-control each time you approached me or placed your hands on my chest to give me one of your effusive thank yous. I would have given everything just to keep you near me, Skeva, even if we'd never been permitted to kiss, to touch, or to love.

Pathe

They found Goria this morning. I had hired guards to search for her everywhere. I knew that she had not run away. I had never mistreated her, never taken a hand to her, and never locked her in her room. I had been liberal in my ownership of her. Shaarvan had told me repeatedly that I was too tolerant. He had said it so often that I stopped listening. Teea and Tevor had spoken almost the same warnings. I had not heard their voices either. I had wanted to give Goria every freedom. Had I caused her death?

Goria had been guarded, of course. Such was fitting for any girl on Altar, but perhaps, I should have doubled the guards or restricted her travel. I had always allowed her to pass through the city to shop or dine as she desired. And, although she was under the protection of the guards, I had not forbidden her to journey wherever she wished. Had I been too lax? It is obvious, now, that I was.

I had warned her several times about dodging the guards, but she did it once too often. Poor Goria.

Goria had gone to Thenos. I know that. They were friends, she'd told me often. Should I have doubted it, knowing Thenos? But I knew he was not interested in Goria. He had long ago tossed her aside, like all the others he'd stolen from Shaarvan. Why should I have been concerned?

I went to him that morning. He denied, of course, that he had met with her. Witnesses, all commoners, since he chooses to surround himself always with such, upheld his story. They said that Thenos and they had dined together and discussed governmental policies.

Why should commoners be so interested in government? I almost asked, but it was superfluous. I was only concerned as to what had befallen my poor, unhappy Goria.

Thenos offered to investigate. There was a strange light in his eyes that I did not like. It is hard to doubt one's brother, but I thought back to the things that my mother had told me and her suspicions of Thenos, and I had to admit that I concurred. Even to one whose Powers were as weak as mine, the feeling of evil around him was a dark field.

I withdrew from his presence and breathed in the fresher air. I would pursue Goria's murderers. Thenos' evil must not distract me. What cared I for his manipulations or the malevolence I felt within his soul? Either he was guilty of Goria's death, or he was not. That alone would hold my interest.

I returned to my house, where Goria's body lay. Fists and hands had been used to beat her; it did not appear that any weapon had been turned on her. An unlucky punch must have ended her struggles. Her skull had been broken. There was evidence that her hands had been tied, her legs secured for her rape. Her capture and subsequent death had been at the hands of commoners, not Shapechanger. No Shapechanger would have needed to resort to tying her, nor would a Shapechanger have been so inclined. Yet, I kept remembering the way Thenos had looked at me. Would he have done this to Goria?

I had examined her body before. My second examination only confirmed my notes. The blood samples I had taken had shown no drugs in her body. The brain scan seemed to confirm that the damage to her brain had been from an errant blow or an overly enthusiastic one. As I had suspected, it was her only serious injury and the cause of her death. Poor Goria. I could only hope that she had not suffered too greatly.

The sample I had taken from her vagina would tell its own story. I set to work with my computer and the knowledge I had gained from my many years of practice. It would not take me long to extract the DNA history in the semen. Then, I would trace it back to its origin. Altarian records were well-kept; only commoners were not aware of how easy it was to trace them.

Shaara

The four moons of Freinana began to cover more and more of the sun's light. By Specto, they would completely cover all the light, and the day would be as dark as night. I hated the dingy, gray fog that covered those periods. It clung to my spirits, weighing them down like weights in a racing saddle. I fretted that my last days of freedom should lack sunshine. Not even the landoors could bring a smile to my depression. It was as if Specto foretold the gloom of my future. It was the day after Specto that Shaarvan came.

I was rehearsing Jastar for his show trials in the following week. Jastar was a young stallion, and it would be his first showing, but he was not doing well. All the gloom was eating away at his spirits, too.

Fence after fence, he pegged until I gave up jumping him and practiced his dressage. Even there, he refused to concentrate. When we rounded from point Z to M, he blew his stack. His bucking frenzy lasted but a moment. I rode him to a halt and watched him breathe great snorts through his nose. He was trembling so much that I wondered if he was becoming sick. I patted his neck, but he flinched at my touch. I dismounted and breathed into his nostrils. "What is it, boy? Why do you fight?" He snorted and pawed at the ground. It was then that I saw that there were two Shapechangers watching at the fence. No wonder Jastar was a mess. I walked him back to his stall and asked Netha to please walk the stallion out for me.

"I don't have to take orders from you," Netha said in his nastiest voice.

"You will walk Jastar out," I said, staring into his eyes and willing his response.

"I will," the groom responded tonelessly, and he walked away, leading Jastar. I was so surprised it had worked that I stared after him. Then I shook my head, ran to Crimson's stall to give him a pat, and slowly went to meet my doom.

Targone was gone. There was only the new Shapechanger. As he walked towards me, his eyes fastened on my face, I knew what he would say.

He was an incredibly handsome male, even more handsome than my beloved Tren. His cheekbones were high, his eyelashes long and lacy, and his skin tone even and fair. In the thick, light brown hair that just barely touched the top of his high collar, there were streaks of gold that carried the light of the sun. I wondered — if I dared to reach out to touch the furry sunbeams, would I be burned? Silly thought.

"I am your husband, Shaara," the Shapechanger said. His voice was soft, almost gentle, but there was a look in his eyes that told me that I should not depend on his forbearance. The tilt of his head, the way he held his body, hinted at arrogance. He had the self-assurance of one who commands many people.

"No," I whispered pleadingly. Let this stranger *not* be the one. Let him be the brother, the son — anyone other than the one who called himself my husband.

In the sevenTide since I had heard of Shaarvan's existence, I had dreaded his arrival. I had hoped that either he would never come or that like a flash of lightning in the darkness of a thundering sky — in that the instant when I saw him — I would know him, and, at the sight of him, my past would flood the memories back into my empty brain. But that did not happened.

He studied me as I studied him. "Do you not remember?" he asked. His eyes, gray as the dingy clouds of Specto, wanted something of me. But there was more. It was in his voice and in the eyes that stared so deeply into my soul. It was as if he was sending his thoughts deep inside me, a melody I could almost hear, but it was being played too softly to identify. I listened, scarcely breathing, needing to hear the mystery song that teased my mind, but I could not grasp it.

I shook my head and shut out what was beginning to irritate my brain. The Shapechanger's eyes grew hard, and his anger burned, but he said nothing, allowing me to study him further. I did not wish to oppose him, but I so urgently needed time to search for something that I could remember, for something familiar in him.

He was a tall Shapechanger, like Targone, but his body was broader in the shoulders and more massive than the others. He was strong. In all ways he was strong, that I could see and sense. Why did I not remember touching those shoulders, feeling the muscles beneath his skin?

The Shapechanger's face was perfectly shaped, all angles and planes, as if chiseled out of granite. Yet, as he smiled . . . Why was he smiling? Hadn't he been angry with me a moment ago? His dimples at the sides, just below his cheekbones, made me sigh. Would I have forgotten those dimples, that smile?

I shook my head sadly. I had no memory of the one before me — not his body, his eyes, his smile, nor what he would expect of me. A trace of bitterness rose in my throat. I wanted to lash out at him for causing me this pain. "I've never seen you before," I said, "but of course, that's rather tough to see since I'm supposed to keep my eyes glued to the ground like a good Shapechanger wife."

He laughed. How could he laugh? He, with his obvious temper, his arrogant look? "Lift up your eyes, Shaara," he said, still chuckling. "Since Targone told you the Shapechanger laws, I am sure that you know that it is safe to meet the eyes of your husband."

All I knew for sure was that Shaarvan was a Shapechanger. He should have been irritated at my tone. I'd been around Targone long enough to know that an angry voice was punishable, yet Shaarvan had only been amused by my belligerence.

I raised my chin and met his eyes fully. "I wasn't afraid for my safety," I boasted.

"You should be," he said with the same quiet, even tone in his voice. I shivered. I had heard no change in the volume of his voice or in his manner, but there had been a difference. His eyes still crinkled at the edges, but my body knew he had given me a warning.

That did it! I'd had enough of Shapechanger dominance. "Why? Because you'll beat me?" I said.

"Shapechangers rarely need to beat their wives," he said calmly.

There was something in his eyes that frightened me. What was it? Why did I know instinctively that he was dangerous? Targone was right — this male had Power, more Power than I'd ever felt. His Power was like a candle casting off heat. The warning in its touch rode the air, and its flame flickered towards my skin. He was curbing it, protecting me from its full force. I could feel his skill at directing it away from me. Yet I knew its presence, the warning of its touch. My anger ran and hid, and fear overran my mind.

"Come," he said, holding out his hand. "We shall sit over there in the shade and see if that temper of yours can cool before it brings you trouble."

His eyes were like diamonds, glittering with a cold, hard center, yet many-faceted and sharp. I had not consciously begun to walk towards him, but my feet brought me there, and I could not look away. He took my hand and led me. I followed at his side, docile as an old landoor but leery as a frightened kelbla. In a moment, I found that I was sitting beside him on the bench. I scarcely remembered how I had traveled there.

I was allowed to look away then. He had freed me from the compulsion. I was so nervous I could not stay still. I started to rise.

"Easy, Shaara," he said. His hand took my hat and tossed it to the ground. Then his hand brushed and smoothed my hair until it lay all around my shoulders and down my back. I wanted to cringe away from his hands, but my body would not obey me. Once again, I could not move.

"I am sorry this is difficult for you," he said, as the hand stroking my hair played freely, running its fingers through the strands, meeting tangles that were gently unraveled one by one. "I had hoped your memories would come back with the sight of me."

His gentle manner reassured me slightly. Again, my anger dared to flow. In irritation, I jerked a tangled curl from between Shaarvan's fingers. It hurt, and my eyes watered at the pain, but there was a victory in taking back what was mine.

"I am not the one who was your wife," I told him. "Whoever I was before, I am no longer."

My rebellion did not take away his smile. His eyes shared the joke. I thrust my chin up higher and continued. "Targone says you will force me to go with you, but my life is here. I will not go."

I expected fireworks, but his voice came quietly. "What about your son?" he asked.

If he had hit me, the shock would not have been so great. "My son?"

"We have a child named Shaarac. He loves you very much, Shaara. He has been in deep sleep since you were stolen."

"I gave birth to a child?" I sputtered.

I didn't know whether I could believe him. Wouldn't I know if I'd borne a son? Wouldn't I feel a mother's loss at being separated from him? I erupted off the bench. "You are lying," I cried out.

"Can a Shapechanger lie, Shaara?" he asked, watching my face.

I stared down at him. I knew the answer, and I could tell that he'd known that I would. How much had Targone told him about me?

The same quiet voice, calm and unbothered by my rebellion, said, "Sit down, Shaara. I shall tell you about him."

"No, you're a Shapechanger," I cried out. "That means you can take any shape you want, doesn't it?"

Shaarvan was watching me intently. He nodded in response to my question.

I stared into his eyes. "I want to see what you really look like."

Shaarvan laughed. Tiny crinkles around his eyes formed. My heart fluttered. He was unbearably beautiful. How could his smile cause me pain?

"Shaara, I am as you see. I was born this way."

I stared, overwhelmed by his presence. There was a sexual charge between us that was making it difficult to think. Even with Tren, I had not been bothered this intensely with my need for a male. I took a deep breath, shut out my other thoughts, and threw the Shapechanger's words back at him. "If you were born that way, your mother must have had a difficult birth."

Shaarvan got it at once. He laughed his beautiful, sexy laugh, and while I was still spellbound by it, he captured my hand. "Ah, Shaara, I have missed you so. Your tongue is as quick and amusing as always. Sit down now and listen."

His words were sweetly coated, but he had issued an order he expected me to obey. I perched on the edge of the bench, as far from him as possible, with my hand still firmly grasped.

He did not force me closer but smiled at me in a friendly, understanding manner. Shaarvan was frightening, but he did not act like the rigid, controlling Shapechanger that Targone's tales had warned me of. Was it an act? Or was it possible that a Shapechanger *could* be a little sympathetic to my feelings? After all, Targone was the only Shapechanger I had ever met.

Shaarvan began to speak. In his voice, there was a hypnotic quality that drew me. Once again, like music, the melody of it was pleasing. "I do not know how much you understand about giving birth, Shaara," he began. "But the baby, inside his mother, is surrounded by fluid. When he is ready to be born, the baby often kicks a hole into this sack of fluid. Shaarac, our son, did this to you.

"You were standing at the window of our cottage, looking out into the morning. You felt the water gushing out of you, and you realized that Shaarac had decided to begin his passage. Tears flowed from your eyes like raindrops dripping from the roof. You longed for his arrival, but at that moment, the forest just outside the window had entranced you, and you were captivated by its power.

"An early morning freeze had turned the trees into a fairyland, as you called it. Icicles, like prisms in the morning's first rays of light, held the slivers of a hundred hues of colors, glimmering a spectrum of glowing lights. Your eyes dreamed of running through that forest under the sparkling diamond icicles, but Shaarac had forced other plans."

Gently, Shaarvan slid me next to him. I was startled at his touch, fearful of his closeness, but his words had woven a spell. I did not flinch as his arm wrapped itself around my shoulder.

"A Shapechanger male does not speak of love, but his heart bonds with his mate, and his blood sings his devotion," he told me.

Engrossed in his words and the smell and feel of him, I swam in the gray of his eyes as they looked into mine. They were soft as a morning mist.

"I carried you out to your heart's desire, Shaara, and you reached up and touched a frozen spear of ice. You laughed, and your laughter stung me. It stung with an ache of tenderness. I wished I never needed to set you down again. I wanted always to hold you in that moment, to savor your joy and the sparkle I saw, not in the sea of icicles, but in your eyes glowing in delight. I yearned to hold you there in my arms forever, listening in wonder to the music of your laughter, but I feared I had allowed you to stay too long in the bitter cold of the morning. I tucked the blanket around you more tightly, and I told you that we must go in."

Both of Shaarvan's hands cupped mine now. I looked down to see the great size of them. One finger was stroking my palm. I shivered, and the finger stilled.

"You begged me to wait, and you told me then, for the first time, that you loved me. Shaara, you changed me that day — three simple words that only a woman can say. Yet, they held the depth of your soul in their voice. I had been strict with you, as Shapechanger training requires. You were stubborn, recklessly defiant, and more difficult than I had ever known a girl to be, but yet, with all my harshness, you had given me your heart. I was awed by the miracle of it. There is still wonder in my soul at the largeness of your gift."

Was there a tear in Shaarvan's eye? He looked up at the sky, and for a moment, he could not speak. I wondered if I should reply to his words, but I did not know what to say. Before I had the chance, he continued.

"We kissed, with a special sweetness in the sharing, and our hunger for each other grew. It was a wrench to pull away from you, my Shaara. Desire was in your eyes, although your body had already begun its labor.

"I ran with you through the forest towards our cottage. Through you, I felt the laughter of the trees. You and I were bonded with that forest, joined in the delight of that one moment in time."

Shaarvan lifted up my hand and brought it to his lips. His touch made me gasp. Waves of longing swept through my body. I was frightened by the intensity of the feelings.

"In our home later," Shaarvan said, seeming to ignore what his touch and his tale were doing to me, "our family gathered round to aid the birth of Shaarac, but the baby lingered, content to remain within you. My brother, Pathe, was your medic. He urged you to walk, and you did, circling and circling until, at last, Pathe sent you back to our bed. You lay down, and I came into the room to lie beside you. I held you in my arms while you slept, and together, we prowled the forest of our dreams. In our Shapechange image, we walked the forest in search of a safe den for our cub. As a Saberey, the tiger of the Old Ones, you delivered our cub. I knew then that Shaarac would come quickly."

Not content to awaken every pore on the skin of my hands, Shaarvan's finger stretched out to touch my face. Again, the contact with him brought shivers down to my soul. The Power of Shaarvan was like the current of the strongest river. Would its force sweep me under?

"We woke. The child was coming," he went on, sending me deeper and deeper into his spell. "You begged me to stay with you, and I did, holding your hand, watching your pain, wishing I could take it away. It was the second miracle I shared with you that day. Shaarac's birth was not easy for you, but your smile when he cried that first breath drew me to you and to Shaarac. A tighter bond, a bond of the love you had named earlier, was formed between us.

"On the bed beside you, I watched you nurse our son, and I knew that fate had smiled upon us. Our destiny would hold the promise of many tomorrows, and our tomorrows would be filled with the shared rhythm of our hearts."

Shaarvan was good at weaving spells. I could feel his hold on me strengthening as I listened. When he finished, I was still enthralled.

I sighed into the silence, at last breaking free from the magic of his voice. "It was not I, Shaarvan. That was another girl you loved. I cannot be that person."

"Feel my hand, Shaara. Really feel it. Know it in your mind. Does the touch of it tell you how large it is compared to yours? It is this hand of mine that battled a make-believe dragon in the forest with a single broken branch. I did that for you. It is this hand that smoothed your hair and comforted you when you cried and when you grew fearful. It is this hand that taunted your body with its caress as it played melodies across every single pore of your skin."

His hand reached up to touch my hair. It brushed a fallen strand out of my eyes and returned to touch my cheek with its hard, rough knuckles. I breathed in sharply. His touch was exhilarating. It felt delicious, but it also hurt with an ache so sharp I wanted to scream. But yet, I didn't want him to stop. His fingers were stroking strange patterns on my cheek. He was confusing me. I couldn't think.

"Stop!" I cried out.

His hand left my face. Such a wrenching loss! It was as if he'd stolen something precious from me and left behind only emptiness. Again, his fingers joined with mine. "Look at my hand, Shaara. Do you see the difference in size? It always amazes me how small the bones of your hand are. Your fingers are half the size of mine yet it is the softness of the skin on your palm that is the true wonder."

His hand was playing with mine, touching, rubbing, massaging. He brought my hand to his mouth. His tongue ran teasingly across the surface. The touch of his tongue, warm and tickly, almost propelled me from the bench, wild with desire.

Shaarvan's eyes were watching me, urging me . . . to do what? I didn't know what he wanted from me. It was all so new. I was frightened of him, but I was drawn to him in a current that was sweeping me along faster and faster.

"Ah, Shaara," Shaarvan groaned. "I have tasted you everywhere. I could close my eyes and touch you with my tongue and know exactly where I was on your body." His lips began to tease my neck.

"Don't," I cried out, pulling back. I fought to clear my mind of the dangerous flow that was rushing me down into forgetfulness. I launched an attack. It was always the best defense. "Targone told me what the scratches on my arm mean. How could you hurt me so badly if you loved me?"

I thought I saw a flash of anger, but if so, it was too quickly gone to be sure. Once more, in Shaarvan's eyes, I saw only gentleness and concern. "You do not understand, Shaara. You were wild and rebellious. You betrayed the Shapechanger. I took you into the pack and made you one of us."

I knew he told the truth as he saw it. I could read that much from his eyes, but I was not through grasping at straws. "Targone says I am bonded to my owner, Tren."

Again, I thought the fire in his eyes flared, but gray eyes, with all the patience of a stone idol, were looking down at me when he answered, "You are bonded to me. I am your owner."

"Targone says…"

"Targone has been helpful in many ways," Shaarvan said, with a voice that allowed no further argument. "I appreciate his efforts in protecting you, but his job is over."

"But Tren? Did he tell you about Tren?"

"I know."

"I belong to Tren," I repeated. I knew that Shaarvan might kill me for saying it, but he must know the truth.

"No, Shaara. You belong to me."

Shaarvan's hand reached up behind my neck and locked there. I couldn't move without pain. I froze and watched as his lips came to me. "No," I wanted to protest, but the hand on my neck would not allow me to speak. The lips met mine, and the hand freed me from the painful grip, but it was too late then. There was music on Shaarvan's lips. I sought to hear it more clearly and was swept away. I knew then that Shaarvan was right. It had never been like this with Tren.

A hunger rode me, overpowering me with its need. It ripped inside and through me. Agony raged up and down my spine. I needed Shaarvan. I wanted him, but the pain . . . I screamed. Tears streamed down my face. I couldn't breathe, I was so frightened.

"Easy, Shaara. It is all right now. Easy." Shaarvan pulled me to him and held me as I cried. "Do you remember, Shaara? Do you remember now?" he asked.

I looked up at him, wanting badly to remember. There was such a feeling of familiarity in the hands that stroked my back, in the fingers that had touched my face and awakened me from my sleep. My body knew his touch, but my mind didn't. I shook my head, an, as I lay my face against his shirt, listening to the sound his heart was making.

"Kiss me, Shaara," he urged. "It will not hurt you now. Meet my lips and feel how our hearts are one."

I was terrified but compelled. I drew closer and touched my lips to Shaarvan's. Sweet, lovely feelings washed over me. I wanted him, I needed him, I craved him. When his tongue entered me, I moaned. Intense joy, as strong as the pain of a moment ago, rocked me with its pleasure.

"Shaara." He broke away to look at me. "Oh, Shaara, I missed you so. My lovely Shaara, my sweet wife." His arms held me tightly against him, squeezing me in an embrace so fierce I thought my ribs would crack. I felt swallowed by it, and suddenly, I was frightened again. Isandor had beaten my body, but he had not touched my soul. He had not made me feel. Shaarvan was demanding more of me than I wanted to give.

He must have read my thoughts. "It will be all right, Shaara. Relax."

I drew a breath and tried to be the Sleena, or Skeva, or whoever I had become before Shaarvan arrived. It wasn't easy, with my heart beating like the fluttering wings of a brownfeather climbing skyward.

"Shaarvan, we are here." I knew the voice was Targone, but I couldn't move. I couldn't tear my eyes from the gray ones that stared into my soul.

Shaarvan released me. "Come, Shaara. I shall meet Tren."

I drew back. "Please, Shaarvan, you will not be angry with him, will you?"

Shaarvan reared back to stare at me. "Shapechanger women do not attempt to interfere," he said icily.

"I don't remember how to be Shapechanger."

Instantly, Shaarvan's eyes softened. "I shall be patent with you, my wife." His knuckles once more brushed against my cheek, and I felt the pull of Shapechanger. His large hand covered mine and urged me up. I stood, and we walked towards the others, but as we went forward, I was very apprehensive. I was suddenly remembering what I'd told Shaarvan.

Chapter Nine

Targone

I had heard that the Warlords of Westla possessed Powers that we lesser Shapechangers could only dream of. The Warlords came so rarely to the minor planets that I had never been in the company of one. If Shaarvan of Altar was a typical example of them, the Legends did not exaggerate. He was as god-like as the Chants proclaimed.

Among us on Freinana, on the western side of the continent, there were many Shapechanger who had taken up residence. Freinana was not known for its high culture, but it had a calm and unusually pleasant climate, even without an expensive climate-control device.

Our planet was especially known for its research facilities, and many came to Freinana to study. Those students often regarded the Warlords as suitable research for their theses, and of course, spoge and krilla can be drunk most pleasantly over such interesting topics of conversation. For this reason, although Shaarvan probably labeled me an uninformed outlander, I was quite familiar with many interesting facts concerning Warlords.

It was widely known, for instance, that Shaarvan was the nephew of the Highest of Westla and that he was probably Westla's future heir. He was also the son of the Head Elder of Altar. It was said that the Trendacons, his family's tree of ancestry, traced their roots to those of the first mutations from the Saberey, and was thus stronger than any who followed.

So, I was fascinated by this opportunity to observe him. Already, I had learned from his wife's arms that there was truth in the rumor that some Trendacons took their wives in the Old Way. No one I had ever known had used that process for hundreds and hundreds of Passes. Some even doubted that it was anything more than a myth, but I had seen that it was true. Shaara wore the scars.

It was for that reason that I also believed the tales that spoke of the Warlords actually walking among the Old Ones in their night visions. If Shaarvan learned how to evoke the Saberey and call up its Power, it was possible that it was they who told him how to do so.

The ripples of the Warlord's Power permeated the air. His wife, Shaara, was not so cocky anymore. I think she had begun to learn the lessons I had tried to teach her. I had no doubt that Shaarvan would train her skillfully. One could assume from his lineage that he would do everything expertly.

Shaara fit him well. I saw at the lake that she had more potential than she had earlier displayed. My Power had given me an inkling suspicion that she was pleasing when exhibited properly. The sight of her in the lake water confirmed it. Shaarvan, a lord of Altar and Westla, would have accepted no less.

And with her promise, the prepubescent stirrings of her Power that I'd felt, someone with Shaarvan's strength would be necessary to control her adequately. I had never come across a woman with Shaara's potential, although I was always careful to hide such knowledge from her. It amazed me to know that her transition was not complete. What would she be like when she reached her fulfillment?

I told Shaara many things in our talks. I hoped they helped her to adapt to the life she would live. Yet, I only gave her hints of her husband's Power. I never explained to her about the Warlords. Was I cowardly in withholding that information? Perhaps so, but it is best not to discuss their strength. In fact, it was safer not to discuss Shapechange lore at all, for the myths also said that the Warlords delivered retribution freely.

I glanced over at Tren. For a commoner, he was amazingly composed and calm before Shaarvan. Was he not able to feel the Power surrounding such a Warlord? Did he not fully understand that Shaarvan, in this meeting, would render judgment over his fate? Tren would live or die at Shaarvan's whim. Would the lord deliver prosperity or punish him?

I had recommended that Tren be rewarded for his intelligence and courage in coming forth to announce Shaara's presence. Most commoners would not have done so. They have only muddled information concerning the Shapechanger and believe, as Shaara once did, that we steal their souls and suck out their memory and their essence. I suppose it is possible that a Warlord could do that, but for what purpose?

Tren had greater knowledge of the true nature of the Shapechanger, far too much for a commoner. I told Shaarvan that, also. I reported all to the Warlord, knowing holding back information would not have been prudent.

My duty in this matter was, therefore, at an end. I would say nothing, no matter the outcome of Shaarvan's sentencing, but I did inform Shaarvan that I was honored to view the commoner as my friend and that I was impressed with Tren's integrity and dignity. It is my hope that the Warlord will show leniency.

As to Shaara — there is nothing more that I can do for her, either. She enchanted me, it was true, but I know that she will soon be back on Altar, and I will never have the opportunity to see her again. I recognize that, and I accept it.

I hope Tren can bow to the loss of her as well. We shall both miss her questions and her smiles.

Shaara

When we stood before them, I could not look at Tren I was ashamed. Yesterday, I had thought I loved him. Today, I hungered for another. And I had endangered Tren by my words. What was wrong with me?

Shaarvan held my hand tightly as if he thought I might pull away. I shot a glance up at his face, but I could read nothing. His eyes were fastened on Tren.

"I am Tren, my lord," said my former love. I did not raise my eyes to his.

"And, I am Shaarvan of Altar, the husband of the Shapechanger, Shaara. I thank you for notifying us of her presence here, for protecting her, and, especially, I thank you for killing Isandor."

My eyes flew once more to my husband's face. He knew about Isandor? Did he know everything?

"I am more than grateful," Shaarvan continued. "I am forever in your debt. Is there some reward I can offer you?"

Was Shaarvan not angry then? Would he forgive my words and what Tren and I had done?

"You can bring me a girl exactly like her, my lord," Tren answered.

I looked into Tren's eyes then. He was wearing his feelings in them. He had never told me. The harsh glare of Shaarvan's eyes warned me that my behavior was unacceptable. Nervously, I fastened my eyes to the ground.

"Tren," Shaarvan continued in his calm, firm voice. "I would like us to be friends, but we have a problem. When a Shapechanger bonds, it is forever, and the bond is in the depth of the soul. I am going to show you something that will hurt, but I think it is important for you to see.

"Shaara, come to me."

I stood beside him. How could I come closer? I looked up, but I did not like the look in his eyes. Did he mean to punish me for my breach of Shapechanger etiquette? Was he going to demonstrate his Power over me in front of Tren? *Please, no.*

Shaarvan's hand slid around my neck and gripped me. He tilted my head until his lips met mine perfectly. I could do nothing but whimper. Such was the pull of the current that held me. Then, Shaarvan's lips devoured me. I was drowning, being pulled under the depths, deeper into the maelstrom. The whirlpool sucked me down, down into the blackness. I could not save myself until I saw the light. I swam to it. Like a beacon in the dark and dangerous water, it was my focus. And then, I saw the light was Shaarvan. His soul reached out to pull me in. The joining was a salvation. There were no deadly currents, only a buoyant peace.

Shaarvan eased my racing heart and calmed me with his hands holding my jaw and face. His fingers lightly brushed my lips, and one hand smoothed back a lock of hair. I was no longer afraid then. I understood how our souls were joined. I could not take my eyes off his. There was only Shaarvan in my world.

"Tren," Shaarvan said, still holding my eyes to his, "I did not show you that to flaunt my Power over Shaara but to show that she is well-claimed. Her Power grows stronger. She is almost fully Shapechanger. You could not have controlled her. I have removed your bond on her. It was painful for her, but it is now gone. The bond she holds on you cannot be removed unless you share our blood and take a

Shapechanger wife. Having known Shaara, you would never be content with less now, anyway.

"Join the Shapechanger, Tren, and I shall give you a woman whose veins run with the same fire as Shaara's."

Shaarvan released my eyes. I could not help darting a quick look in Tren's direction before I dropped them. Tren's were full of pain, but it lessened him none. He was still a man full of pride and strength, a commoner who had dared a Shapechanger.

"Thank you for your offer, my lord Shaarvan, and for the demonstration. I no longer have any uncertainty that she is yours; I can see that Shaara has been returned to her rightful owner. But there is another matter that I must discuss with you if you will permit it."

I felt Shaarvan's nod.

What are you doing, Tren? I wanted to say it out loud. But I kept silent and sent up a prayer. *Barquel, please protect him.* Would Barquel grant the prayers of one that only half believed in him?

"I want it open between us," Tren continued. "I kissed your wife. I did not believe you were alive. I had agreed to become Shapechanger and was ready to take Shaara as my wife with full honors. Targone is the witness of my pledge. I ask your pardon, my lord Shaarvan, and that your punishment be swiftly given."

I gasped. It was worse than I had imagined. Why had he told Shaarvan everything? There was nothing I could do that would not make it worse. I kept my eyes lowered. I bit my lip with worry.

Shaarvan watched me for a moment. His finger touched my lip. Was it a reminder to be silent? He turned to Tren. "Targone had informed me, but I thank you for your honesty. As I said, I have removed your touch from Shaara."

Once again, Shaarvan was watching me. I raised my eyes to look at him. *Please don't hurt, Tren*, I wanted to say, but I didn't. If I spoke, my defense of Tren would only harm him.

I was frightened of Shaarvan's vengeance. Everyone knew that Shapechanger killed for even a lesser cause. I could see that Shaarvan was still considering all the information that he'd heard. He had still not passed his judgment.

Shaarvan's eyes continued to study me. Once more, his knuckles stroked my cheek. He didn't look away when he began to speak. "We of the Shapechanger do not take lightly the contamination of our bond. I would have killed you, Tren, for the lips you placed on my wife, but you have done much good for her. As it stands, we shall call it even — your life for Isandor's. The offer I granted you still stands."

I breathed a sigh of relief. Shaarvan lifted up my chin. "This time, I shall not even punish my wife for swimming nude with another."

I could not help my gasp. The grip of Shaarvan's hand on my chin tightened. For a long moment, the force of his eyes let me know him.

When he saw that I had understood, he let go of my chin. Immediately, my eyes lowered to the ground. At last, I understood what Targone had tried to tell me. Shaarvan's punishments would not be something I could shut out with a journey to the forest. I shuddered.

Tren was speaking. As was fitting, he ignored the training he had just witnessed. "Targone has offered to take me with him to meet others of your blood, my lord Shaarvan. I shall make my decision, then. Thank you, my lord." Tren bowed his respect to Shaarvan and walked away. He gave me not a final word or glance.

I wanted to call out a goodbye, but Shaarvan's hand repeated the silence command. I could say nothing.

Shaarvan stood a moment, watching Tren walk down the long path on his way back to the casino. Then he turned to Targone. "You are correct. He is all that you said he was. He possesses too many Shapechanger secrets and the force of him belongs to Shapechanger. Make sure he becomes one of us."

"Shaarvan!" I cried out at the unfairness and opened my mouth to dispute such injustice, but his hand seized my neck. His strong grip delivered no punishment, but I was warned.

"Thank you for your service to me, Targone," Shaarvan said. "I have transferred a large credit to your account. It is little reward for what you have done. Should you ever need me, I shall come."

Targone said his goodbyes to Shaarvan. He, like Tren, said nothing to me. I had watched two friends walk away without a goodbye, all because a man I did not know now claimed me as his wife. How had my life changed so abruptly, slipping beyond my control?

"You will show me where you have stayed, Shaara," Shaarvan ordered.

I could not look at him. My abrupt isolation from the others and the renewed awareness of my vulnerability robbed me of any courage I still possessed. Without a word, I led him to the house where I lived, but my thoughts were pinpricks of dread and uncertainty. What if this were all a lie? What if Shaarvan were not who he said he was? What proof did I have?

As I came closer to the house, my heart began to pound. I knew that my doubts were fabrications: Shaarvan was who he said he was. My body had told me that, and besides, he was Shapechanger, so he could not lie. But what would he expect of me now? Would he punish me alone in the room, free from the eyes of Targone and Tren? Would he change into a cat and rake me again with his claws? Would he force me to join with him? How did a Shapechanger join with a woman? Would it be in his man's body or . . . ?

We had reached the entrance. Shaarvan stepped forward and placed his hand on the door. I started to point out the latch, but he was already opening it. His other hand still gripped my arm. I could not move forward until he had examined the door.

"It does not lock," he stated.

Was that a question? I shook my head.

I was listening for the sound of Flar and Frieda. I did not feel their presence. The believers must still be in the cycle of the Wheel. They were probably with friends, toasting Barquel with drink and lumpy, cold congealed food.

Shaarvan said nothing more, but he was still frowning about the door. Had he wished to lock me in or bar others from entry?

We climbed the stairs. I was used to them; I could have run up the whole three floors and not been out of breath, but my steps grew slower as we approached the top.

My room seemed small with the huge Shapechanger in it. Who was this male who now ruled my life? Was he Isandor or Targone? Was he Tren? Or was he different from everyone I had ever known?

"Sit down," he commanded, and I didn't dare argue. He continued to stand, a giant whose head was not a finger's distance away from the ceiling. Would the length of the bed handle his span, or would his feet dangle over the edge?

Shaarvan's eyes were darting around the room, probably puzzling over how little of me there was in it. Even with Isandor dead, I had changed nothing. Not even a vase of flowers cheered the room. Frieda had repeatedly offered them, but I had told her that I had the green of the pastures and the wildflowers there. I had also refused her offer of curtains or other frills. I kept my room immaculate. The window that opened outward, I cleaned every night. It was the only important thing. The rest of my room was only for sleeping.

Shaarvan's eyes returned to me. "Good," he said. "In this, you remain a true Shapechanger."

I could tell that he was pleased with me. I took a deep breath and blurted out my chief anxiety, at least at this moment. As Targone had told me, it was better to know. "Isandor used to make me come here in the middle of the day. He raped me then. Is that your intent?"

Shaarvan ignored my question and went to the window to look out. The glass shone. I could see Shaarvan's reflection as he admired my view of the landoors.

His eyes continued to gaze across the green of the pastures as he began to speak. "You have changed in some ways, Shaara. Before, you would never have had the courage to say those words. You would have worried and fretted until I read the question in your mind." He turned back to look at me. "I am not Isandor, Shaara. No Shapechanger rapes for sport." He sounded miserable and cautious about his wording.

He came towards me and sat down. I stilled myself not to cringe away from him, but I could not stop my trembling. I thought he would start to draw the patterns that would make me desire him, but he only took my hand.

"I have been searching for you on many planets, Shaara. I would have searched fifty more and never given up. You once trusted me, and I let you down. I am very sorry, my wife."

"How did you let me down?"

"By not protecting you enough."

"Shaarvan," I whispered, "I don't know what happened. Would you please tell me?"

He nodded and began to acquaint me with the parts of the story he had pieced together. "Our ship had landed on the planet Watha, and the engineer went to find a part we needed. When he did not return, I decided to go out and search for him. You asked to go planetside with me, and I permitted it. I did not think that we would find the engineer, but we did need to locate the part.

"I only allowed you to accompany me because I had decided to take you to see the volcano. You would have loved that, would you not?"

I nodded, but I wasn't too sure what a volcano was.

"I promise I shall still take you there someday, my wife." Shaarvan's hand brushed back my hair. He found the spot exactly in the middle of my forehead and touched his lips to it. Then he continued to tell me of that day.

"We walked towards the bubblecruiser, you and I and the guards. Shaarac, our son, stayed on board, thankfully. I was armed, and the guards were loaded down with pipes and knives, but the slaver, the one who sold you, threw a chemical bomb at our feet. The gases took our consciousness, and we slept as if our beds were on that concrete landing site. Before the chemical cloud subsided, the slaver injected me with a slow-acting poison, and he stole you away.

"When I woke, I discovered that my crew had risked flying the ship with a worn-out part. They had taken me to Westla. There, the medics had an antidote for the poison, but I almost died from the delay. If you had been killed, my wife, I would not have fought to live. But your life gave meaning to mine. I knew you needed me. It took me almost a halfPass to recover, but during that time, Shapechanger from Westla searched for you. On Altar, both men and Shapechanger took crews and planet-hopped, seeking you. My father visited traders and traffickers. Your name was never forgotten a moment by your family and friends and by the officials of Altar and Westla.

"When I was well enough, I flew back to the planet where you had been stolen. There was no trail to hunt for you, my wife. It was as if Kada and the trader had never existed. There were no records of rented bubblecruisers, no chemical bombs sold, and no sight by anyone of anything that could have been connected to your abduction.

"The endless days of travel, the fruitless investigations, the fact that I did not even know if you were alive, Shaara — it has been an eternity without you. My heart, beating with the rhythm of your name, has been all that has kept me going. Do you understand how much I feared for you? I couldn't sleep nights, wondering if you were all right. I knew you were resilient, intelligent, and brave, but I also knew the dangers for a woman who talked too much, who argued, and who was so stubborn. Even for me, you were almost unteachable.

"It is strange, Shaara. I thought during that twoPass I had owned you, that I had trained you. In truth, it was you who had trained me. I was no longer the one I used to be. My heart no longer beats the way it did before. For now, every rush of blood whispers your name, 'Shaara, Shaara, Shaara.'

"By all the stars in heaven, I am so grateful that the worst that happened to you was one man's abuse. I know. I see your eyes burning with arguments. Isandor beat you and raped you, but although he assaulted you maliciously, the hurt inside you will heal. I do not mean that I belittle the harm he did you. I only mean that you are strong. He damaged your pride and your inner soul, Shaara, but I shall help you to forget.

As your husband, I shall comfort you and lend you support. Whenever you have a need, I shall listen and hear your words of anger and of grief for the horror you lived through. Sharing my bed will bring you no pain or suffering, only pleasure, and our joining will be your pillar, your tree of stability. I shall heal your soul, Shaara, and ease the ache in your heart.

"You have survived, and you are well and physically healthy. That is what is most important, my darling one. Isandor did not break your bones or, burn scars across your body, or blind you, or cut you so you could not walk again. I have seen things like that done. It sickened me, the things that I have seen."

Shaarvan kissed my hand, but I do not think he knew he did it. His eyes were seeing only his memories. He was lost in the world of his torment.

"Shaara," he said, continuing. For a moment, his eyes focused on me. "Shaara, have you ever heard the sound when the winds rush through the mountain crags and whistle through the pines?"

I shook my head, but I don't think he noticed.

"It is an eerie sound, a wail of loneliness and sorrow. Such was the beat of my heart crying your name as I searched through every brothel and slave trader's market, longing to find you but afraid to find you half-dead from neglect, disuse, or harmed in some way by a man's cruelty. To find you sound and healthy, and full of life, Shaara..." He crushed me to him, and the arms encircling me did not frighten me. I felt safe.

My head pressed against his chest, listening to the sound of his heartbeat. I did not hear my name as he had said I would. The name I heard was "Shaarvan, Shaarvan, Shaarvan."

Did the puzzle pieces all suddenly fit together, then? Not at all. To be married to a stranger, to have a missing son, a family, a home world I didn't know, to supposedly be part of a frightening species with Powers beyond my understanding . . . I was Alice down a rabbit hole, completely lost and shrinking, shrinking, shrinking.

The Shaarvan Series continues with:

Book Four

Shaara of Westla

www.ingramcontent.com/pod-product-compliance
Lightning Source LLC
Chambersburg PA
CBHW070859250626
47159CB00003B/1126